Georges Bernanos

JOY

TRANSLATION BY
LOUISE VARÈSE

Pantheon Books

41 Washington Square, New York 12, N. Y.

FIRST PRINTING
August 1946

SECOND PRINTING
November 1946

Manufactured in the United States of America
American Book–Stratford Press, Inc., New York, N. Y.

FIRST PART

1

SOFTLY she opened the door and stood for a moment motionless on the threshold, holding up a black-mittened hand. Then, with cautious tiny steps and blinking eyes, she entered the room, her little old head hidden by the triple folds of a woolen shawl, as solitary as a corpse in the dazzling light. Across the room a sunbeam stretched from one end to the other. When she stood still the luminous shadow of the linden tree continued to dance on the wall.

"What are you doing here, Mama," cried Monsieur de Clergerie, "and at such an hour! So early in the morning! What can Francine be thinking of?"

He had appeared at the other end of the room with his horn-rimmed glasses and his little cloth cap, a frogged smoking-jacket over his night-shirt. But she kept on staring at him as though trying to make sure that she recognized him, trying to find a place for him in the relentless concatenation of her thoughts. With a shrug of his shoulders he came up to her and without a word took hold of her arm, gripping it firmly.

"The keys?" she said.

"Perhaps you left them on your bedside table? Yesterday, Mama, don't you remember? . . . But wait, I think I feel them in your pocket. Here they are!"

The wrinkled hand darted at them with the agility of a little animal. She held them up to her ear making them tinkle, then smiled maliciously. Her son's voice, the pressure of his fingers, his mere presence always succeeded in calming her. But this time her features relaxed only for an instant and once more she began talking softly to herself.

"I know what is bothering you," he said, and could feel through her sleeve the impotent resistance of her arm which he had not relinquished. "Yes, yes, I know. But you must not worry. *She* will not be getting up today. *She* will not leave her room. I count on you, Mama, entirely on you."

"What delicate health, my poor boy!" replied the old lady after deep reflection. "What delicate health! . . . Never mind. I will see to everything, my son, leave it to me. It is unbelievable how fresh and vigorous I feel today. We will supervise the washing. Has Edmund brought back the key to the granary? Oh, it is a heavy responsibility for me, a house like ours . . . Your father is very low, very low."

She had pushed aside a corner of her shawl and her suspicious gray eyes looked out, reassured now. And her arm no longer resisted his grasp but relaxed, and as though set free, she began to laugh.

"Why do you try to hide from me that she is dead,

my boy?" she said. "This is her trousseau of keys. She will not get up today, you say, poor girl. Ah, no! She will certainly not get up. What a frightful farce! Do you think I am mad?"

"Of course not, Mama!" said Monsieur de Clergerie blushing, "I see that you are now fully awake. Don't bother your head any longer. Have you written out our menu for today? Let me have it and I'll send it to the kitchen."

"Here it is, here it is," she said quickly, taking out of her waist a scrap of paper covered with incomprehensible signs. "I am very hungry. I am quite starved. In *her* day—oh, I'm not blaming her, poor child, it was like that, and that's all—the cook did just as she pleased; what food! . . . And that reminds me, . . . that reminds me, my dear . . ."

She tapped her chin several times with the end of her index finger, her cheeks suddenly flushed with anger. Her eyes were uneasy again.

"Yesterday she ate half of the dish all by herself, I saw her—the whole piece of kidney so fat and shiny, all by herself—a sin, a veritable sin. Who ever heard of sick people having such an appetite! But you are as innocent as a child."

He dared not interrupt her, he no longer even dared to touch her fragile body trembling all over with anger. The voice which old age had made so strangely bitter without, for all that, having changed its timbre, was the same voice that, as a little boy, he had learned to fear, but it was also the voice that had never failed to calm his terrors, settle, with a word, his doubts, answer for him to the world; and it seemed that she guarded the secret of his mediocre life, his pathetic joys, his regrets, that she would take his secret with her to the land of shades. He loved her. He loved her above all because she was the only living thing he understood completely, whom he understood with a profound animal sympathy akin to passion. At the hour of death he would like to hear that voice—just as it was, unsoftened, with that same emphasis, that same vibration of restrained fury or scorn, which had in the past so often calmed his nerves when, during his wretched adolescence, he would suddenly wake in the night in a frenzy of dread. "Imbecile," he would hear the longed-for, liberating voice exclaim, "you didn't see anything at all. And if you wake your father you'll get it, let me tell you!" Then relishing his shame, he would bury his nose under the covers, relieved of an immense burden.

Monsieur de Clergerie was a little man, dark and mournful, with the head of a rat. And his uneasiness was also that of a rat, with the same little precise movements and the perpetual agitation of their kind. Twelve boring volumes were written on his narrow face, where a secret vigilant preoccupation was always at work, now become so intimate a part of himself that he was not even aware of its existence, could not put it into intelligible words. He plotted the downfall of his rivals in his scrupulous and laborious way but without the least expenditure of hate. He believed that he was merely weighing his chances. For he had the honor of belonging to the Academy of Moral Sciences, and was now maneuvering to become a member of *the* Academy pure and simple.

But divine pity, which is present in all things, had seen to it that this little man, according to the law of his nature, would never do more than nibble and gnaw, always exercising his avid teeth on things of no value. Greatness of any kind amazed him and he avoided it in bewilderment. He hardly dared contemplate it even from a distance, and then without relish, nervously stroking his short gray beard. His malevolence, which was more like ingenious folly, was harmful only to fools less ingenious than himself. For the only strength of this ambitious midget was to admire nothing and nobody, even looking upon himself as a poor thing, but eagerly bent on hiding his nonentity. He instinctively sought out mediocrities like himself, treating them as such with a sort of terrible candor. He saw through their duplicity and was not put off for an instant by any of their pitiful defences whose flimsiness he knew so well. Every human being, no matter how miserable he may seem, has, nevertheless, his own truth. But what is the truth of others to a man who has never undertaken to discover his own?

Among his friends of the Academy and his colleagues in the world of journalism who were impressed by the grand staircase of his house in the Rue de Luynes, he was looked upon as rather an aristocrat.

Aristocrat in town, bumpkin in the country. The old village philosophers, florid with experience and many a binge, who could tell at a glance the weight of a sack of flour or the generous capacity of the belly of a young heifer, were not duped by him. Like them he was a peasant, only a peasant without lustiness, who had become a simple spectator, a bitter, disconsolate spectator of the enormous fecundity of the earth. His niggardliness delighted them. His legendary pusillanimity—for he was supposed to be equally afraid of drunks and poachers—excited their pity. They derived a malicious amusement from what they read of his works and his successes in the local papers, and without believing a word of it, they calculated the price of so much publicity. "A chip off the old block," they would say, "Nobody's fool—but a milksop"—their idea being too subtle for them to express except by a chuckle or just a wink.

There is no doubt that when fame is withheld from genius the result is a tragic experience. But unrecognized mediocrity has its calvary as well. It had been too heavy a burden for Monsieur de Clergerie. Without his suspecting it, it had been crushing him for years, and he even, unwittingly, sought diversion and a sort of morbid delectation in the memories of his youth (unhappy though they were) when at the college of Coutance he had been a scrawny boy, secretive and sickly. At that time, as a humble revenge over his lustier comrades, he had longed for nothing so much as the opulent life of a landed proprietor, or to be the mayor of his village or a county councilor. His first scholastic successes, however, had decided otherwise. After the brilliant delivery of his thesis on "The Quarrel Over Investitures," the Bishop of Bayeux, making his confirmation rounds, had deigned to take the trip to Courville, personally to congratulate the young doctor. From that moment, secretly terrified at so sudden an advancement, he began willy-nilly to play the role of a learned gentleman, benevolent counselor of orthodox society and future academician. His father's admiration gave him no rest. Although born to have a career and not a life, he nevertheless at the age of thirty married Louise d'Alliges, a lovely little fay from Provence with sea-blue eyes, sacrificed by a stupid guardian on the altar of history and archeology. She loved him with a spotless heart. Shortly afterwards she died of homesickness as she thought, but in reality out of remorse at finding him, in spite of herself, so ugly and dull and herself unworthy of him. She left a baby daughter of eighteen months, Chantal, whom grandmother de Clergerie immediately pounced upon as though retrieving stolen goods. For the old lady had always despised—but with peasant ruse and caution, and never an offensive word nor even an imprudent gesture—the sad-eyed stranger who never weighed the butter and who left her keys lying about on a corner of the table—the keys. . . .

"Mama," he said at length, "you make me very unhappy. Why do you behave like this? When you please you can be just as sensible as anyone. Francine can hear us, do you want her to laugh at you?"

"Anyone can walk right in here as though it were a mill!" the old lady remarked ponderously. "It has always been like that. You are too trusting. Like your father . . . During his lifetime, what disorder! But tell me, my boy, why am I trembling like this? Am I cold?"

"Simply because you have worked yourself into a rage, that's why."

"I can't seem to remember now," she said after a moment of silence. "Against whom? Is it possible? I have never been one to talk without due reflection. You, my son, are unhappy, very unhappy, and I know it. You have no backbone—that's the word—no more backbone than a jellyfish. And neither did *she*."

"Of whom are you talking, Mama?"

She looked at him slyly for a moment.

"The heat is not good for you, my boy," she said. "Your ears are red, all the blood is in your head. That's the whole trouble. It is nothing, nothing at all. Bah! you have never thought of anything but yourself and your health. I am sure you take your temperature twice a day the way you did when you were twenty, you remember? I threw the thermometer out of the window! You with an invalid wife, good Lord! It was the ruin of this house."

"Of whom are you talking, Mama?"

"Don't play the simpleton. What a question!"

Unconsciously he took the black-mittened hand resting on the table and held it in his own.

"You mustn't talk like that. Be nice now, Mama. I am going to ring for Francine and she will take you for a little walk before breakfast. Come!"

"You want to change the subject," she said, shaking her finger at him. "You're a sly one. Lord, but I'm tired! You see, I don't always understand your tricks right away but they come to me later. I'm used to that. It's ten years now that Louise is dead, maybe twenty! When you said to me just now: 'Don't worry, she will not be getting up today . . .' did you think I believed you? Poor darling! There is no danger of my meeting her in the halls with her beautiful white teeth and my trousseau of keys in her hand! Little fool! A trousseau of keys! Will you tell me what good they were to her? She never locked a closet, she never locked up anything."

"Why do you keep talking about it? You disliked her and that settles it."

"How can you say I disliked her!" cried the old lady nervously crossing the ends of her shawl over her breast. "It is true, though, she was greedy! What choice morsels she used to pick out of the dish right under my nose! I didn't even notice at the time . . . and now I keep thinking about them, I keep seeing them. They make me hungry. It is an obsession . . . and at my age! . . . As for you, let me tell you, you haven't the kind of health a man should have. You eat like a glutton but it doesn't do you any good. It

turns to bile. She had a horror of your yellow complexion, my poor darling. A mother sees everything. She surely blamed herself for it and confessed it as a sin. You, my boy, have never understood anything about women."

"It is possible," he said with a shrug glancing impatiently toward the door. "I only wonder what pleasure you get out of tormenting me. I have so much to do, Mama, and you know it, such a lot of work."

"Pooh!" she cried, "work! You've got to work—you've got to work to relieve your nerves. Otherwise your liver would smother you and that's what I've always said. You are not like your father. You take after my family."

She stopped suddenly and listened. As soon as the door opened her face froze and she lowered her eyes to the floor.

"Francine," said Monsieur de Clergerie blushing, "my mother will take her walk a little earlier than usual today. Be sure to keep out of the sun and take the left side of the avenue. You will go as far as the crossroad and come back slowly along the shaded walk and the hazel wood. In case Madame de Clergerie would like to rest in the shade, you had better take her cape along to throw over her shoulders."

While he was talking the old lady had become suddenly livid, and probably humiliated to the depths of her pitiful, obscure soul; she drew herself up very straight while she tried to hide the trembling of her hands under her shawl.

"I am sorry to disturb you so early, Francine," she said, "and on a Thursday too! There is so much work today. And tomorrow we have the washing. I . . ."

Slowly she stroked her temples with the ends of her pointed fingers, trying for a moment to hold back, or perhaps to recover, all those ideas floating in her tired brain, formless, colorless, and without weight or, suddenly, clamorous and buzzing like flies.

"I must go and see how the mason is getting on. Another week and he'll be busy with his work in the city and we'll never lay eyes on him again. You know very well it is always like that at this season of the year . . . We used to go ourselves to the brickyard for our supply of bricks. Figure it out for yourself . . . A hundred bricks came to ten *sous*. The Dervault's barn, including the roof, cost us three thousand *francs.*"

Again her hands began to tremble with fatigue and disappeared under the knitted wool. With a final effort that made the yellow-haired maid smile cruelly, she pressed her lips tightly together to keep back the absurd words, the dangerous and importunate words that she felt rising to her lips and that her will could no longer control; her forehead damp and her eyes clouded again but still hard, she gave her son a vague smile, and, inscrutable, walked slowly out of the room with little steps.

Monsieur de Clergerie beckoned to Francine and in lowered voice said:

"Let my mother walk ahead of you if she likes, do not seem to be watching her, keep away from her unless she calls you. And I must also beg you once more to speak cautiously among yourselves in her presence. Old age has undoubtedly weakened her memory, but her intelligence and will remain intact; she understands everything, will understand everything you are saying when you would least expect it. You know that, don't you? I am sure I can rely on you, Francine . . . And will you please tell Mademoiselle Chantal when she returns from mass that I wish to see her."

"Yes, Sir . . . Indeed, Sir, I promise you may count on me, Sir . . ." the girl repeated, shaking her blond head with a comically wise air.

She left the room and catching up with her mistress at the door of the kitchen, with perfect composure, and without raising or lowering her voice said coolly:

"You'll have to finish the stairs, François, I must take the old vixen for a walk."

The valet turned his pale face toward her for an instant and then went on staring at his resplendent leather slippers.

"All right," he said, "and you might throw her into the frog pond while you're about it. You'll get a smile from Fiodor."

The old lady had gone to her usual place in a dark corner of the kitchen, her face turned toward the window, on the alert. For days and days she had shared in this morning diversion, her heart faint with wretchedness, the insulting words that she understood perfectly striking her like so many blows. But, although she made a desperate effort, she found it impossible to separate them from her reveries, from the monotonous ruminations of her clouded memory. Had they really been spoken? Or did she only imagine them as she imagined so many things known only to herself and incommunicable? In vain, from under her cautiously lowered eyelids, she watched their lips, in vain she tried to catch the insult on the wing, almost before it was formed, spending in this immense effort all her patience and her guile. Useless struggle. She saw the sardonic twist of the lips of those impassible faces and long after, it seemed to her, the brutal words struck her—too late, much too late. In spite of herself, she was deceived by their deferential attitude that lied. The incredibility of such a torture made it seem like a nightmare. Except when she was in the presence of her son her life presented such enigmas she dared not try to solve, fearing to feel her reason totter. One day, her patience exhausted, she had slapped the yellow-haired chambermaid and the general consternation and the pity she read in all their faces wounded her pride more cruelly than any insult. Since then she suffered without complaining with the vigilance and tenacity of an animal.

"Listen to what I say," continued the valet, "and don't forget it, Beautiful. Even without the vixen this house is getting to be impossible. Me for Paris! Fiodor cleaned me out last night. We played until morning."

"You better take a look at yourself in the glass," replied the girl coolly. "You're ruining your health.

The boy from Falaise with his lantern that wants to show Monsieur Fiodor what's what!"

"*Monsieur* Fiodor, . . . *Monsieur* Fiodor . . . Why Monsieur? . . . A former Russian officer—and so what? You think I'm just a hayseed, don't you? Why, at the Baroness Voinard's, I saw guys just as classy as Fiodor, like the head butler. He was from Mont-de-Marsan, and had been a seminarist. He paid five louis apiece for his ties."

"Come, come, François," said a soft melodious voice at the door, "don't bother about me, old man. What's the good of getting jealous. It's vulgar . . . Mademoiselle Chantal has just come in. I suppose you have to take out the old lady, Francine?"

The chambermaid blushed, shrugged her shoulders and taking her mistress by the arm went slowly up the steps to the garden.

"That little girl is a fool," François remarked shaking the sand out of his precious slippers.

"Not at all," replied Fiodor. "Why a fool? The trouble is she is losing her naturalness . . . how do you say it? . . . anyway, she is losing her nature . . . And it's hideous. How I adored her! She was like something that came out of a box of toys with a dairy, trees and little wooden cows. I assure you she positively smelt of varnish."

François was so surprised he nearly forgot his slippers for an instant.

"Well, that's a bit thick," he exclaimed. "Who bought her eye pencils and powder and rouge anyway, I'd like to know! You hypocrite! And now you've made her drink ether. She pretty nearly killed herself."

"Whose fault is it?" Fiodor went on in his soft voice. "That is my nature, I admit it. Everyone should defend his nature. That's ethics. Why didn't she defend hers? Here no one defends his nature, it makes me sick, neither Francine, nor you, nor Monsieur de Clergerie, no one. As for our historian, I have read his books. He is undoubtedly a man of some consequence, but without the slightest insight! (Oh, damn those odious slippers, can't you think of anything else?) Now listen to me, this bourgeois house that seems so dignified and sound is eaten up by insects."

"What!" . . .

"Insects!" repeated the chauffeur angrily. "Exactly!"

"Monsieur Fiodor," said François, "you're killing yourself with dope; you ought to be locked up—yes—for your own sake. I have always said that it's the government's duty to protect a man from his own weakness. A superior guy like you going in for such stuff, it's all wrong!"

"You don't quite get me," replied the former Russian officer, languidly tapping his mouth with his finger tips to hide a yawn. "You don't understand insects. My own immense country has been devoured by insects. Insects will finally get the better of the whole earth, remember that. You, my friend, are gentlemanly by nature, but if you will pardon me, you lack education. I am afraid to go on speaking so frankly."

"What insects are you talking about? Mildew? Weevils? Or what?"

"I am not joking. As I see it, there are two persons here who live according to their natures, good or bad: the old lady and the young lady. The others are insects."

"You're kidding, Monsieur Fiodor."

"Not at all, I assure you. By no means. They are simply outside of life. I myself am outside, but, I beg to point out, with me it is voluntary. I wonder if one day I shall enter life again. At the moment we can do nothing but devour one another. Such is the power of deceit! What could that respectable old gentleman have been thinking of to introduce a servant like me into his home? Is this a place for me will you tell me? And yet he wouldn't think of putting his nose inside a night club. He goes to bed at nine-thirty! But, naturally, as I was recommended by Countess Daveluy. . . . What a snob! And he wants to be magnanimous. Have you heard the way he talks to me? But he is afraid of me, too . . . I drive like the devil when I'm in the mood. What a life! The rest of you are afraid of me too, and I, in a way, I am afraid of you. We are mutually afraid of one another because we only know one another's lies. What are they hiding? What trap? Why do you play poker and get drunk on whisky and horrible dry champagne—aping the gentlemen at the club? And that charming child, why ether? Why these lies? I admit that neither the old lady nor the young lady are afraid. That's because, the one is full of hate and sin; the other is a child. She'd only have to whistle through her milk teeth and you'd see an angel appear on the top of the wall, a real little angel as light as thistledown."

"You're drunk," calmly remarked the valet who for some time had been cleaning his nails with his penknife. "Every man to his own vice. But you'll have to admit that wine, after all, isn't as bad."

Monsieur Fiodor opened his red mouth in a silent laugh.

"I am not afraid of wine either," he said. "What nonsense! I've been babbling too much, and I am sorry to have bored you. Now I must go and have a look at the old bus. I am to meet the 6:30 train—a guest."

"Who is it? I haven't had any orders, neither has Francine."

"You will, don't get excited, my friend, be calm. You ought rather to be sympathizing with me. I have to make some tedious repairs. I'll be swimming in grease. But if you like, I'll give you the orders myself. You are to make up the—what the devil do you call it—the canary-room, that's it! What a name! At any rate, the room that opens into the library, the bedroom for the guests who work."

"I get you," said the valet. "I know who you mean. There aren't so many writers coming here, and since the Auvergnian is dead there are only two others you could be talking about, either Mazenet or Abbé Cénabre."

"You win. It's Abbé Cénabre. I even have to take him around through Dorville. And by the way, why plain Mazenet, François, bu *Abbé* Cénabre?"

"Why, I don't know," said the other blushing. "Just a notion. It came out like that. Aren't you the slick one—always looking for things . . ."

Fiodor stretched his arms toward the ceiling with a little groan of pleasure and walked over to the window which was still in the shade. The reflection from the green lawn bathed in sunlight made his smooth-shaven cheeks look paler than ever, his face more melancholy. The immense stretch of garden was reflected for a second at the back of his expressionless eyes. Then a bee struck the window pane with the sound of a bullet.

"Look at them," he said and his voice was soft again. "Look, over there, my friend, coming around the hedge, both of them. I am sure the old lady is listening to the birds, and she is hard pressed to love them, for truly, her stony old heart has never felt anything for anybody . . . Seriously, what do you make of this house and its masters, François? What do you think?"

"What do I think? Why, nothing. What should I think? It's a better run house than most. Scholars, academicians, rich landowners, almost no women—it's all right."

"I tell you it is being eaten away by insects," Monsieur Fiodor persisted with the same confidential air. "Yes, believe me, you are going to see astonishing things."

"It's already screwy enough to see you here," answered the valet, reddening again.

"François!" said Mademoiselle de Clergerie.

She had just put her head in at the half-open door and only her ash-blond hair, her bright eyes, and the brighter glow of her teeth could be seen.

"I wanted to ask you to call Francine," she said, "but she is probably out with my grandmother. It was only to tell her to get the canary-room ready for this evening. That was all. Or perhaps Fiodor has already told you?"

She had walked over to the table while she was speaking, resting her hand on the edge, and now looked at the handsome Russian with serene eyes.

"I am sorry, Mademoiselle Chantal," he said stiffly. "It was not in my line of duties. I had no orders."

"Heavens!" she cried. "Orders—you didn't need orders! Anyway, I'm sure you acted for the best as usual. You knew already, didn't you, François?"

"You have guessed right, Mademoiselle Chantal," the valet replied quickly with a smile. "I know that Abbé Cénabre is arriving by the 6:30 train."

"Very well! So that's settled. We need say no more about it. You will find sheets in the linen closet and toilet articles and soap. But what awful soap! The whole place reeks of it."

"Francine chose it herself the other day at Falaise," said François, "I made exactly the same observation. I know about such things. But the last order from Guerlain's came yesterday. I'll get a hammer and open the case right away."

He disappeared so quickly (intentionally, perhaps) that Mademoiselle de Clergerie could not suppress a movement of surprise—perhaps of dread. But almost at once she put her little hand down quietly on the table again.

"I must tell you," began the strange chauffeur, not a muscle of his impassive face moving, "I owe you an explanation . . ."

"You owe me no explanation, Fiodor," she interrupted. "My father is satisfied. That is enough. Do you wish to complain of anyone?"

"No," the man said, "but allow me to point out that I cannot without your permission risk offending you by an excess of frankness, an ill-advised frankness."

She shook her head. "Frankness is never ill-advised," she said. "Frankness cannot offend me."

He met her pure and scarcely troubled gaze, and tried to hold it with his own, but only succeeded in making a kind of grimace, painful and at the same time cruel.

"I cannot leave this house!" he murmured, "and yet, I cannot endure your scorn any longer."

The blood rushed to her cheeks.

"And I," she said, without trying to dissimulate the altered tone of her voice, "I have done nothing that gives you the right to say such things to me. No, I have done nothing. You must at least realize that the very tone of your voice is a bitter humiliation and wholly unmerited. Are you not ashamed to take advantage like this of a pretended secret which is yours only because you have stolen it? You must, you must go away!"

"Where should I go?" he said, and the childlike cadence of his voice contrasted strangely with the obstinate and crafty expression of his face. "Where do you want me to go? If there is the least chance left for me to redeem my soul, that chance is here. You can perform that miracle whenever you like. For those holy hands, anything is possible."

"These holy hands!" she murmured bravely, forcing herself to smile while her eyes filled with tears.

Suddenly she blushed furiously, but it was as much from anger as from shame.

"You cannot have spoken! No, it is not possible that you have dared to speak!"

"To whom would I have spoken?" he replied quietly. "Who is there here who would understand? And again, allow me to point out—you said just now, 'frankness never offends me,' I believed you. My words may displease you, but I acted in good faith. What I have seen, I have seen. What difference does it make whether I was worthy of seeing it or not? Am I already so lost to grace in this world that I have not even the right to admire God's works? We are children—all of us Russians are children."

"God knows," she said in a low voice, "the evil you do in wilfully pronouncing His name because of me. God's works! If there is the least grace left in your baptized soul, remorse would now seal your lips. Besides, there is no question of God's works. There is only a poor sick girl whom you caught unaware, and on whom you have spied ever since with diabolical malice, yes! . . . or at least with the most cruel curiosity. Not that I am afraid of being ridiculous! I really don't care about that. But don't you understand, I am needed here? I am still, for my father, both common sense and reason, as well as a sure ally. I know how easily he is terrified, how apprehensive he is. He would think that I was completely crazy, and perhaps he would be right . . . But you . . . What possible interest can you have in . . . in . . ."

"In miracles?" he said. "Real miracles that fall from you like flowers. I am a vile wretch, I do not believe in God. Yet why was it I who found you that first night when I was not even looking for you, why was it I rather than someone else? For anyone might have opened the door. Why was it I? And if words like *saint* and *ecstasy* have any meaning, you were a saint in ecstasy."

Discouraged, she shook her head, but without anger.

"How can I trust you? The nonsense you hold back today you will reveal tomorrow, in self-interest or through vanity or for the simple pleasure of doing harm. What a coward I am to contend with you over this miserable secret. How much better to acknowledge everything at once, if only I had the courage. I have been told that my poor mother suffered from such nervous attacks—the same or others, what difference does it make? Then why not speak? But you see I haven't the courage, the least ordeal is too much for me."

She wiped away the tears running down her cheeks with both hands, like a little girl.

"I can't stand it any longer. This perpetual restraint is killing me. I hardly dare to breathe. To have to play a part like this, unwillingly, in spite of myself—how horrible! I am not a child and I know very well how disgraceful such a breach of confidence is in a man. If you were the man you pretend to be you would already be far away from here."

At these words she grew suddenly so pale that compassion got the better of him, and, out of decency, he turned his eyes away.

"Humiliate me!" he said. "I am a vile wretch, I know, full of vices, but I am also an unhappy one. You have pity for everything and everybody, you smile at everything, even at the leaves of the trees, even at the flies. And yet for me you have only words of contempt."

"No, not contempt," she cried, "pity! Because I know you to be a liar, and there is nothing that God hates so much as a liar. I may not have had much experience or be very clever, but I know that you hate your own soul and that you would kill it if you could."

"It is truly a rather heavy burden," he replied coldly. "Nevertheless, what I have seen here in the past three weeks makes it easier to bear. You are pleased to say that I spy on you. You should realize, rather, that without me what you want so much to hide would already be known to everybody . . . Yesterday again . . ."

"It isn't true!" she said, trembling. "You only want to frighten me."

"Very well, I will say no more. Let me only add this: I am, after all, merely a servant in your house like any other. One word from you and your father would discharge me. You know that very well too. It would not be difficult to find a pretext."

Again she forced him to lower his eyes.

"I am not capable of such a thing and you know it," she said sadly. "Besides, my father is not a man to discharge anyone . . . And if I don't think of his peace of mind, who will? The tiniest worry is too much for him, you know that too."

Her expression softened suddenly and he saw with surprise, almost with terror, an indefinable look come into her eyes, both shrewd and mocking, as strange as a word in a foreign language.

"You will get tired of waiting for miracles," she said. "You will even get tired of inventing them. You will get tired of everything, even of other people's pain. It seems to me that evil is much less complicated than you would like to believe. Here or anywhere else there is only one sin."

"What sin?"

"To tempt God," she said. "And what's the use? I think you are really very stupid. God looks where he pleases. If he has not yet looked at you, what is the use of tempting him?"

"I . . . well really . . . I never thought of that."

He tried to laugh, but his face was contorted by the same painful grimace. Chantal's expression had regained its calm and her eyes shone with a light so pure that no one would have imagined they had ever been troubled.

At that moment the cook came into the kitchen carrying in her arms an enormous bunch of carrots still covered with rich brown earth.

"Ah, no, Fernande!" cried the young girl laughing. "Not creamed carrots again. Really! My father can't bear the sight of them."

"But I showed the master the menu for today, and he said it was all right," said the wily Norman, as rose and gold as her carrots.

"And he never even read your menu, I am sure. My poor Fernande, from now on we'll just bury all creamed dishes, you and I. We must respect other people's tastes. But I don't have to tell you that, you, a cook of the old school. And besides, between ourselves, Fernande, isn't Norman cooking a bit—what would you say—a bit naïve, a bit insipid! We are accused of being too prodigal of home recipes that reek of the farm. You can gorge on them, but that isn't eating."

"Eating . . . Will you please tell me what difference that makes to Monsieur de Clergerie? He nibbles on some toast and then drowns it in a quart of mineral water. And you, Mademoiselle, it's beyond me how anyone with such refined tastes can take so little pleasure in her food. For the last two months you've eaten like a bird."

"Oh, it's only because I am more of a *gourmet* than you think!"

"*Gourmet!* And those *filets de sole au Chambertin* last Friday? The famous *filets de sole au Chambertin* that I had dinned into my ears all one morning. Be careful of this and be careful of that. And at dinner you didn't hardly touch a mouthful . . . Well, Mademoiselle, do you want me to tell you something?"

"No, don't tell me, Fernande! My father for the moment is very much concerned with the reputation of his table. And he is right. God knows that we should not despise anything. We must do our best. Have you noticed how all of us, how especially men, are sad as soon as they stop talking, as soon as they are alone? Would you believe it, Fernande, when I was little I used to cry sometimes to see them so sad . . . Yes, men are sad. Women, you see, have all sorts of little desires, silly joys. So a cook who takes pride in her cooking and knows her job, is not useless, far from it. Our good dinners may not be worth a sermon, but what of that? Civic duties differ! And ours today is not an easy one! Eleven guests tonight, my poor Fernande, on a Friday, too! Never mind. Monsieur de Clergerie will be satisfied, you'll see. So here is our dinner menu and I'll not change another comma. To begin with, *Potage de Carême . . .*"

"Ah, no . . . not that!"

"Sh! don't worry. It will turn out all right this time. You must not forget the *croûtons au parmesan.* Don't let your dough get altogether cold, that's very important, otherwise it will be too brittle, hard to shape, and will look horrid. And be sure to moisten your butter with white wine before putting in your carp roe and skate livers. So, that's that for the soup. Then there'll be broiled shad with sorrel, and a *pâté de saumon* in honor of Monsignor Espelette who adores it."

The cook was carefully rolling up her sleeves above the elbow and, without taking her eyes off her young mistress's face, said simply:

"You'll never convince me, Mademoiselle, that you are the least bit interested in all that. You're only pretending."

"Pretending what, Fernande?"

"Well, that's my idea," repeated the fat cook shaking her head. "Besides this house is getting impossible . . . Monsieur de Clergerie has, of course, the right to choose his servants where he pleases, but I can't, for the life of me, see why he goes to Paris agencies instead of getting them right around here like his late father always did. Believe me, Mademoiselle, I've had plenty of experience, I've been a widow twice . . . I know something about life. But people like that one, I just can't understand—the one just went out. I tell you, Mademoiselle, he's crazy, completely gone. He ought to be locked up. Oh, I'm not taken in by all his fine talk, not at my age, I'm not! Naturally they don't say much when I'm around—they're all innocence! But I've got sharp ears and I keep them open. You mark my words, we're going to see such things as never happen even in books."

"Oh, Fernande, please!" said Chantal in a choking voice.

She had been unable to control a sudden start, perhaps of nervousness, perhaps of fear, and now stood there very pale, her eyes grown somber and almost hard.

"You frighten me, Fernande," she answered. "I really don't know what is the matter with me. It is you who are crazy."

But the cook looked at her for a moment without replying, her head cocked on one side with frank peasant curiosity.

"My, how you reminded me of your mother," she said finally. "I would have sworn it was her in those last days, poor lady, so jumpy and upset for nothing at all, her poor little hand always on her heart—she was a saint. Your grandmother was a fine, tall woman at that time . . . Oh me, Oh my! You can say what you like but there's nothing like health. Health gets around anything."

"You will call me for luncheon, Fernande," Chantal cut short, her voice still unsteady. "Please call me promptly at eleven o'clock."

And she noiselessly closed the door.

2

THE joy of day, day in flower, a dazzling August morning with all its overtones and luster (but already autumn's perfidious aromatics in the oppressive air) burst into all the windows of the endless sunporch with their red and green panes. It was the joy of day, but through some inexplicably perishable splendor it was also the joy of just one day, that unique day, so delicate and fragile in its implacable serenity, when for the first time, at the very height of the summer, the insidious mist appeared still floating above the horizon, but which in a few weeks would descend over the exhausted earth, the dried-up fields, the dormant water full of the odor of dead leaves.

With her light, even and unhurried step, the young girl crossed the flood of sunlight and only stopped when she reached the shady entrance-hall with its closed shutters. She was listening to her heart beating, surely not in terror, nor in vain curiosity, since for weeks and weeks now, without her even being aware of it, each hour of her life was full and perfect, and it seemed to her that nothing she might do could add anything or take anything away . . . Hours out of the past, so like hours of her childhood—even that marvelous feeling of suspense was not lacking that used to give her the sensation of running breathlessly on the edge of an enchanted precipice. Deep delights, more secret than the deep heart's beat! High up in the Pyrenees, on a dizzy path, looking down out of the coach windows into the rosy chasm where eagles were always circling, joyously, the favorite daughter of Sainte Thérèse would exclaim: "I can only fall into God!" Hours out of the past, perhaps, but she had lost any desire to seize them as they went by, to look for whatever joy or sadness they might contain, as one breaks a fruit in half.

At first she had thought, and that is what she wanted to go on believing, that this sort of happy indifference, this happy somnolence of desire, was nothing more than a child's miraculous carefreeness and purity. But the death of her confessor, Abbé Chevance, had irreparably marked, marked forever, the decisive step; and no matter how she tried to ignore it, the corpse like a vigilant guardian kept watch on the threshold of this new peace. "I give you my joy," she had said. She had truly given him her joy and had received another from his old, death-tied hands. She accused herself, it is true, of indifference, coldness, but try as she would, it did not trouble her, she felt no remorse. Her conscience was clear, she did not feel at fault,—or, if fault there were, it was nature's fault, her ineffable poverty. But who can be troubled by poverty in the hands of a Lord richer than any king. Long before she had confided in anyone, before she had been aware of it herself, poverty, a supernatural, fundamental poverty, had shone over her childhood like a little friendly star with a soft and steady light. As far back as she could remember the exquisite feeling of her own weakness had been a great comfort to her and a marvelous consolation. It seemed to her like an ineffable sign of the presence of God, God himself who shone in her heart. She believed that she had never desired anything beyond her power to accomplish, and yet, any effort in the end was always easier than she had anticipated, as though divine compassion had miraculously gone before.

Until now, until the last few weeks at least, there had been nothing to endanger this humble felicity, nor to trouble her certainty of having been born for easy labors scorned by greater souls, nor to test that sort of quizzical intuitiveness which always surprised the less thoughtful, and whose secret was known to Abbé Chevance alone. And it had taken that simple, stubborn old man a long time to penetrate this secret, for he had been afraid to question her, dreaded above all (in his impatience to understand and to admire) to wound such a soul in that most vulnerable place where, unknown to anyone, and in a silence purer than the immense stellar silence, the divine union, the incomparable acquiescence, is consummated. He may even at one time have run the risk of being caught in the snare innocently spread by that clear and profound conscience, of thinking that his little penitent was less indifferent to society than he had supposed, to worldly success, to the bourgeois luxury of her father's academic drawing-room that the former parish priest of Costerel-sur-Meuse ingenuously considered (as it was by reputation) magnificent. Anyone else might have been unduly worried by the gowns signed *Berthe Hermance*, the *Rose et Lewis* hats, and even the gray squirrel coat which she had such a charming way of wrapping around her with one of those quick, confident movements of her slender arms . . . But by some premonition of genius he had already recognized in her what he had so long been seeking in the empty, noisy world where he wandered like a stranger—the spirit, the radiant spirit of trust and complete surrender. "What do you want me to do?" she would say to him. "Am I able to choose? I should never dare. I accept each hour of the day God gives me because I should never have the strength to refuse it. I accept it with closed eyes, the way I used to listen every Saturday evening, when I was still at the convent, to the reading of my weekly report. When I open my eyes I see that I have been spared once more, safe for another while." And she also said: "I am lucky to be a little short of breath, it makes me walk slowly up the hills."

She had not changed since then, but in whom now could she confide? The old priest had taken something away with him. Or at least, it was as though a precious part of herself had been engulfed in his silent and solemn death which had been so incomprehensible to her. Not divine hope which was the very source of her life, not that innocent sense of security subtler and more certain than any calculations of uneasy souls. But he had gone, the rude master, who in receiving her joy had, until then, kept her from feeling the full weight of this supernatural burden. Now she must accept it, take possession of it, possess it altogether. O fountain of suavity!

She had accepted this ordeal with her usual simple grace, and without the least fear. Being convinced that peace was hers only because of an extraordinary caprice of God, she felt no complaisance over this unlooked-for discovery in which, unsuspected by her, lurked an insidious peril. To keep nothing for herself, to spend from day to day the alms that fell from heaven, had been for so long her one anxiety and only care—and why should she be parsimonious—what for? The only thing that mattered was to keep an accurate accounting for the old priest. And, impenetrable in his extraordinary gentleness, he waited patiently for the measure to be full, for God to reveal himself to that heart which already overflowed with him unaware. Sometimes this confessor of men would shrug his shoulders, half serious, half jesting, saying in his Meusian accent: "You were indeed born prodigal, my daughter! The rest of us, you see, know too many pious souls who hoard and have to be taught to spend. That warps our judgment. What a pity! Nothing is worse than to disdain God's grace, but it should not be economized penny by penny either, ah no! Because, you understand, my daughter, our Master is very rich."

And another day he said an even stranger thing which, although she failed to grasp its full meaning, marvelously consoled her, and seemed to give her a glimpse into the future where she discovered, beyond the inevitable trials whose nature and duration it was impossible to guess, security and peace.

"Certain people would find me too weak with you, or too presumptuous; that suits me perfectly. I am not sorry. My daughter, if I should come to fail you too soon, I forbid you to change hastily anything in the ordering of our modest life. Remember that ours is a modest life. It must be written in a colloquial style whose only key, if there be a key, God holds."

Once or twice, when she had adroitly avoided an opportunity of pleasing or winning admiration (for her shrewd wit and vivacity made her popular), she was astonished at his disapproval. "But after all," she said, "what do you know about the world, an old hermit like you! Do you want me to become vain and flirtatious or what?" Blushing he had replied: "I will tell you, my daughter. I used to try very hard to be admired, to be liked. That is the world!" Then, with that profound finesse which no one had ever had the wit to recognize in the former priest of Costerel-sur-

Meuse, he at once added, "I had more to fear from the world than you have."

That was an evening of the winter before. The pale light glowed on the window pane of his modest room, crept up to the shabby table where he leaned on his elbows, one hand making a vague gesture in the air. And suddenly all the light of the dying day shone in his eyes and in a clear, strong voice, he had said to her:

"My little daughter, I know what is necessary for you. It will come in good time, for souls have their seasons. Yes, their own seasons. I am an old Meusian peasant and I know each season. Frost comes even in May. Does it prevent our plum trees flowering? Does the dear God husband his springtime, measure the sun and the showers? Let him be lavish, squander his substance. I am only an old fellow without much judgment or experience, but at least I know that, and it is something the Reverend Father Riancourt has never thought of . . . Or should I say, *perhaps* he never thought of it . . . Oh! the Jesuits, how subtle and clever they are! They are certainly an honor to the church. But look at it this way now: they are like agricultural engineers, they have methods, they are very scientific, they have their methods . . . The poor tenant farmer also has good ideas provided he doesn't go beyond his field. Ah yes, my daughter, there comes a time when we should aid our Lord in his prodigalities. We receive a hundred favors for one. What is the use, the world reasons, of paying three times the price for such a simple, ordinary life that seems to be at everybody's disposal? Ah! one mustn't be too hasty! One never pays too high a price for the favor of living unnoticed!— For the moment, at least, God wishes people to see only your flowers! Yes, it is God's wish, my daughter, that you finish blossoming to the full. There is no fruit without pain, and no matter how gentle the hand, when the fruit is picked, you will feel it. Until then try to be so docile and so supple in the divine hands that no one will suspect. For it is the mark of a great love that it remains hidden for a long time. . . . Look at the girls of my province, the girls of Lorraine. . . ."

When she burst out laughing, saying she hadn't such good eyesight as that, he shrugged with mock impatience.

"You can laugh, my daughter . . . but the joke is on the Paris girls. They sing before the sun has risen, like the blackbirds. But our girls of Lorraine, Ah! how thoughtful they are, how wise! My late mother, three years before she was even betrothed, said to our great-uncle, the Dean of Mondreville: "I will never marry anyone but Gilbert, the cooper!" (My late father was a cooper by trade.) And Gilbert himself didn't know a thing about it; she had never even dared look straight at him, holy daughter of God! But they were a good couple in life and in death, right to the end, because the root went deep; the root had grown underground before the branch had flowered. That is the way God wants us to love him. Let them say of you: 'She is so gentle, so good, and so gay! It is a pleasure to see her. She makes everybody want to be good!' I pray that even when you belong altogether to our Lord, no one will dream in whose hands you are held."

Alas, since then she had seen her old friend's eyes gradually grow dim and finally turn away toward the other side of the night. She had heard his voice mixed with the death-rattle suddenly become that of a stranger, and that death, so lonely, so denuded, was not at all as she had imagined it would be. Had it been the supreme test of the obscure saint, the forsaken man, or only the master's final lesson to his little pupil, the solemn warning? Feeling himself borne so quickly toward the night, had he feared that there was too little time to prepare the heroic child for the arduous experiences of the inner life, for the fundamental deception which sooner or later must temper a heart predestined for God. It is true that she had until now, through a sure instinct, refused to let her thoughts dwell too long on a problem whose solution she knew would always escape her, was out of reach of reason and all human hypotheses—could be found only in God. Yet out of that frenzy of sadness, that immense solitude, still hardly more than a presage, as she kept watch by the corpse she honored as that of a saint, a sort of phantom had appeared which lacked some of the features of the living man, and whose silent appeal was not as clear to her. She remembered certain things he had said as, for example, that although divine love was a thousand times more strict and obdurate than justice, yet God might for a long time grant us the grace of loving us as we love little children . . . But the time comes when we learn—at the price of what anguish!—that the most inhuman of man's passions finds its ineffable image in Him, and that, as the ancient Jews divined without understanding, He is a jealous God.

A jealous God! . . . In God that brooding, rigorous passion, that fierce avidity of his creature? She could not yet believe it—or perhaps it was too bold, too sublime a vision from which she had turned away her eyes. Besides the word had no meaning for her, seemed almost mad. She was not jealous of anyone, and it seemed to her, after the most searching self-questioning, that she could never be the object of jealousy, even of divine jealousy, for day by day she felt herself less capable of refusing anything, certain that she possessed nothing. Her life was so simple, governed by monotonous daily duties, that she thought she was in no danger—more through necessity than virtue—of ever getting far from the exact place where the most exacting master would look for her. For that was another of Abbé Chevance's profoundly sagacious teachings: the importance of remaining as near as possible to the precise spot where God has left us, and where he can find us at his pleasure. Man's supreme misfortune is his instability.

In her new solitude, therefore, she had scrupulously

tried not to take a single step beyond the familiar path until she should have found another guide comparable to the one she had lost. To do easy things perfectly was not only the desire but the need of this gentle and inflexible will which Abbé Chevance had made more supple with such infinite art. It is true that she certainly had no idea of so marvelous a power, and now the unforgotten voice that could command it at will was silent. How can an intrepid heart tell what is easy when the impossible is not beyond its reach? And what temptation could have been more subtle and perfidious? How could she have known that, for months and months, the only care of her humble friend had been to moderate the momentum of her mighty ascension or, at least, to keep her from perceiving the immense arc of her flight, and the void growing little by little under her wings? That serenity which she had always accepted as the sign of her weakness, of her nature's mediocrity, she began to fear. Then, having made an effort to tear herself from that equanimity, once she had lost it she would look for it once more; but then, discovering in it new delights, yesterday unknown, would flee it again.

What delights other than a supernatural sadness, in which sensibility played no part—consumed entirely in the soul's most secret depths. "You have never been so gay," Monsieur de Clergerie would sometimes remark with unaccountable irritation. Was it true then? What was this invisible spring, this bitter freshness that was hers alone? What name would Abbé

Chevance have given it? Whenever she tried to question her lost friend, so useless to her now, there arose in the tenderest place in her memory that final image of him—the somber eyes that seemed emptied of all tears, the line of the mouth, the enormous weariness of the arms flung out on the blood-stained quilt. Ah no! that was not where she must look for him . . . Then, without intending to, without understanding, because she rejected that ardent sadness, that vain gift of tears whose illusion she feared, because she could no longer hope to find the old priest anywhere but in his eternal rest—in God—she would slip into prayer as into an enchanted sleep.

Prayers? But were they? To tell the truth she did not know, nor would she have dared give a name to what was for her only a strange suspension of pain and joy, a slow melting of the one and the other into a unique, indefinable sentiment made up of tenderness and trust, an uneasy and yet suave quest, and something else resembling that same sublime pity she had so often seen shining in her old master's tired eyes. Moreover she admitted willingly that she could never keep her mind on those little themes proffered by pious authors, too enamored of definitions and formulas, whose imaginations are not equal to their zeal. "Don't ask me," Abbé Chevance would say, "What's the use? What difference does it make to you whether they are prayers or not? What difference does it make to me so long as I realize in you, day by day, the order of charity. *Ingressa igitur cuncta per ordinem ostia* . . . After Esther had passed through all the doors in order, she presented herself before the king where he resided."

Alas! Who would open the doors for her now? Who would hold out a friendly hand at each new threshold? Had not the final grief of the dying man been to realize too late that the sweet ignorance in which he had allowed his daughter to remain would suddenly when he was gone be changed into a fearful solitude. "How well God has hidden Himself in you!" in a trembling voice he had once exclaimed. "Let Him rest there!" He had taken with him into the shadows of death his portion of her secret, and her own she would now be incapable of revealing to anyone, for she herself was too far from understanding what was being accomplished in her. It is true that the apparent mediocrity of her confessions, their insignificance, worried her a little, and she blamed herself for enlightening the Dean of Idouville so badly. He had known her since childhood and still treated her each summer as though she were a school girl on vacation . . . But what should she tell him? How describe a submission to God so perfect, so ingenuous that it could hardly be distinguished from the modest tenor of her life . . . She could find nothing new that was worth revealing except that sort of agitation of the soul, too fundamental, too profound for words, comparable to a thunderstorm of which nothing remains but a furtive light in the limpid sky, and an almost imperceptible vibration in the glowing air.

And yet, without realizing it, she had already taken the decisive step and had started through a strange country, outside the frontiers of her ancient paradise, alone. Anyone but this fearless little girl would undoubtedly have been overwhelmed by the realization of her solitude, and, terrified, would have fled to the final refuge of a convent. But too long accustomed to seek peace only in God, she was incapable of running away, incapable of evasion before the appointed hour, ready to meet it face to face, her gaze as firm and determined in its implacable purity as that of a brave man. Her admirable efforts, spontaneous and almost unconscious, not to retreat within herself, not to depreciate herself, the necessity of enlisting all at once all the forces of her heart, like a general-in-chief his regiments against an enemy whose position and plans he does not know, had in a few weeks completely transformed her. Like a man who, having fallen asleep at sunrise, wakes in the brutal light of noon with the serenity of dawn still in his eyes, the world, which had been no more than a mysterious word to her, was through intuition and the flowering and radiation of pity, now revealed not to her experience, but to her charity. Only the blind of spirit believe that evil is known to those wretches alone who let themselves, little by little, be devoured by it, who at the end of their mournful labors have only known sin's precarious pleasures, its dull melancholy, its obscure and sterile rumination. Oh vain fall, oh cries never to be heard by the living, cold messengers of the shoreless night. If hell has no answer for the questioning dead, it is not because it refuses to answer (for rigorous, alas, in observance, is the imperishable fire), but it is because hell has nothing to say, will say nothing eternally.

Only a certain purity, a certain simplicity, the divine ignorance of saints, catching evil off its guard, can penetrate its thickness, penetrate the thickness of immemorial deceit. To know man's truth one must, through a miracle of compassion, embrace his pain, and what does it matter whether one knows its impure source or not? "All I know about sin," the Saint of Ars would say, "I have learned from the lips of sinners." And what had he heard, the venerable and sublime child, among all those shameful confidences, all the inexhaustible babble, but the groan and death rattle of spent passion which in the end breaks the hardest hearts. And can any understanding of evil equal insight into pain? Is there anything that can go beyond pity?

Thus Chantal thought that her peace was still intact, her joy untarnished, when already the mysterious wound had opened from which flowed a more human, a more carnal charity, revealing God in man, confounding through the same supernatural compassion the one with the other. Too personal, too deep a transformation of the soul's life to show any outward signs, it had come gradually, imperceptibly, had arisen slowly in her heart. She was not, it is true, ignorant of evil and had never pretended to be. She was both too sensitive and too spirited to try to hide from herself, like so many would-be innocents, certain doubts and disgusts; her rectitude had always proved too strong. Her premonition of sin with all its degradation and its wretchedness had until now been vague and indeterminate, because it takes the heartbreaking experience of being deceived in our admirations or our friendships to reveal the tragic secret of evil, to lay bare its hidden spring, that fundamental hypocrisy, not of attitudes but of intentions, which makes the life of many men a hideous drama whose key they have lost, a prodigy of fraud and duplicity, a living death. But who can deceive anyone who believes that she possesses nothing, deserves nothing, depending wholly on the indulgence and charity of others? Who can deceive such joyous humility? The dying agony of the old priest had, nevertheless, accomplished this miracle.

That was, indeed, the only deception Chantal had ever known, and the only one that could have found the vulnerable spot, could have daunted her naïve felicity. She had never thought that God could ever fail her, and yet on that memorable night had she not looked for him in vain? He remained invisible and silent. Just as babies who have seen only smiling human faces look at the first frown with amazed curiosity but without the least fear, the bitterness of such a death had in no way weakened her trust, even though the memory of it was like a shadow between herself and the divine presence, unique source of all her joy. What then was falsehood's power that it could so alter before men's miserable eyes even the countenance of saints? And suddenly, like those too bright, too dazzling landscapes suddenly submerged by the twilight, which, when slowly they reappear as though risen out of the night, are unrecognizable, the narrow familiar universe in which she had been born, in which she had lived, took on a new aspect. It seemed to her that even the objects around her had become strangers, all the ostentatious and oldfashioned furnishings, sumptuous without imagination, severe without dignity, academic and bourgeois, of a millionaire professor. She had often smiled at them indulgently as one smiles at venerable old persons, pompous and ridiculous, whom one has always known and who are inseparable from one's childhood memories.

And now through the damask and the gold their lamentable abjection and poverty appeared. She could not see them any longer without an indefinable uneasiness and a sort of shrinking dread. How many vanished confidences she had made to those cold and cautious witnesses—those false witnesses! And did she know that the same vain confidences had been made to them twenty years before by another young woman with sad eyes? It wasn't that she dreamed of hating or despising them; she was only tempted to pity them as slaves who had been trained to lie, who lie on command. She felt that more than witnesses they were accomplices—accomplices of a life in their own image, narrow, stubborn, calculating without love and without honor, of a hypocritical gravity and dubious decorum. And, as before her eyes places and things were being transformed, people also—their faces, their voices, their gestures—gave themselves away, gave up a part of their secret. Too impassioned herself to conceive their mediocrity or too pure ever to realize their ignominy, she only felt their sadness, the sadness of so many lost hours, of useless efforts, of spite, of hostility, of ambitions as hard as stone and lighter than dreams. For a while her filial tenderness had resisted, then gradually had changed into a more complex sentiment . . . Her former image of her father lost one by one its familiar features, melted as it were, and disappeared . . . How far away from her they were, all of them! How groping and unhappy! Why? To them, as to her dying friend, she had only her poor joy to give, her joy which was as mysterious as their sadness. And give it to them she would, even though she gave in vain!

Moreover, it would be a mistake to suppose that this inner revelation had at first made any outward change in the even course of her humble life. She had accepted this sadness as she accepted everything, careful not to dwell on it unduly. To see her, to hear her limpid laughter, to watch her as she ran after her two great dogs, Pyramus and Thisbe, her blue shadow on the wall, it would have been impossible for the most attentive observer to imagine that she had just discovered a world where moralists advance on leaden feet, had suddenly, in a breath, and almost as though in divine play, penetrated so far into man's pain. She herself thought she was seeing with the same eyes these comic or tragic personages whose names and faces were so familiar to her, and was surprised to find herself thinking of them with so much pity. But how resist such pity, both so heartbreaking and so gentle, that it began to shine in her eyes, to transfigure her to the point of troubling certain of her more discerning friends. She did not give herself up to it without reserve, for moments she would try to shut it out of her soul, but little by little, imperceptibly, like a diligent little spring, the same supernatural compassion, uselessly restrained, would burst out in prayer. For her prayers had never been so sweet, her union with God so close as after these vain struggles in which, without her realizing it, all her moral forces were engaged. O prayer, that was but an ineffable deliverance or, as it were, the groan of nature taken out of itself, overcome by grace! Who was there to tell her at that moment its perfection and all its peril?

Yet weeks and weeks passed after the death of Abbé Chevance without her realizing that her prayers had changed, attuned to a completely new, entirely inner experience, transcendent and full of realities never dreamed of before. This misapprehension was natural enough since she continued to perform the same duties, to supervise the household with the same gaiety which was so like a child's that it had even disarmed the insolence of an unbelievable array of constantly changing servants, collected according to Monsieur de Clergerie's whim and the most preposterous recommendations. Indeed, in the choice of his servants the little man showed an absurd optimism very quickly poisoned by avarice and suspicion, but nevertheless so notorious that a certain number of perfidious friends were diligent in providing him each season with new recruits whose worth they knew from sad experience, and whom they were not anxious to get rid of too unceremoniously. For, to discharge such enigmatic personages with resounding names and black and watchful eyes, from far-off cities not on any map, is not to be lightly undertaken. "You are worn out," the future Academician would occasionally say to her. "It is too heavy a responsibility for you! It was too much for your poor mother!" But as she would reply with one of her lovely, gallant laughs, he was satisfied, and simply thought, "How young she is!"

Then she would whistle to her dogs, or perhaps hurry to her own room to dream in peace of her old friend. O that pure cool silence! How she loved it! Too much, perhaps! Her prayers at present were not like those of which she used to say to Abbé Chevance: "I talk to God all the time. I know very well how to talk to Him. I think I talk to Him infinitely better than I pray to Him." But now, at least during those rare moments of blessed peace, her words would vanish on her lips without her knowing it. The hidden sadness, the pity or rather that sort of painful apprehension full of compassion that she now felt whenever she looked at any human face, would burst all at once in her heart on a single profound tone. At first she attached no importance to this singular phenomenon: "I just fall asleep while I am praying . . ." she thought. For it was the only explanation she could find to reassure herself, until the day. . . .

Of all those disturbing faces, the Russian's had aroused an irresistible distrust which closely resembled repulsion, had Chantal been capable of repulsion. Twice, three times perhaps, he had come to the house, humble and aloof, eyes lowered, his long restless fingers with their polished nails toying with enormous leather gloves, his voice halting and a little husky and his slight Russian accent scarcely more than a kind of pensive sing-song, a little too soft and caressing. Among many other references he brought a very flattering one from the old Baroness de Montanel, who, as everyone knew, had at her disposal six splendid academic votes, and who every fortnight quenched with weak tea the thirst of the whole editorial staff of the *Revue Internationale.* She could vouch for his perfect education, his honesty, and especially his marvelous cautiousness which made him unique as a chauffeur, as reliable as an old dowager's coachman. Moreover he had belonged to the Tsar's regiment of Pages, he had served in the Guards and later under Denikine, and not to starve had been forced to sell his priceless family jewels. But the best recommendation of all was that he had remembered a long article he had read in the *Messager Russe* before the war, consecrated to the important and erudite works of Monsieur de Clergerie.

In this silent personage Chantal had, from the first day, sensed an enemy—a man to be feared, though less dangerous for her than for the simple creatures he at once captivated by his insinuating manners and his infinite acquiescence. She did not understand him. She never could and never would understand him, being as invulnerable in her truthfulness as he in his falseness. And yet, she hated him unconsciously with a jealous hatred—for what other name, alas, could be given to that revolt of her pure conscience, so well armed and, at the same time, so defenseless? She hated him instinctively as though he already possessed the incomparable secret with which to menace her, to menace God Himself.

"What have you against him?" Monsieur de Clergerie asked. "He seems a little furtive, I admit, but of course he is not in his proper sphere, and I don't suppose these Slavs are angels. But a young girl like you cannot possibly judge. And after all we can't very well get our servants from a Patronage, my child."

To this she found nothing to reply for, although her sound judgment and youthful wisdom, her natural clearsighted horror of falsehood, and a certain mocking gaiety, were sufficient to put her on her guard, they could not furnish her with any precise reasons. At times she would even blame herself for being unfair to this latest recruit, probably no better and no worse than any of the others, and she made a great effort to overcome her dread, and to treat him with her habitual kindness and subtle charity. But unlike other people who knew her—with the exception of one only who was no longer there—this ambiguous stranger, in whose pale eyes one could see falsehood stirring like a wreck under stagnant water, this vile man was not satisfied simply to submit to her spell, but sought to discover its secret cause. Any truly pure heart will defend itself even against the curiosity of a friend, but what torture to feel that you are an open book to someone you despise!

Because of her simple ignorance of her own inner life, which she supposed too humble and transparent to be safe from anyone's curiosity, she thought he had seen through her. But, after all, what difference did that make? What frightened her was that patient, assiduous, inexplicable curiosity which only she was aware of, so insidious that she could not accuse him without making herself ridiculous, and so furtive that only by chance had she surprised its studied vigilance—yes, obscurely she felt the treachery of that curiosity. Even to have been the object of such a man's desire would not have disturbed her so much, because in this old Latin country of ours the most innocent young girl always has her wits about her, and knows instinctively how to act, and Abbé Chevance's gentle penitent would have extricated herself easily enough from such a predicament with that dignity, tinged with mockery, which every woman of our race inherits from her grandmothers. But passion is not so calm, so watchful, and above all, so indifferent to pleasing! What she read in his cold eyes was more like that curiosity so often seen in the eyes of trained animals or the ones corrupted by too indulgent masters, when on the road they meet their free and happy brothers! What was he contemplating with such envy? What was he looking for that she could give him? She often laughed at her fears, and at such times found them absurd, powerless as she was to justify them or even to express them in sensible language. But it was no use! She felt a web being cautiously spun around her, thread by thread—and not around her alone, for she was vaguely conscious that weaker ones than herself were already caught in the same snare. How she longed to protect them!

When Monsieur de Clergerie had insisted on his daughter's taking charge of his household as soon as she left the convent, he did not realize what a weight such a responsibility was for such shoulders, nor that the daily supervision of six or seven servants, collected from the Devil knew where, and discharged as casually, was a rude and perilous school for a seventeen-year-old girl who would never be altogether the dupe of her own candor, more often hurt by what she guessed than by what she saw. But she had protected herself in her own way by a miraculous goodness, quietly and without any visible effort that could attract attention or inspire either praise or blame. And now it seemed that she was caught in the snare of that goodness, whose enchanted source, always fresh and inexhaustible, she had thought was known to herself alone. This stranger, apparently so irreproachable, whom she could accuse of no definite fault, no deliberate or wilful lapse, who, after all, was for everyone simply a paid servant, an anonymity, a passer-by (and had she been less pure she might have blushed to give him so much thought)—this stranger was the first to make her doubt whether she was up to her humble task, to make her fear that simple gentleness alone was not enough to overcome those obscure, pitiless forces that were menacing, that such a weapon against a certain malevolence, hitherto unknown, was but a child's toy . . . A fear that she rejected at once with all the power of her soul! A fear, moreover, without bitterness, that even melted into a sort of felicity when, poorer and more alone than ever, surrounded by hostile and closed faces, she gave, she lavished, she threw out to them with both her hands, like a thing of little consequence, her incomparable, her sublime hope! And then, such was the blessed exhaustion of her charity, her sweet distress, that she would hurry to take refuge in her room, making an effort to hold back her tears, and there, intoxicated with fatigue and supplication, her lips murmuring a prayer she did not hear, not daring to take her eyes from the crucifix, she felt herself slowly gliding, then suddenly falling into sleep. . . . Only, she was falling into God.

And that is how he found her that day, the stranger, standing there beside her, his face convulsed, his arm outstretched, having just touched her shoulder . . . What time is it? The window is full of the night, the hall is bright behind the half-open door. "What are you doing here? Why?" In vain she searches for words, for a cry of indignation, of anger; all she can find is blank surprise. He has not turned away his eyes in which she cannot detect the least offensive curiosity, nor any surprise to equal hers, but, in spite of his astonishing calm, a sort of covert complicity burning to declare itself—about to declare itself. "What are you doing . . . how dare you!" she cried, and he: "It is a long time since dinner was announced. No one thought of coming in—the door was not locked. They are looking for Mademoiselle Chantal in the park, they have sent the gardener to young Arnaud's house." She had risen, trembling all over, and stammered: "I . . . I fell asleep." And then he looked at her steadily, too steadily, with reproach—yes, actually with reproach in his lying eyes. "I acted for the best, Mademoiselle will understand—they might have found her . . . No one would understand . . . They are simple animals, happy animals. Excuse me if I say Mademoiselle should be careful. For my part, I know . . . only angels sleep like that! You must excuse me, but at Goutchivo I saw an orthodox nun, a little daughter of God, who resembled you; our soldiers had broken her legs, she was lying on the ground in front of the icon, almost naked, with nothing to eat for days and days—an angel from heaven, a sweet prodigy, a child's tale whiter than the snow . . . I do not believe in God, but that whiteness! How is it possible not to believe in that, not to love it? For there is more whiteness than you think in this black world. I should not, of course, address you in this language but I cannot do otherwise—excuse me—for you must know who this man is who has surprised your secret, not today, but weeks ago. For it has happened before that you . . . that you . . . what shall I say—well, that this thing has happened unknown to you in front of me, for a minute, a breath, and so often that, stupid as they are, I wonder by what miracle (a miracle would cost you nothing), by what miracle they have noticed nothing."

At that he had bowed very low and had slipped from the room without waiting for a reply, leaving the door wide open with the idea, perhaps, that the light from the hall would succeed in rousing her completely . . . Some time passed before she heard his distant footsteps, muffled voices, then turning her head, pale with shame, she caught sight of her eyes in the glass, immense, fathomless and unrecognizable. Her eyes? But wasn't that look one she already knew only too well, whose dark fixity she could hardly endure, where there floated a formless dream without color or contour, the corpse of a dream, a dream that had decayed. Yes, those were her grandmother's eyes, her grandmother's very eyes! Anguish like a lightning flash pierced her breast and shone through every fiber. Of all the blows she might have dreaded, might have looked for, that was the worst, the most unexpected, the one she could not parry. The extreme, the supernatural simplicity of her life, her humble piety, her ingenuous horror of confusion, of disorder, of anything that might trouble the transparent sincerity of words, actions, intentions, that steady wisdom and agile reason which the old priest had formed with such prudence and such love—nothing had prepared her for an ordeal like this. Perhaps her grandmother's madness, that strange silent delirium crossed by flashes of lucidity, had affected her adolescence more cruelly than she supposed. The doubt that had just arisen in her poor brain, still drowned in ecstasy, stabbed into the wound with such precision and so profoundly that she never thought to doubt, or at least to weigh, the sole testimony of this stranger. Neither his words nor his equally equivocal designs, nor his calm insolence, his boldness, made her hesitate a moment; she was only conscious of that nightmare resemblance, the tragic proof that stared at her from the mirror. "We are nervous cases all of us—we are neurotics," Monsieur de Clergerie was wont to say, thus justifying his dyspepsia. He was, moreover, completely seduced by the new psychiatry in fashion . . . In the past, Father de Riancourt, chaplain of *Sacré Cœur*, had warned Chantal against a tendency toward childish mysticism, too soft a piety which he taught her to be ashamed of, even taxing it with hiding a certain ostentation which she had naturally always heartily despised. Since then how Abbé Chevance had reassured her! He had known how to put his finger on the spot, adroitly untangle her scruples and set her on the road again by way of a safe discreet little path that could not arouse anybody's envy. True, only through the old priest's tender solicitude had she been able to cling to her fragile peace . . . Even at the deathbed of this righteous man, she had felt herself, not yet, it is true, in revolt, but taken out of herself, tempted by something terribly grave and powerful she did not understand, a total sacrifice . . . O Illusion! And since then . . .

"I was here at five-thirty," she said to herself without daring to take her eyes off the mirror as though afraid of losing the only proof, the decisive proof of her frightful experience. "I had just given Granny her tea and toast, and now it is eight-thirty . . . When he touched my shoulder I was in exactly the same spot, the same position, with my arms outstretched! It isn't possible!" The stiffness of her muscles was still so painful that she was afraid to move her legs for fear of falling. Whenever she turned her eyeballs lightning flashes shot across her blurred vision. "I shall never be able to go downstairs alone, never. Will they come and find me here?" She remembered hearing Dr. Michauld say that her mother a few weeks before her death, suffering from complete nervous exhaustion, had been subject to these lethargic attacks, the same probably, or of the same general nature. Although an incomparable joy still stirred in the depth of her heart, she did not dream of looking for a less humiliating reason for the discovery she had just made. She knew how rare, how precious are God's gifts. She was not ignorant of all their vulgar counterfeits that so outraged Abbé Chevance in his honesty, and of which he spoke with such contempt—too much contempt perhaps?—the simulacrums, the half-sincere attitudes and worse still, those more secret taints half spiritual, half sensual that seem to be just at the articulation of body and spirit, and which science has solemnly classified and catalogued, devastating to find names for them the whole garden of Greek roots, and that were already familiar to the old Flemish mystics of the 12th and 13th centuries who owed nothing to the strange erudition of Sigmund Freud. She was, besides, too simple, too self-indifferent, too armed against an immediate recoil of hurt pride, to have thought of introducing the black angel into her lamentable adventure. Besides she had never worried very much about the Devil and his machinations, feeling sure that through her excessive insignificance she would escape his notice. For the One whose patience penetrates most things, that immense gaping gaze whose avidity is without measure, brooding darkly even over the glory of God, watches in vain through the ages with all his colossal attention, turns and turns in vain in his braziers, like a little unalterable stone, pure and chaste Humility.

Who knows what she went through in that brief

moment? Only by a sudden surprise can a magnanimous will be caught off its guard, but even in the tumult of her heart and mind, through an impulse of her soul stronger than her terror and her shame, Chantal, poor child, felt that if she failed immediately to break the enchanted circle she was lost. Coming closer to the mirror, her elbows on the marble mantelpiece, still trembling, she forced herself to smile, she smiled at her pale image in the glass. That tragic face, drawn with anguish, inspired in her less pity than disgust. "I shall decide one way or another before I go downstairs," she said to herself. "I must decide now or never . . . In the first place I am ridiculous . . . the whole thing is ridiculous! . . ." She thought of a temptation she had once had, and remembered how, when she had confessed it to Abbé Chevance with bitter tears, he had listened to her, smiling exactly as she had just smiled at herself in the glass. Then he had said gently: "You must go home to dinner now. Look, it is seven o'clock! You mustn't keep Monsieur de Clergerie waiting for that." And she had gone home at peace with herself. "Why decide? I shall not decide at all, what's the use? Now it is time for dinner, too!" She thought of the charming reply of Louis de Gonzague to his little playmates who, during recess, were discussing what they would do if they were told that the end of the world would come in a quarter of an hour. "I should like to finish our game of hop-scotch," he had said.

The blood beat in her temples again, and she rubbed

her cheeks to bring back the color more quickly. "It is nothing, perhaps less than nothing. Only it humiliated me terribly. I still thought myself too wise. What does one ache more or less matter to God? It is good to be weak in his hands. It is better to be weak. And who could be weaker than I from now on? Literally I can no longer hope to find my way alone. I am at the mercy of this Russian!" She tried to laugh, but this time she had counted beyond her strength. In a flash she saw the stranger again as he had stood there beside her, with that equivocal expression on his face, and the stab of shame she felt was so painful she could hardly suppress a groan. "It is my fault," she stammered while the powder puff trembled in her hand. "One should foresee everything, one should foresee the worst, resign oneself to it in advance and not think about it any more. At present what is done is done. Naturally, it is not easy to keep one's life simple, but complications always come from outside. Simplicity comes from within. What is simpler now than to go downstairs, reassure my family and have dinner? There—I look a little more presentable. Luckily Annette forgot her rouge. I am made up like a dancer . . . Let's hope Granny doesn't notice . . . or Francine. They are a bit alike. They have an eye on all of us and not such an indulgent one either. Thursday, God willing, I'll confess everything to the Dean of Idouville. He will say that I was dreaming, that I am crazy, that poor Abbé Chevance has turned my head. What of it? That is better than honoring God with hysterics and swoonings like a lunatic, and scandalizing the neighbors . . . *a sweet prodigy, a child's tale, whiter than the snow* . . . How ghastly!"

She was already going shakily down the stairs, her little hand gripping the banisters so tightly that at each step she had to make an effort to loosen her fingers. From the open door of the drawing-room the discreet noise of conversation reached her, but strangely magnified. She went on talking to herself softly, almost tenderly, as one reassures a child or a crazy person. Was she absolutely sincere? Did she really condemn with such severity, did she reject once and for all, what had been for so many weeks—she realized it now—her mysterious nourishment? "Beware of things that trouble you." This counsel that her old friend Abbé Chevance repeated so often, still echoed in her heart. There is nothing more profound than the first revolt of a pure soul against the designs of the spirit. That she was troubled, and had been for a long time without realizing it, she could no longer doubt. What greater proof could she have than the testimony of her body's collapse? Too sensible to indulge in vain regret that would only tighten her bonds, she only longed to take up her daily tasks again, the exercise of her household duties—simple, categorical, authentic—and, mortified, to re-enter that universal asylum and only refuge for saints and sinners, a disciplined life, where she looked to find peace, like a lamb lost in a storm . . . But as she descended slowly toward the light and the voices, the realization of the solitude into which, in spite of herself, she was entering, a solitude in which no doubt she would die, struck her with such force that suddenly, naïvely, she stood still as though the next step would decide her miserable fate. Alas! if it were true that she was ill, one of those poor things betrayed by their flesh and blood, who pique the curiosity of doctors and psychiatrists and of whom the true servants of God speak with less pity than aversion, what then would she have left that really belonged to her? Nothing, not even her prayers, not a single heart beat! The thought, like a luminous dart, literally pierced her through and through. From now on she had nothing to offer God without apprehension, without reserve, or even without shame. The excellence, the perfection of such destitution, the omnipotence of God over so lamentable a poverty, the certainty of being at the mercy of what men call chance, and which is only one of the most secret forms of divine pity, all this overwhelmed her with a sadness that was full of love, and suddenly, with dazzling joy.

Then she fled toward the light and the voices, not stopping again until she stood in the doorway, one hand on her young breast, her cheeks flushed, eyes shining, and so radiant that Monsieur de Clergerie exclaimed:

"I haven't the heart to scold you. You are the image

of your mother—her very image! Your long sleep has done you good."

But as Fernande was grumbling because the delay had spoiled her dinner, Chantal ran gaily out to the kitchen to whip up another chocolate *soufflé*.

3

SINCE that decisive night, weeks, as short as days, had gone by. She had spoken to no one, not even to the Dean of Idouville. Knowing that Abbé Cénabre was soon to visit them, she decided to wait until he came. He had been absent from Paris for four months so that she had not seen him since the death of Abbé Chevance, much to the regret of Monsieur de Clergerie who thought his daughter not unworthy of the spiritual guidance of that powerful intellect. She was certainly without any prejudice against Tauler's illustrious biographer whom she hardly knew, although he had been a frequent visitor at their house in Paris, and had always treated her with a kind of severe benevolence whose restrained courtesy pleased her, for, despite her simplicity, she had always, even as a little girl, detested familiarity. Of his books she knew only the titles and although she had heard all the gossip about him and even more insidious slander, she felt an obscure sympathy, tinged with timidity, for this distinguished man who, in spite of his celebrity, seemed to despise fame, who lived free and alone, perhaps poor as well, in a fierce independence. Why, she wondered, had the name of this former schoolfellow which he had so rarely pronounced in her presence before, returned incessantly to the dying lips of Abbé Chevance? Was he, in his mind, confiding his daughter to Abbé Cénabre as Monsieur de Clergerie still believed? "I ought to love him," she thought.

He would arrive tonight for a week's stay, and now, instead of awaiting the occasion patiently as usual—God's gracious succor that always came in good time—here she was allowing herself to be demoralized by a few careless words uttered by Fernande, perhaps out of malice or mere stupidity. "*We are going to see extraordinary things here, Mademoiselle, things that don't happen even in books.*" But why? Were such things really possible in this familiar house where everything reminded her of her childhood, and on a glorious summer day? In Paris it might be barely conceivable, but here! And what things? "How nervous, how uneasy I am!" she thought, "it is disgraceful. In the first place *extraordinary* is one of those senseless words of which Abbé Chevance used to say that they could not have been given by God in Paradise, but must have been born on the other side of the seven rivers, out of the daily experience of evil's domination. There is nothing outside of order. In the end everything returns to God's order. And, besides, is one ever alone? Can one be afraid? Afraid of what? "Let your father discharge me. It is not difficult to find a pretext," the man had said. What was the use?

When she had recovered from her first surprise, Chantal felt for him as much horror as pity. Was he really so different from the others who had preceded him or who would come after? So many bold, equivocal strangers, both insolent and servile, who pleased the master of the house for a week and then one morning left as they had come, with their eyes full of resentment, a long beard, a short jacket, tan shoes and their canvas traveling bags in their hands! For Monsieur de Clergerie through whim and also through a secret dislike of the whole sardonic race of French valets, had engaged one after the other, long-legged bony Czechs, Poles with shaven heads, an Hungarian recommended by the papal Nuncio, and even a Levantine Greek more sinister than all the others put together, who had quietly disappeared with the new roadster. At least this Russian rarely spoke, although he had succeeded more than once, with singular address, in engaging his unwilling young mistress in those conversations full of double meaning and insidious allusions which, in the end, make of the two interlocutors two accomplices, accomplices of the same secret. At the first attempt she thought that she would die of shame. After all, what was she but a child? "God always acts for the best," Monsieur de Clergerie would often say. "For example, it would have been hard for a more frivolous girl, or one more romantically inclined, to have been without a mother's care." Alas!

No, it was not the Russian, nor any of the others, nor that trivial incident, nor the strange fear she felt of her own eyes, of the expression of her pale mouth, or of those hands that so often trembled now, of that whole body—of all that complicated apparatus of flesh and blood and nerves which she could no longer control, the treacherous, humiliated, melancholy animal on whom she forced, like a golden bridle, her joy, faith, hope and charity. Ten times, twenty times, perhaps, she had almost given in to that marvelous vertigo, rolling to the very edge of the luminous abyss, and only by an intolerable effort had been able to terminate quietly her prayers. Or had it happened unknown to her? "Allow me to point out that if it had not been for me, what you so much wish to hide would already be known. Again yesterday . . ." Those were the words he had just spoken and even if he had not said them, his meaning was clear in his impassible smile. She linked those enigmatic words with Fernande's stupid prediction: *Extraordinary things . . . things that don't even happen in books* . . . And was that part of her life which she longed to hide in God, in God alone eternally, together with the pitiful secret of her hereditary taint, to be held up to derision, the subject of backstairs gossip and curiosity! *Miracles, real miracles that fall from you like flowers.* "I shock them," she said, "that is how one makes a mockery of God."

Then why—by what prodigy—did this supreme dread, as soon as she stopped trying to understand

and to resist it, open up in her so fresh, so pure a spring? It was as though she had found in the idea of the completeness of her distress, in the failure of all human hope, in fierce disillusionment, the very principle of her consolation! To seem ridiculous in her own eyes succeeded in breaking the last shackles of pride, in liberating her. "I was happy that God himself would have taken the trouble to strip me with so much care that it was impossible to be poorer than I. I compared myself to a wretch who, having only a few pennies in his pocket, suddenly discovers that those are the very pennies that are not in circulation any more."

The shadow of a cloud dimmed, one by one, the first red and green panes of the sun porch, then they all went out together and the immense garden behind them seemed suddenly colorless. "I have been dreaming here for ten minutes. It's absurd. Am I going to decide to go in or not? . . ." Through the door she could hear her father's nervous little cough, and even the clink of his pen against the crystal inkwell. "If I were brave, I'd tell him everything right away! Have I the right to hide from him all this time that I am ill? Isn't it only fair that he should be told even before Abbé Cénabre, a stranger? For, whatever I do or whatever I say, I have to face the facts. After all to be sick isn't a moral issue!" And she entered.

From behind a rampart of books and papers, Monsieur de Clergerie lifted a knitted brow.

"So, there you are," he said. "It must be fifteen minutes at least I have heard you trotting around the hall like a little mouse. It is a curious thing. When I am exhausted and suffering, as at present, from my recurrent insomnia, I have observed an extraordinary sharpening of my sense of hearing. I must make a note of that for Professor La Pérouse. Why do you laugh?"

"Oh, nothing, really. Or because just the name of Professor La Pérouse makes me want to laugh. Jean-François de Galaup, Count de la Pérouse, Commander of the Compass and the Astrolabe, eaten by the aborigines of the island of Vanikoro!"

"Come, come, Chantal . . ."

"And besides, forgive me, Papa, but all the theories of Professor La Pérouse, true or false, have not helped your headaches in the least. You looked better before we left Paris."

"Do you think so? Oh! I haven't too much hope . . . all these theories on cosmic rays, telluric radiations, cortical nervous energy, all these new methods of treatment in which the doctor, strictly speaking, gives precedence to the physicist . . . I am a little bewildered I admit. Perhaps I should try homeopathy? We are such children when it comes to scientific matters. The most distinguished man of my generation could take lessons of a mere college boy. It is ridiculous. And yet a humanist, a real humanist, trained in the best methods of grammatical, juridic or historical exegesis, is better qualified than anyone to broach these weighty problems. My old master, Ferdinand Brunetière, was sufficient proof of that. What do you call, for example, a copper wire coiled in a spiral?"

"Why, naturally, a copper wire coiled in a spiral, that's all."

"I am asking you the scientific name, which has slipped my mind."

"A solenoid, if you prefer."

"That's it, exactly; *solen*—pipe, *eidos*—form . . ."

"And we say that the current is open or closed! I didn't know I was so learned. But I had an astonishing examiner when I took my oral, a real sport, up to the minute; he said to me, 'Give me the theory of the magneto!' "

"You are a child of your times! The theory of La Pérouse, it would seem, is very ingenious. Even Dorval admits that. To a layman like myself it appears . . . what shall I say?—fantastic. The idea is, I believe, to protect the sympathetic nervous system from the action of certain rays about which nothing is known except that they do exist. La Pérouse, then, proposes placing the patient—particularly anxious types—inside a copper wire coiled in a spiral, forming a protective solenoid with open circuit, to act as insulator in relation to the cosmic rays."

"Proposes?"

"Yes. That seems ridiculous to you. His experiments have, nevertheless, met with success . . . Oh, in an entirely different domain, it is true. He has cured vegetable tumors—a sort of cancer of the pelargonium. Don't shrug your shoulders. The pelargonium is not, as you think, a plant that grows only for these gentlemen in laboratories. It is simply the geranium."

"My poor geraniums! Won't they even let our flowers alone?"

"That is a poet's point of view. My dear child, you mustn't think that I take these intellectual speculations too much to heart. But they bother me. Yesterday's paradox is tomorrow's truth. We old people may resist and object as much as we please; we have to adapt ourselves as best we can. Old age arrives with all its infirmities—rheumatism, insomnia, the frightful symptoms of nervous exhaustion, and I don't know what all! Just as we are about to reach the goal, life fails us. At twenty the poet is always right; at sixty the doctor is never wrong. He knows the secret of our ills."

"Ills! Heavens, I should be so happy to be old! I should love to be an old woman with spectacles and a stick, quite, quite close to the cemetery and the little grave, knitting a woolen stocking with a wicked twinkle in her eye."

"Of course, but meantime you never stop singing all day long!"

"There are so many old women who sing. The trouble is nobody listens to them."

"You are extraordinary. Really! If I did not know you I would accuse you of affectation. You see, darling, every man traces beforehand the road he is to follow, starts on his career and awaits the consecration of a final decisive success: a position, a public office, a title or sometimes—fame. There is one thing I can say for myself, no matter what happens, at least I have made you happy. I have made your girlhood an enchantment, a holiday, a lovely summer morning like this one today. Troubles will come soon enough. Ah! if only your dear mother had known how to smile! I would not be as I am. In spite of appearances I was essentially healthy. I had the rugged constitution of my father—of a peasant, of a Norman. But what a nervous system! So precarious . . . You can understand then, my child, what that grief—a long agony, twenty months of sorrow . . . Why are you crying?" he asked innocently.

"I am not crying!" she protested, shaking her pretty head. "What made you think I was crying? Ah, you are a much too indulgent father. I even wish you were more strict with me. It is not easy, no, it is not easy, to tell you anything that is not already in your head at the very moment . . . And you reproach me for being too gay! Yet you admitted just now that I had to smile for two."

Calm and limpid, her eyes rested on him now, and he no longer recognized the sound—the soul— of her voice as she said:

"I think I had better go on smiling."

Just as in the past—in the same place perhaps—in the days of another summer, while before his eyes a young life, frail as a November bee, was being consumed, he seemed to feel through the thickness of his studied egotism, the approach of some misfortune, a steely chill, and on every side a growing hate that knew no fear. What fresh blow was about to fall upon him? It was over in a flash.

His daughter had stood up, had already crossed the room in silence. Her hand lifted above her head, holding back the curtains, she looked out across the lawn still in shadow, toward the blazing garden designed by Jeumont, with its *Second Empire* shrubberies and their somewhat disheveled charm, the *Empress* flower borders and, lying in the full glare of the relentless sunlight, the wide, tawny avenues dappled in violet. Through the thin foliage of the shady path, walking with slow steps in front of the lighter shadow of Francine, she saw the black figure of her grandmother.

"Chantal," said Monsieur de Clergerie (suddenly he felt a need for emotional release, a strange desire to let himself go), "sometimes I blame myself for neglecting you a little. I live isolated by my work, by my anxieties . . . for I have anxieties, serious anxieties. Your grandmother, poor thing, can no longer be of any help to me. Besides, you know what confidence I have in you, the esteem—yes, the esteem—I have for your precocious intelligence, your judgment, your loyalty. You have no need of anyone. You grow straight—like a lily! I understand such souls, I admire them. I have no intention of trying to influence you. Happily you are among those who are marvelously able to benefit from the guidance of a wise, holy and enlightened priest. Your decisions will always spring from lofty, unworldly motives . . . What peace of mind for a father! I had the very highest regard for Abbé Chevance. I only criticize him—recognizing, of course, his most magnificent gifts—for his lack of worldly experience, an excessive timidity. Don't misunderstand me, it was not a question of education, of manners—quite unimportant. What worried me a little was his taste for middle-course solutions, and I always feared that, at the crucial moment, he would lack decision, firmness, boldness. He treated you as though you were a child. Do not deny it."

"But I deny nothing. How can I know? Come, Papa, be fair! If I had known as much about Abbé Chevance as he knew about me, I . . . well, I could have done without a spiritual director . . . But I don't want to prevent you from admiring me. It makes you so happy!"

"I do admire you . . . to tell the truth, I envy you. I am accused of being ambitious. Why not? There are legitimate ambitions. Mine, I think, are that. You know what they are. The Academy represents for me merely the final consecration of a career that has been more than honorable, of a life given to science, to the disinterested cult of science. Naturally a man of my education, of my social standing, enjoying a certain fortune, must pay his tribute to the world, must respect its customs, its prejudices, if you like. In the eyes of a Cénabre, of a Chevance (I cannot separate the two names), duties of that sort seem frivolous. They are less so than is generally thought. They impose innumerable sacrifices on us. A constant self-control—salutary—yes, very salutary! Discipline is, in itself, a beautiful thing. It deserves your respect, my child. And do you think that it is easy to resign oneself with a light heart to certain compromises which the thoughtless, with their customary obduracy, are quick to stigmatize. Compromises! But there are compromises that are more onerous than intransigence. The uncompromising are paid a hundred times over in popular admiration. For the general public responds instinctively to the categorical yes or no, to the theatrical gesture. Your poor mother used to think she was being sacrificed. She was so young—and from the South besides—a humming bird of May, a poet, indescribably fragile—a melody! She did not understand that I was sacrificing myself too—sacrificing myself to my ultimate goal. You understand? Each one of us brings his share. I have not a word to say against your grandmother . . . She has given me everything, absolutely everything. God will reward her. She was an exceptional woman. Sometimes, even now, in spite of her disordered brain, she makes the shrewdest remarks full of common sense, from which I can derive benefit. People will tell you that she never loved anyone but me, that to everyone else she was a hard, unfeeling woman. It is true that she guarded me jealously as she guarded her fields, her house, everything that belonged to her. You should respect her too, my child—even more than you do me. That she made your mother suffer unjustly, as perhaps spiteful people will insinuate, is, I believe, pure fiction. At least she has never shown the least sign of remorse, and has kept her secret, if secret there be, with admirable dignity. It cannot be denied that you have been surrounded by 'good examples' as they say."

"Heavens, Papa!" she cried, turning toward him her half-closed eyes still dazzled by the sunlit garden. "How serious you are! And eloquent! Now I am sure that something is bothering you. Oh, yes, I am!"

"Let me finish," he said, and she noticed, suddenly, how pale he was. "Today I must hear you say that I have made you happy."

"I'll say it a hundred times for one! Isn't it plain enough? It must be! Oh, Papa, I am serious. I have never hoped to be a perfect daughter, not even a very good daughter. But if you doubt for a moment that I have been happy, then I really am worth less than I thought . . ."

He noticed the convulsive movement of her little hand grasping the handle of the French window, and was surprised.

"How nervous you are, you too! You, Chantal . . . But please do not jump like that. It startles me. I must keep calm, composed. Not through selfishness but through necessity. What an unfortunate constitution! I pay for a single emotional moment with a whole night of insomnia. It is hardly fair. But people judge only by appearances. Well, then, I have made you happy? That is what I want to hear. That is the essential. Besides you are, I admit, very easy to please.

You have the sense of abnegation, of sacrifice . . . I might almost say, the instinct for it. What grace of God! To know how to find one's joy in other people's joy, that is the secret of happiness. I remember when you were a little girl of seven, passing the plate of cakes you would forget to take one for yourself, not apparently on purpose but unconsciously. Your grandmother used to say with her rather homespun good sense: 'It is only because she doesn't like sweets. She is like me.' But I knew that you loved them, poor darling. Yes, anything satisfies you and your father thanks you for it. I have been able to give all my attention to the day's work, to my writing, to my career. Had I loved you less I might have forgotten your presence entirely. Those days are past. No vain regrets. We must be reasonable. I am only very much afraid that our dear Abbé Chevance has not prepared you for other duties."

"But he has! I *am* prepared . . . that is, he didn't like making plans too far ahead . . . (I can almost hear him!) Oh, Papa, it is, you know, so easy to obey! . . . I realize I am a little too lively, I see the funny side of things, I have some wit, I amuse people. That deceives them. On the other hand, you mustn't, no really you mustn't, take me for one of those determined, energetic girls who have, once and for all, taken their bearings and set their course. I do not go by the compass. I have been given only the most simple, empirical directions, probably because I was not meant for long voyages. I must never lose sight of the coast . . . I too, Papa, I have my worries— Oh, naturally, little worries made to fit me. Just the same they are worries, you know! I bear what I can. You give me a cold chill when you speak of my precocious intelligence. I am instantaneously old. I feel pouches under my eyes, wrinkles, I am a wizened old woman. The truth is there isn't much I can do. I can obey. I can make the best of what is given me. I do piece work, as it were. Don't you see? Oh, Papa! don't, please, suddenly have the idea of putting me, just as I am, without method, without even any preparation, without advice, at the head of my life like an American heroine. Please make the effort, Papa! I am sure if you would watch me,—really put your mind on me for a little while, a week or two—you would not admire me quite so much . . ."

Then, with a sad, tender smile, she added:

"But, perhaps, you would love me more."

"Now, now Chantal!" he said. "Why, you are not only intelligent, darling, you are the very personification of energy. How many young girls of your age would have been able to drive our old *Voisin* along the Tantonville road, as you did one evening, at eighty miles an hour, I was told—absolutely top speed! Even the chauffeur couldn't get over it."

"Couldn't get over it is right! He was stuck outside Liaucourt! The motor would start, would run a few yards and then stop, choked of course . . . The exhaust muffler was blocked. Afterwards I drove fast because we were expecting Baroness Walsh for dinner, you remember? But I am boring you. You hate automobiles! Abbé Chevance hated them too."

"I don't understand you. All this talk of mufflers, exhausts, these break-neck speeds, coupled with your self-effacement, your taste for the inner life, that fervent filial piety that I sense in you—why, take for instance your sudden appreciation of certain culinary refinements that you cared nothing about before . . . (yes, dear child, I know it is for my sake, out of obedience . . . Yet, I can't help thinking there must be some natural predisposition, an inclination). I am completely dazed by all these contrasts. Where am I to find time to give you my undivided attention? I have confidence in you. Confidence! It is absolutely necessary to me—it should be in the very air I breathe—you will agree, considering the precarious state of my health! You too, darling, try to do this for me—let me go on loving you blindly! What peace in the midst of so many cares!"

"All right, Papa, but don't look too close, that's all. I am very happy like this, why change?"

"Why change! Just as though you did not know very well that life is nothing but change, a becoming, a perpetual becoming . . . Circumstances . . . Oh! you will do me that much justice . . . I have not acted on impulse . . . I have weighed everything carefully . . ."

He wiped his livid forehead, and continued:

"This is one of the most painful moments I have known since your mother's death. And besides, at that time, I was not so impressionable, not so exhausted, not so completely exhausted . . . Well, let's get it over! Providence took from me in my youth a tenderly loved companion. It has pleased Providence in my maturity to give me back, better than a companion, a friend, a partner, a veritable intellectual ally. I have asked Baroness de Montanel to be my wife."

He immediately let his eyes fall and in the silence that followed while his yellowing fingers toyed with the pages of the open book and the clock filled his ears with its inexorable ticking, he could find no other words, and kept repeating with a sort of stupid indifference:

"Not on impulse, no . . . I have weighed everything . . . not at all on impulse."

The same silence continued. He had the impression that he was plunging into it head first.

"You know Baroness de Montanel. We are of the same age, we have the same tastes, our plans for the future are the same. This is the moment, just before three important Academic elections which will perhaps decide my own (the Duc de Janville will not be a candidate next year for Monsieur Houdedot's chair . . . that will be an excellent chance for me), this, then, is the moment for me to come out of my retirement. A real mistress of the house will be indispensable . . . a hostess. We will entertain enormously next winter. My . . . your . . . that is Baroness de Montanel brings me several infinitely precious left wing votes. Her mother was born Lepreux-Cadaillac, and was closely connected with the best radical families. She herself is the goddaughter of Waldeck-Rousseau. Of course my marriage is not merely one of convenience, but I will not go into my more disinterested personal motives . . ."

To his complete surprise (for he had not yet dared to lift his eyes) he felt a cool arm around his neck—so childlike—and against his shoulders the light living burden of his daughter's trembling body.

"Chantal, my darling!" he cried taking her icy little hand in his.

But she gently freed herself, and he was conscious of the faint odor of her hair as it brushed his cheek.

"Dear Papa," she said. "Please, not another word . . . Don't explain, don't act as though you had to justify yourself . . . It hurts me. You can't imagine how it hurts me!"

He replied coldly:

"Justify myself? And why should I, if you please?"

"Don't be angry. Since your mind is made up do let me at least have the credit of submitting with a good grace, of thinking only of you, of your security, of your life. Calm is so essential to you. The rest will come of itself . . . Aren't we absurd—you afraid of hurting me, I afraid of hurting you! We are carrying on two separate monologues—it's really funny, isn't it? My conclusion was a kiss."

A malicious twinkle came into her eyes:

"It was perhaps the only way out," she said.

"My dear child, I thought you more sensible." His voice was trembling. "Don't speak of the security of my life! I admit that often circumstances have been favorable. But Providence has given me a heavy cross to bear. Oh! I am not blaming anyone, it has been like that and that is all there is to it . . . a fatality. Every man has his own. It is strange, nevertheless, that I have never been able to share without reservation, the joy of my successes with anyone! In spite of the best intentions, seeking only the most modest, the most solid connections, and only by absolutely legitimate means, in short acting as anyone would in my place—it seems, nevertheless, that my happiness is destined to be the counterpart of other people's sorrow, that I am unable to be happy except at someone else's expense."

She was looking at him sadly (was it sadness or the acquiescence of a heart now without defense?). . . .

"You are right, Papa. Many people sacrifice themselves who would not have the courage to give themselves."

The growing agitation of Monsieur de Clergerie could be seen not so much by the trembling of his knees under the light woolen blanket which, summer or winter, invariably covered them, as by his dull, staring eyes.

"I know, I know. A very touching thought, better than touching—it is true, profoundly true. To give oneself, to give oneself in that way as by a sort of spontaneous impulse, my God, even if it were not the noblest way to live, wouldn't it be the most sensible, the wisest? Don't we have to come to it in the end, anyway, whether we want to or not? Since we can never do as we please! . . . Ah, well, in short, my little girl, this . . . this happy event, far from separating us, will only bring us closer together. For many years a place has remained empty here. Now it will be filled."

He struck the table with the palm of his hand with simulated cheerfulness. Chantal's calm face had become a little drawn, and the smile still lingering on her pale lips seemed slowly to fade.

"You see, Papa," she said after a silence, "I had not expected . . . Really I had never dreamed . . . Perhaps you were right. Poor Abbé Chevance! He spoiled me so. You go on and on, you think you are letting the good Lord carry you and you say to yourself: I shall always have enough sense not to struggle, to make myself as light as possible—the way I used to at Trouville when the swimming master had his arm under my shoulders . . . The little waves are fun. And a ground swell? Oh, well, it only lifts you higher. But a moment comes when you can't just float any longer. You finally have to go somewhere, take a direction. Where? What should I do now? An empty place, an occupied place, that sounds very simple . . . But it is really an adventure, an enormous adventure, my poor Papa. You don't seem to have the least suspicion of that."

"No, indeed I haven't," he cried. "You are not going to tell me that your presence here is impossible with Baroness de Montanel . . ."

"Oh! It isn't that!" she replied, shaking her head. "Only you seem to forget what it is to be a young girl . . . Alas! my poor Papa, we are a very unhappy species, and we are fast disappearing. People are so busy they don't know what to do with us any longer. It is not for lack of money but for lack of time . . . We demand the most particular care, always the same, for centuries the same, for we are slower to sprout and blossom than the tulips of Holland. We defy the laws of economy. Modern life beats all the records of speed, and we are still jog-trotting along like our grandmothers. We are as ridiculous and old-fashioned among you as a poor silkworm's cocoon in a factory of artificial silk."

"Chantal," cried Monsieur de Clergerie with unfeigned surprise, "what am I to understand by all this? I don't recognize you any longer. What bitterness!"

"It's over . . . over for good and all. I think I was going to be a little jealous— Oh, not of Baroness de Montanel nor of you—of no one in particular . . . I am jealous as we are jealous when we are very hungry and a hurried butler forgets to pass us our favorite dish . . . It's over . . . Oh, I am sure, Papa, that I shall be no less dear to you tomorrow and day after tomorrow. For you nothing has changed. But after all, we are not pure spirits! We have to do something with our head, our arms, our legs and also, sometimes, our heart . . . You see I have not, alas, yet reached the stage of being able to love like the angels. I need to put myself out, take a lot of trouble, and when I have worked hard (there is lots of work here, you know, servants are so scatterbrained, so careless!) at the end of the day I measure my tenderness by the aches in my back and knees, and even by that touch of rheumatism in my left shoulder that I can't get rid of. You have just taken away my job. You have made me a minister without a portfolio."

She smiled again.

"Be careful! Unemployment demoralizes the working classes, that is what you wrote in the last number of the *Revue*. I read it!"

"God, this is what I feared more than anything," groaned Monsieur de Clergerie. "Complications, always, always . . . What am I asking of you after all? You pretend that all you want is my happiness, my peace of mind. Will two of you be too many to assure it? Of course, you understand, I am only answering your own arguments, speaking your language. In any case it will only be a temporary solution. Sooner or later you will have to choose, my child. May I add—you know how I always respect another person's conscience, I have no right to insist, I merely suggest,—well I should have thought, I still think that God intended you for the religious life . . . Oh! I don't mean one of the contemplative orders, of course . . . But your piety seems too sincere, too profound, too deliberate to . . . to . . ."

He kept tapping his foot under the table with a strange incomprehensible fury that suddenly burst:

"I blame Abbé Chevance for having wilfully kept you in a state of indifference through a ridiculous obstinacy . . . yes, ridiculous—for which he has surely answered to God by now—in a state of absurd, childish ignorance—you of all girls, so calm, so sensible, I should even say discreet." (He was stuttering now.) "You have the necessary experience to run a house like this, you have firmness, magnificent willpower, and yet you act as though you had made a wager to live in this world with the simplicity, the innocence and submissiveness of a little child. What a contradiction! What a responsibility for a father! I am overwhelmed by so many cares. I should be able to lean on you but you evade me with your unalterable smile. I swear, there are days when I should like to see you weep . . ."

She looked at him stupefied, and already in her startled eyes appeared the shadow of a sorrow so intense that it resembled terror.

"My God, Papa, what is the matter? What have I done?" she cried in a trembling voice.

But nothing could stop Monsieur de Clergerie now. He was ashamed of himself and that was enough to make him furious.

"I am not a saint, far from it! I am just an ordinary man. I don't understand you, you are beyond me. So be it. Let's not discuss it. You have the advantage—our roles are reversed, and what's more, let me tell you, yes, I admit it, your sweetness, your patience will end by making me mean, contemptible, unfair. I should prefer your reproaches. Look at your grandmother, she has always treated me harshly. There is nothing that is more like pity than a certain blind obedience, and nothing resembles contempt more than pity. What the devil! At eighteen a girl ought to know her own mind. For two years I have been waiting. From week to week I have been waiting for the word that would clarify your situation, decide your future. Why do you refuse to speak the word? Why this silence? I am not speaking egotistically—after all a suitable marriage would be the best thing for me, for my career—you could marry anyone. But your vocation is too clear, everybody sees that. Again yesterday our venerated Dean of Idouville . . ."

"Please! That is something I'd rather not discuss," she said in a proud tone she had been unable to repress. "I was happy here—why not? I thought I was useful to you—and why pretend—I really was. I owe you the truth, Papa. Neither you, nor the Dean of Idouville, nor anyone else in the world, not even an angel, will force me into a convent one hour too soon. That I discharge my little duties day by day to the best of my ability, and, alas, according to my mood and my strength—what does that prove? Convents are not asylums nor sanatoriums—at least not for me. I am not looking for repose . . . Only, you are right to think that the moment has come for me to make a choice. I agree with you, and that is what I said at the beginning . . . But in all this there is not the shadow of an excuse for your speaking as you have of Abbé Chevance and me."

He had listened to her with growing agitation.

"One would think I was putting you out of the house! What are you driving at?"

"I think I should leave you now—at least until you are calmer. How could I have irritated you to such a point?"

But he himself was suffering too cruelly to hear that cry of pain, that last appeal for pity. Without meaning to she had uncovered his selfishness as rigorously shielded as a chrysalis in its silk sheath. He believed, of course, that he loved his daughter. Perhaps he did love her. Perhaps years ago he had also loved that quiet shadow, invisibly present still, that gentle, radiant stranger. Away from them, out of their presence he would surely have loved them both, worshipped them, prayed to them as angels. What he found unbearable was to discover himself, to recognize his wretchedness and his torments, his own life the color of ashes, through their twin destinies . . .

Very pale, she came up to him again, put one of her hands on his shoulder and the other lightly over his mouth.

"Don't be unjust, don't make me unhappy, you will be so sorry later."

"I am not unjust. . . . I only want to protect you . . . protect you against yourself. Precisely! You have more common sense than all the Abbé Chevances in the world; you come of a long line of landowners who knew the value of things, and in the supernatural order it is not such a bad idea to know the difference between a good and a bad bargain. You are not naïve, no, but you are pure, unbelievably pure. Of course, I am just a boor who knows nothing about souls, who has ruined one saint's life and is about to ruin yours. That's what they'll say, that's what they'll write. I must bear, as though it were a shameful burden, thirty years of relentless labor, all the innumerable humiliations I've had to swallow, the terrible disappointments, and they hound me like a pestiferous rat."

And because she had just drawn away from him, because he still felt the caress of her cool trembling fingers on his lips, almost unconsciously, excited by an obscure jealousy he could not have explained, he spoke.

"I had decided not to say anything about this. Why alarm you? But, after all, it is perhaps better to put you on your guard . . . against . . . well against perils that simple common sense or even the keenest judgment sometimes fails to discern. Alas, one must have a certain knowledge of evil . . . or at least a presentiment . . . in short, let's speak plainly—you see Colonel Fiodor every day—haven't you noticed anything?"

"Oh, yes . . . yes, of course! I mistrust that sort of colonel, Papa! But it was you, not I, who engaged him."

"I know, I know," he said testily. "I engaged him, it is true, on the recommendation of Baroness de Montanel . . . Well, that idiot is wantonly compromising you."

Terror got the better of her shame and Chantal could not suppress an anguished cry:

"What did he say?"

"Say! What did he say? Ah, that would be the last straw! What innocence! No, he is satisfied to make an odious spectacle of himself. He follows you about like a shadow, is respectful to the point of absurdity, a willing slave to your slightest wish. It seems that he devours you with his eyes . . ."

"It seems! What do you mean? Then you yourself have never . . . Oh, really Papa, . . . listening to gossip!"

"That is not true. I simply thought it was my duty to take into account a report, an accusation, if you like, but one that appears to be perfectly disinterested—for the young woman knows what she risks in . . . in interfering—in short, Francine has spoken to me. What was I to do? She is a good child, healthy and simple and devoted to us. She adores your grandmother. Anyway, we mustn't take it too seriously, my child . . . It is really a much more commonplace affair than you think."

Chantal had turned toward the window, toward the golden light as toward a friendly face, the white circle under her tearless eyes reaching almost to her cheeks. The old man's stammering was in her ears like a drone without meaning, a sort of childish complaining. She was trying with all her might, not to keep back her tears, but to dominate her pride.

"I think," she said suddenly in a perfectly calm voice, "it was a mistake for you to listen to Francine, Papa, and also to worry about me."

"You know nothing of the world, you do not wish to know anything. It is so much simpler! Your mother, too, thought she could cross muddy roads in her little Cinderella slippers. Yes, sooner or later you had to find out that the world was not made for angels. I am a good Catholic, I have dedicated part of my life to writing a history of the Church, and I say: The world was not made for angels. So much the worse for angels, I might add, if they are rash enough to venture into it unprepared! It won't help you any to look at me with those pure eyes. They are pure because they have seen nothing, fathomed nothing. Everyone of us has his secret, his secrets, a multitude of secrets rotting in his conscience, slowly, slowly decomposing. Even you, Chantal, yes, even you, if you live long enough will, perhaps, feel at the hour of death, that weight, that stirring of the slime under the deep water . . . What is expected of us? The impossible. First of all, we have to trace our road, step by step, from childhood to old age—groping along every inch of the way, springing all the traps, groveling, groveling, always groveling. Good Lord! To get oneself heard, recognized, one has to put oneself on a level with other people. You can't talk standing up to people lying down. When you stand up you find yourself alone. And are we made to live alone? Answer me that! First of all, could we live alone? Ah! Ah! Ah! Yes, that's it—could we! I have said that there are days when your confidence, your cheerfulness, your unbelievable serenity make me furious, drive me mad. A base sentiment, isn't it? Oh, really base! I am sure you think it utterly base, don't you? Come, can't you, at least, answer me?"

She kept her eyelids tightly closed to avoid seeing the unfortunate little man, maddened by an unutterable loathing for himself, opening like a ripe fruit.

"You don't want to answer me? . . . Perhaps it *is* a base sentiment . . . in a sense . . . And who says that I have not tried to fight it? And now circumstances are such, I am at so decisive a turning point in my life that I feel the need of frankness, of fresh air . . . Do answer me!"

"But, Papa, I love you," she cried, dismayed. "I love you!"

For by a supreme effort she had succeeded in quieting the revolt in her heart. Her frail trembling hands seemed to want to cover, to efface something, and in her glance shone that sort of pity that is only seen in a mother's eyes.

Suddenly his nervous frenzy subsided and Monsieur de Clergerie began carefully rubbing his pinkish bald spot with a corner of his handkerchief.

"I love you too," he said in a broken voice. "Forgive me! Where are we now? Where were we going?

. . . What nonsense. I am so overworked, my insomnia, this thunderstorm that is threatening . . . Your father is a sick man, my poor child, you must take that into account. A sick man . . . supersensitive. I want to see only happy faces around me, hear words of joy, of gratitude . . . The supersensitive are always disappointed."

He watched her timidly, with apprehension, through his lowered eyelashes. He was surprised to find her still there in front of him, her head drooping slightly over her right shoulder, and on her delicate face, as tender as before with its arched eyebrows and the faint line between, was the sign of a pure, indomitable will, an almost military firmness . . . "She is only a child," he thought, "my child . . ."

"Speak to me," he said. "I have hurt you. But you seem so confident, so pure. One feels that you have not sufficient pity for the poor wretches who wallow, like me, in the mud of this world . . . I repeat—this whole story of Fiodor is trivial, ridiculous . . . You mustn't give it another thought. Only speak to me, my darling! Won't you answer me?"

But from that moment he longed to suffer through her, to be humiliated by her.

"I was thinking, Papa," she said sadly, "although you have not given me much time for that . . . Never mind. One cannot always see the details of simple things right away, but the most difficult come to one in a flash. Only you must be careful, Papa, not to count on me too much. You must not lean too heavily on my poor shoulders. Serenity, confidence . . . Oh, that's all very well! But I see now . . . that is, I think I understand, that God gives them to us only on credit, never for nothing. Afterward . . . be sure we have to pay both capital and interest to the last penny! My word! You will soon all be expecting me not only to gather the stars, but to stoop down to pick them off the ground! Fiodor and all Francine's gossip are nothing to me. I am not as simple as you think . . . Would you like to know what really makes me unhappy in all this? It is that I cannot make you happy, all, all of you. It seems to me that for centuries I have been working for nothing else, and I am still no further along than on the first day. But according to you, I almost lost my courage in a second, in a breath. Oh, Papa, I too can be sad—not afflicted, not sorrowful nor even desolate, for it was Our Lady who was desolate at the foot of the cross—but sad with a sadness that is as cold as hell! Now that I have experienced it I shall never forget it, never! There is an intoxication in sadness, a vile intoxication! It is like foam on the lips. I have eaten of the forbidden fruit. Oh, it is horrible! . . . I envy those who succeed in loving sadness without offending God, without sinning against hope. I never could! Sadness came into the world with Satan—that world our Saviour never prayed for, the world you say I do not know. Oh, it is not so difficult to recognize: it is the world that prefers cold to warmth! What can God find to say to those who, of their own free will, of their own weight incline toward sadness and turn instinctively toward the night? Ah, Papa, we calculate the time left for me to stay with you, we make a hundred plans for the future, and yet we are going down, down, we are in a hollow, our strip of sky is shrinking, our horizon lifting. I should warn you! You must not lean too much on me. I am not too steady on my legs any longer. Yes, yes, you may laugh if you like. I am asking mercy—no, not mercy—but a truce, a simple truce, the customary truce for burying the dead. Yes, I mean it, the dead. There is no battle without corpses. You all seem to think I am a saint. It is amazing! A saint is at ease always and everywhere . . . How really funny . . . here your marriage has hardly been decided, and gently and prudently you push me toward a convent. What convent? No one knows. The name doesn't matter; just so that it is a great building made of yellow stone, with walls twenty-five feet high, an enormous entrance, and the turnbox sister at her wicket. But how about my dogs? Could I take them with me?"

Twenty times Clergerie had raised his hand in protest, irritated, questioning, imploring. Such words, that voice grown almost hard, that mysterious tenderness in revolt, were for him so many enigmas. And yet, in a flash, he felt again the strange premonition that had so upset him. What was she defending that was so precious, with such savage energy? What unknown part of her life? At her last words he was completely dumbfounded.

"Can it really be you, Chantal, talking like that? Your dogs!"

"Yes, my dogs!" she cried, laughing with a heart-breaking laugh. "My dogs need me too—like all of you! And you must remember this, Papa, poor Papa, soon, it is very possible, I may be of no use to them or to any of you."

She made a vague parting gesture, and was gone without giving him time to reply or even to call her back.

4

MONSIEUR DE CLERGERIE would undoubtedly have called in vain; Chantal was already in the shade of the lindens on the other side of the lawn. For an instant only he caught a glimpse of her light skirt. The two dogs went by like arrows, shoulder to shoulder, leaving two silver furrows behind them in the thick grass. She was walking like someone escaping, rapidly yet furtively and with caution, along the narrow path that, running through the oleanders and seringas, made a sudden turn toward the meadows and the little farm, now in ruins, with its single poplar, its mossy trough and its pond choked with reeds, in the middle of a guileless little valley. Water, left by the last storm, still shone in the ruts. A startled blackbird began making a great commotion in the leaves and finally, freeing itself, gave one of its strident cries and flew away. Perhaps for the first time in her life Chantal dismissed her dogs abruptly without even a caress. And as they dragged themselves off as slowly as possible toward the wooden gate at the end of the path where they crouched down whimpering, she even pretended to pick up an imaginary stone among the pine needles. She was not angry, but to her great surprise—for usually when she was very much disturbed or even a little worried she had always instinctively detested solitude and idleness—today she had suddenly felt an imperative need of silence and repose, an unaccountable dread of being seen. Halfway along the path, becoming impatient of all its useless windings, she pushed her way through the hedge, tearing her stockings as she went, and came out of the park onto the burning meadows. At the same rapid pace she made straight for the shade of the poplar, and with a tired sigh sank down on the grass in the shade.

For a long time her ears were filled with the hum of the sweltering earth. Since dawn the birds had taken cover, even the crickets were silent. Nothing stirred but one frail butterfly hovering over the tops of the wild oats. She closed her eyes.

The words that had just been spoken had no longer any meaning for her; there remained only the remembrance of an acute pain almost equally incomprehensible at present, and a feeling of remorse that she was trying little by little to understand, to drag into the light of her conscience. What she had said did not matter, not even if her habitual patience and gentleness had failed her. Like all truly pure souls she quickly resigned herself to past faults, thought only of how to repair whatever harm they had done. "Of all my daughters, you are certainly the least bothered by scruples of conscience!" Abbé Chevance used to say.

What did words matter? Even sin, once the will is detached and no longer nourishes it, withers and dies sterile. It is in the secret of intentions, like in a decomposing humus, in the dark forest of future sins, unpardoned sins, half dead half living, that new poisons are distilled. She could not, it is true, have expressed it, because until this moment every time she so desired, her soul would simply open to God's light as a man takes into his lungs all the air there is to breathe, breathes deeply. Why this obscurity today? "What have I done?" she said.

A clock in the distance was gravely striking ten. But in vain she tried to fix her mind on her humble daily tasks: luncheon to see to, the provisions brought from Lillebonne, Fernande's accounts, and then the basket of *bigarreaux*—those brownish cherries that had to be picked over so carefully because Monsignor Espelette had a horror of worms. Ah, no! Work would be of no help to her at this moment, since she would accomplish it without joy, unwillingly. To weigh what one gives is to give nothing. And all morning she had really done nothing but weigh and calculate—even worse, she had got so hopelessly confused in her calculations that she no longer knew what she wanted or where she was going. She had sought out her father through lassitude, through fear of a vague peril, like a coward she had wanted to unload her pain on to other shoulders, and the tables had been justly turned, and to her own burden had been added the hesitations, the remorse, all the pitiful secrets of the little man. She thought to find relief, but it was he whom she had relieved at the cost of her own peace.

With an impatient gesture she pushed away the high grass tickling her cheeks, for she was lying flat on her stomach at the edge of the pond. The shadow of the poplar had gradually gone around, and the sun fell relentlessly on her shoulders through her thin silk blouse. As far as the eye could see there was not a ripple, not a wrinkle, in the ruthless light; it no longer quivered even over the reeds, around the clay walls that had taken on the ruddy color of the rocks of the Avre valley. The faded thatch of the roofs, the gaping doorways, a shutter still hanging on one of its hinges, the unnatural immobility of those walls that were once alive, their nakedness, all made up a scheme of complete desolation, crushed under the immense weight of the blue sky . . . "What have I done?" she repeated sadly. "What fault have I committed?"

The idea never occurred to her that perhaps her suffering was without reason, without an aim, that there was no possible reply to her question, that her anguish was made to be lost with so many others in universal serenity, just as a cry goes no farther than a certain circle in space and beyond that circle there is nothing. She reviewed meticulously all the events of the morning one by one and—strange to say—it seemed to her that they fitted together so closely, so compactly that no power of will could have broken their implacable logic, that they had been born of inexorable necessity just as they were, in that rigorous succession. And others, apparently no less futile (for her tiny destiny mattered to no one but God), would certainly follow against which her soul would be just as defenseless. Had she not always thought that sufficient to each day is the sorrow thereof? But the day comes when life shatters forever the divine heedlessness of the humble, suddenly demands a decisive choice, substitutes, in a second, resignation for joy.

"I am not resigned," she used to say to her old friend. "Resignation is sad. How can one be resigned to the will of God? Does one resign oneself to being loved?" It seemed perfectly plain to her, too plain. But in God's will there must be some portion that sad human love is unable to convert, change completely, to incorporate perfectly with its own substance. The great thirst—the eternal Thirst—that turned away from living springs, asked only for vinegar and gall, only for bitterness.

And this was not the first time that Chantal had felt herself drawn toward the frontier of a new world so different from the one in which she had been trying to live. But she had always turned quickly away, refusing even to let her thoughts dwell on it. Now it seemed to her that events were pushing her toward it, that she had even crossed the border, had entered it already. The trials of the last few days had thrown open the gates. Should she go forward, go back, remain where she was, wait? No one could be less inclined to indulge in exaggerations, to dramatize all the little experiences of her life, than this simple and sincere little girl. She had always tried, not without malice, to see the funny side of all her trials and disappointments, that touch of absurdity which is hidden even in sorrow, from which even majestic sorrow is not altogether exempt. The gaiety of saints, so reassuring because of its homely kindliness, is certainly no less profound than their sadness, but we are too apt to think it naïve since there is no evidence of that probing, that effort, that painful delving into the heart which makes Molière's irony pinch just at the point where someone else's absurdity touches our own. "Oh, my daughter," Abbé Chevance would exclaim, "sometimes just a simple smile brings peace and comfort, the soul begins to breathe again . . . Take care not to be like the proud—poor things—don't make elaborate preparations in advance for great perils that will never happen . . . There are no great perils, it is only man's presumption that is great."

"I have been overconfident," she said aloud, trying to steady her voice. "That's it! You can't forever just slip through the net; you have to know how to disentangle yourself gently without doing any harm. That has always been the best way for me . . . I must always take my time, never get panicky . . . Naturally this marriage is going to complicate everything—at least for a while—I should have expected it. What an idiot I am! After all, Baroness de Montanel will be able to put up with me for a few months, for a year. But Papa is so jealous of his freedom, so suspicious, so susceptible! I must not even let him think that he is losing me, I must slip through his hands without his noticing it, like an eel . . . Where should I go? I am afraid of convents. They are perhaps a temptation of the devil! The truth is I don't like being too obviously protected. I should hate being in a besieged fortress, but I should not mind fighting in the open, plundering a little and sleeping on the ground rolled up in my cloak, in God's keeping . . . Is that a temptation too? After all I might go to China, Africa! There are missions just for poor girls like me, whom Providence can only use for those monotonous, menial tasks like sweeping out missionaries' huts or weeding the vegetable garden, wiping black babies' noses and hearing their catechism . . . The point is—am I strong enough? And as the answer is, I certainly am not, that is definitely out."

So with a wave of her hand she rejected once and for all that mad dream. Not that she worried as much as might be supposed over those strange nervous attacks whose secret had been discovered, and which humiliated her more than they frightened her. In truth there were only two things she dreaded henceforth—a scandal and the curiosity of doctors.

Going back over the years, one by one, she could not remember ever having either rebelled against or taken advantage of anything that had ever happened to her, being sure that, with her constitution, resistance would simply exhaust her, and also that any event, no matter how unpleasant, could, with gentleness and ruse, be minimized and reduced to the proportion of her simple, diligent common sense. "It seems to me," she had confided to Abbé Cénabre one day, "that it is possible to act like an adult, keeping up one's little place in the world, defending one's legitimate interests, and at the same time view the essential, elementary things —joy, sorrow, death—with the eyes of a child." And indeed, even now, a sort of curiosity, as fresh and new as a child's, finally got the better of her loathing, and she tried to look at her own experience as a spectator. "This poor Russian," she thought, "is quite mad too, and one of these fine mornings is sure to ask me to turn water into wine, or to raise the dead. What difference does it make whether he talks or not. In our family one neurotic more or less hardly counts. For if one is to believe Papa, we are all neurotics. It's inevitable!"

She tried to laugh, but quickly smothered the sound with her clasped hands. She stared stubbornly, stupidly at the top of a yew tree, level with the reddish grass on the crest of the little hill, and in the distance, beyond the black tree top, the bright slope of the roof and a lazy feather of transparent smoke . . . The clatter of a bucket against the stone rim of the well, a banging door, a young clear voice calling out . . . a single moment suspended in the limpid sky . . . And suddenly with a violent mutation of her soul, so unexpected that it almost made her faint, the house so cherished until now had, in that instant, become a stranger, almost an enemy. For the first time it seemed to her that she had been torn away from herself, that, all at once, she had escaped from the mysterious prestige of things grown too familiar, dilapidated as it were by too many eyes, things inconspicuous, and that foil all vigilance and betray us in the end. Long before she could give a name to so unfamiliar a sensation, she felt, by the tension of her whole being, the force of the ties that had just been sundered. It was like the sudden revelation of the treachery of a friend, not so much discovered as divined by the supernatural intuition of love—in the turning-away of eyes, in a hand that avoids ours, or an imperceptible shadow passing over the face . . . In her childhood—in those radiant vacations of her childhood—when from the top of the last hill after Arromanches, she first caught sight of the sloping slate roof among the green domes of the lindens, instantaneously she would also see the black and white tiles of the entrance hall, the stone stairway and the flowered chintz of her bedroom, would smell the cool musty odor of the corridors where the shutters were kept half closed, would embrace, across the distance, the entire house, just as the least gesture of a loved hand is for a lover the assurance of the presence of the beloved herself, a kind of possession.

Today she looked with distrust at the thin line of smoke against the blue, the imperceptible sign of the living house which, still a shelter, had ceased to be for her a refuge; where people came and went whom she had ceased to understand and who continued to carry out their obscure designs among themselves. And certainly she loved them still, but now her pity would no longer rush forth to meet them, would henceforth approach them cautiously; she feared their snares.

With less remorse than a heartbreaking curiosity, she realized little by little that for a long time now she had quite unconsciously been judging her father, that the deep root of that half filial, half maternal sentiment—so hopeless and so tender—plunged into the soul just to that agonizing point where the germ of contempt, which no flame of charity can altogether purify, lies buried. The voice she had been listening to, the voice of that unfortunate little man, hard and cringing by turns, still rang in her ears like a horrible confession. O God! Why this terror, this disgust? She had known that he was as weak as a child with his frivolous ambitions, his vindictiveness, his childish egotism, his terror of death. But she had never feared him before. Pity or contempt, what did it matter? At least she had loved him. She had thought only of serving him, of serving all of them, and first of all the most disinherited whose emptiness, whose nothingness her infallible pity had sensed. She knew that they were empty. "Poor sinners!" Abbé Chevance used to say. "How empty they are!" Which sinners? Out of charity she would not name them, would not select any particular ones out of that pale troop of phantoms. Why should she? All she had to do was to remain obedient to God, to make herself clearer day by day so that those miserable closed eyes might be opened and rejoice; more ardent, that she might warm them in their shrouds, awaken their sleeping hearts. "If God would show Himself to them," she thought, "perhaps they would love Him even more than I do! But they drag themselves through the night calling to each other, until one of us catches and reflects a single ray of the divine star . . ." No, no, she had never feared them, her indulgence toward each one of them had been like a child's, just as spontaneous, pure and free. And although their lives, so strange to her, so useless and, as it were, superfluous, were enough to revolt a young mind like hers, she had been until now too unaware of their secret motives, the passions devouring them, to fear either their example or their contact . . . Then whence had come this sudden estrangement? Who had uttered that cry of terror? "You don't know much about sin," her old friend would sometimes say to her with a sad smile. "No, you really don't know much about sin." And, incapable of finding one of those sublime metaphors so popular with preachers, he added like a peasant thinking of protecting his grain against vermin: "You see, sins are as hungry and cruel as rats. And people who love them are as cruel as they are, or they become so in the long run. Cruelty, my daughter . . ."

Cruelty! He said no more, shut his lips tightly over the mysterious word. What pure soul could readily distinguish between cruelty and madness, would not be tempted to confuse them? How could it believe that man would want to share with hell that horrible bread? She could not, of course, doubt the old priest's word, nor his humble experience which had been of such priceless benefit to her. And yet she had never dared insist, had not dared to question him further. It seemed to her that she could not have endured, that she would have died of such a terrible blow to her innocent charity, and that of all imaginable vices that was the only one she could not have kept herself from loathing. Yes, sin is cruel. No one can deny it. But what of its miserable victims? Isn't it bad enough that, by some hideous mistake, they should hold in their arms, hug to their bleeding breasts an armed beast like that—should we not pity them? Just the thought of such an absurd mistake filled her heart with pity. If they only knew! She was not, of course, so naïve as to think that this knowledge, the awakening of conscience, would be enough to reform them completely; for the very delicacy of her compassion inspired in her a distrust of glib advice and homilies. She hoped to win them through tenderness and patience alone, as one subdues a fierce and wounded animal. But Abbé Chevance had also told her: "My daughter, wounded pride cares nothing for patience and tenderness . . . a drop of water on a red hot iron!" Then braving him with her peaceful eyes she had said: "If patience and tenderness are useless, joy will suffice, God's joy, of which we are so parsimonious. Yes, people who receive it are too tempted to keep it for themselves, consuming all its consolations, whereas it should be radiating from them all the time! Isn't that true, isn't it?

Don't you agree with me? Think of the saints . . . how transparent they make themselves! The trouble with me is that I am opaque. Sometimes I reflect a little light, but dimly, stingily. Doesn't God ask more than that? One should be all crystal, pure water through which anyone can see God!" And so, until now each new disappointment had left her stronger in her fragile peace. And, in reality, it was the very idea of this fragility that was her strength; she felt no need of props or fulcrums, nor of those logical constructions in which the weak and presumptuous confine their lives—they would have stifled her like prison walls. Like all flying things her equilibrium was a miracle of skill and volition, aerial acrobatics. Treachery in a friend, or worse, the discovery of a certain baseness, had always caused her acute suffering which she invariably concealed. "I am so light," she would admit. "I should like to be a speck of impalpable dust suspended in the will of God."

But today, at this moment, like a bird caught in the storm, she had even lost her sense of flight. From what heights then had she fallen to feel herself so heavy on the earth she hugged with hands and knees? In her amazement she was afraid to move, afraid to leave this intolerable, desolate place. She hardly dared open her eyes, to look at the vaporous and obdurate line of the hills that she felt were closing in on her. The slopes intersected by flowering hedges, the white road, the shadowy little valley of the Souette in the distance, and farther still the last copse of the forest of Seigneville set like a hat askew on the crown of the hill, all this peaceful landscape appeared to her now transformed in the unswerving light, enormous, alert, like an animal ready to spring. She had always felt the same shock of terror, quickly suppressed, when she looked at the vast agglomeration of cities, and no less avid is the land formed in the image of man's desires, kneaded by sin, and rekneaded—land of sin. "I have been so naïve! One must not be naïve," she repeated sadly, for she could find no other words for this new anguish. And it is true that at that moment her pain was still that of a child, although soon, in that very spot, under that torrid sky, she was to have the revelation of man's force and cruelty, the infinite resourcefulness of his guile and the ferocity of evil.

Now she was to know, perhaps the only temptation of her life, and the unexpected shock came with such swiftness that it was impossible to evade it. In that instant she recognized her terrifying, fundamental loneliness, the loneliness of the children of God. She was certainly still very far from having any abstract knowledge of that solitude, supposing of course that it is possible to conceive the magisterial absurdity, the sublime challenge of that handful of thinking animals who bring nothing to the world but the good news of Pain become God! But she felt in the depths of her soul, and in the very marrow of her bones, that holy abandonment which is the threshold and the portal of all sainthood. Her surprise was so great that it brought her to her knees, and childishly she looked to measure the distance that separated her from the Seigneville road where the train for Avancourt passes. Yes! in the twinkling of an eye this intrepid, sensible young girl, always so considerate of other people, was seized with the mad idea of running away, just as she was, no matter where, fleeing like a thief. "I will never see them again!" And even at that moment she saw with supernatural acuity each one of those faces which that morning had still been so closely, so intimately linked with all the other images of her life that they seemed to belong to her by the same right as her own thoughts. Now they appeared in a pitiless light that had no mercy for a single doubtful wrinkle, that turned a shrewd smile into an evil grimace, revealed the cast in every eye. They frightened her now, and she no longer felt any pity for them. She thought of certain words, read and reread, that verse in the book of Job where the terrible cry is torn from that hard Jewish heart by the world's malevolence and the desperate irony of the psalms. And all this testimony come down through the ages with a sepulchral odor, that the pious sleepily spell over to the wheeze of the harmonium, took on for her its eternal meaning. Throwing herself flat on the ground she buried her face in the thick grass and wept as she had never wept before.

"What a catastrophe!" a voice behind her said at that moment . . . "I might have known it. One has to keep an eye on everything. We are being ruined, my girl."

Chantal jumped to her feet trembling all over, and with both hands hastily wiped away her tears.

"Heavens, Granny! Who let you come way out here alone? Where were you going? The sun would kill you . . . Francine . . ."

"Don't bother about Francine," said the old lady deliberately. "And which one, may I ask, do you call Francine? My son engages more servants than we can ever pay. I don't want all these imbeciles devouring our bread. They eat like she-lions."

Her hands were wringing wet but pale, almost gray, in the folds of the black shawl. The hem of her long skirt was white with dust, as well as the cloth shoes whose round tips alone were visible. In the opening of the woolen shawl which, in spite of the heat, she kept tightly clasped around her throat, her thin face was visible with dark red spots on her flaming cheeks, and one eye as sharp and cutting as a bit of broken mirror.

"Please, Granny, be sensible!" Chantal stammered, "I beg you, let me take you back to the house. What a state you are in! Where did you leave Francine? What happened?"

"Do try to regain your composure, first of all," replied the madwoman in the same toneless voice. "Am I disturbing you? What a pother! There's nothing to get excited about. Can't I go and come as I please? Just look at that building—by autumn there won't be a thing left but the rafters. And the pond's good for nothing—just mud and frogs. If they'd listened to me they'd have gone to the expense of digging a well at the time of the Seigneville strike when the cost of labor was so low! What an opportunity we have missed! In two years the Valettes' property has doubled in value—and here the pastures flooded every spring, a perfect swamp that makes the cows swell and give more water than milk! . . . But who'd listen to me? That year you saw nothing but doctors and druggists and nurses in the house—to ruin a family they outdo even priests and lawyers."

She was speaking in a mechanical voice, with a constantly accelerated tempo, using up the last bit of her waning strength. It was evident that she could hardly stand on her feet, and Chantal who had timidly slipped one arm around her shoulders could see that her old legs were shaking under the black skirt.

"You have told me that before, Granny, you have told me a hundred times. Do be sensible. You simply can't stay out in this heat. We are going to walk slowly back to the house, and you will lie down in the shade for a moment or two while I find Francine . . ."

"The house, your house! The stones are sure to fall on my head. I prefer sitting beside the pond under the chestnut tree. Then I shall go back myself. Walking always does me a powerful lot of good! Fatigue purifies the blood."

"The chestnut tree! What chestnut tree, Granny? There is no chestnut tree here any more."

"Of course, of course," the old lady continued. "Right here like this, the chestnut tree gives quite enough shade for me."

She gave a little angry cough leaning with all her weight against Chantal.

"I've never felt sprier, I'm very comfortable here, the sun is nice and hot . . . We'll have a second crop . . . what a second crop! And now tell me, my girl, what were you doing there lying flat on your stomach? You see, you like the earth after all! You'll come to it, everybody comes to it . . . Land of your own, land that works for your profit, to a real woman, a thrifty woman, it speaks. She loves the care of it, it's better than a man. Dear me, the times I've lain there myself, just where you were . . . no, a little farther on, from where you can see the big piece of land of La Loupe and the two fields below. The earth is as good as a feather bed—you stick to it."

"Won't you just follow me to the edge of the park," implored Chantal. "We will cross the field together, only the field, I promise! After that you will do just as you please."

"Fiddlesticks! No, no, you can't fool me. Do you think at my age I can go alone through the fields? I am mad, my sweet, raving mad. Do you know, at this very minute while I am talking to you, I see a great big blue fly, yes, blue! . . . Tell me, my pretty, do you know what they call me in the kitchen, those great fellows—handsome devils they are, too! . . . The vixen! That's what they call me. Oh, I notice everything, I hear everything, but the trouble is, don't you see, I'm never quite sure! Never! I am not sure of my son. He's always shying off and sidestepping like a young horse just put to the plow. You can't trust anybody in this world, not even the dead. Ah, I know what I'm talking about! Our worst troubles come from the dead, they're cunning, mighty cunning!"

"Granny!" cried the poor girl. "Don't frighten me. Do be good. You understand. Yes, yes, you do! You understand very well when you want to . . . I know that . . . You are not bad, Granny, you are unhappy, that isn't my fault. I want so much to love you."

"Unhappy? I, unhappy! Oh, don't you believe it! I am very sorry to disappoint you but I am less unhappy than you are. I, you see, have endured! Yes, I have endured. Have you any idea what that means, to endure? All you wanted was to sing . . . such giddiness! One day, do you remember, I made you scour the pots . . . a matter of principle . . . and you broke your nails. But now, today, who is this talking to you, just as steady on her legs as ever? While you—you look skinnier and frailer than I've ever seen you before."

She paused shaking her narrow head contemptuously.

"But, Granny, who do you think I am? Aren't you taking me for someone else?" Chantal asked pleadingly, as pale as her little white collar. "Please, Granny, aren't you tired of playing this horrible game? For it is a game you've made up. I know, a frightful game. Look at me. Look me straight in the eyes . . . Oh, Granny, darling, Granny, please don't tempt me too far."

She started to throw herself on her knees but this gesture of humility struck her as so vain, puerile and almost silly, that she straightened up immediately and turned her imploring gaze on the deserted fields, the horizon, the liquid fire of the sky. For the second time the idea of escape came to her, she would run away wildly, whatever the cost, like a condemned man fleeing his destiny. But it was already too late. So now, instinctively, by some vital reflex, because she felt her power of resistance failing, felt that one more effort and her heart would break, naïvely she sought to hold her ground in order to dissipate this growing nightmare while there was still time, before it appeared in all its horror in the full light of noon.

"You are talking to Chantal, to me, Chantal. I am not Mama, and you know it! Yes, you know it very well . . . Oh, Granny, you have acted out this terrible farce for Papa, for Francine, for many others, but never before for me, never! You have never dared. I forbid you . . . I don't want to know, I haven't the courage to listen . . . at least not today. Can't you see that I am unhappy? I was at the end of my endurance when you came, it was the final blow, yes, it is as though you had stabbed me in the back. My God, what have you against me? All of you? What have I done to you?"

"Are you crazy?" said the old lady coldly. "Can I believe my ears, daughter, making a scene like that, you! Well, perhaps I *have* imagined that you were dead or dying, how do I know! What's the harm, anyway? Can we choose our dreams? Since you came here nobody talks of anything but doctors, potions and plasters! Pugh! No wonder I dream of death—of dying and funerals! Are you looking for a quarrel, my girl? . . . Well, I'll not give you the satisfaction of falling into your trap! It's too plain, much too plain, let me tell you. I prefer to retire."

She attempted to step backwards, almost lost her balance, tottered and, red with shame, straightened herself again, trying to hide from her adversary the increased shaking of her knees. Chantal closed her eyes.

"Granny," she said in a despairing voice, "be quiet! I don't want to know what you are going to say. Those are things of the past. Yes, they hurt you, I know . . . They trouble your poor heart. Do you think they would trouble you less if I were to learn them in my turn? At least, not today, Granny, not right away!"

She pressed her fingers against her eyelids until her eyes ached. She really feared the threatened avowals less than the sight of the tiny black figure standing in the middle of that hostile landscape as at the center of her own temptation; that fragile and mysterious body on which she imagined she could touch, could feel—like the springy moss covering the pebbles that the sounding-cylinder brings up—the humble and tragic secret submerged for so many years now suddenly risen to the surface.

"Louise," the madwoman continued with a certain stress. "I hate mystification, I always come right to the point. I have always been as frank as a man in all my dealings. Yes, or no, have I ever wronged you, my girl?"

She coughed as she always used to at the end of those interminable bargainings when the farmer, completely muddled by all the figures and the heavy cider, surrendering, would dip his pen in the inkwell and wipe it on his sleeve.

"I must know for sure. It is not enough for you just to keep quiet. I can read your thoughts. Oh, you'll never hide anything from me, you can make up your mind to that! No one has ever fooled me, big words don't scare me, I call a spade a spade—I nonplus people, as they say. It's no use your trying all your tricks, lowering your eyes like that, holding your tongue, it doesn't go down with me. I just push open the door whenever I please, I walk right in, my darling, and poke around among all your little mysteries. You're like people who lock their doors and leave the windows open. You think I am a mean old woman, don't you? Now what are you muttering to yourself?"

"Granny, poor Granny," Chantal kept repeating wearily, "poor Granny."

She still covered her eyes with her hands as though the darkness would bring her closer to her dead mother whose secrets that feeble voice—like a hand wandering over the keys of a piano searching for a lost melody—was dragging out of the darkness one by one, those humble tear-drenched secrets.

"Poor, you say! What do you mean by bringing that up. Have I ever reproached you for your poverty, my dear? We may not be English lords but we do marry dowerless girls . . . Never mind that, there's plenty of work here . . . Oh, my, my! Am I a cannibal, a dragon? We'll not even mention your pitiful health —my son's such a simpleton, he has just what he deserves! We are paying what's necessary. . . . That is we did—formerly— At any rate we will pay . . . Bah! There! You see I have all my wits about me. An old woman could teach the devil himself. Even a ghost wouldn't frighten me. And, why shouldn't I say so— the funeral cost two hundred *écus*, and whether I'm crazy or not I'll not gainsay it even in front of you."

Neither anger nor disgust could make Chantal uncover her eyes, although, in truth, she felt neither anger nor disgust at this moment . . . It seemed rather that a supernatural silence suddenly filled her heart —but very different from the silence that is the prelude to great soul-struggles—a silence of a new order that she did not yet recognize. Each word reached her ears intact and whole, she understood its meaning and yet she heard it with stupid indifference—or even worse—with the feeling that her hope had been deceived. Was that creature whose image she could still see behind her closed eyelids—so ridiculously black and tiny under the immense summer sky, really her grandmother or an insect? She thought how easy it would be to crush that quavering voice under her heel, to erase that miserable form with the back of her hand as though it had been a line written in charcoal, an extravagant phrase, on the inexorable azure screen . . . But she was without desire. She felt only a melancholy curiosity that her numbed conscience obscurely realized might well be dangerous. For the hand of fear gripping man's heart is not more icy. Even the corpse of hate is warmer.

No, it was neither anger nor disgust that finally made Chantal drop her hands, open her eyes . . . She simply obeyed the law of her nature, followed the dictates of her pride. She simply faced it. For an hour perhaps, certainly for too long, she had been there, in that deserted meadow, she could not say why, humiliated by evasive phantoms, deceived by familiar images now grown inimical, caught in the flaming countryside like a little fly in the center of a dazzling spiderweb . . . She faced it.

The old lady had not moved an inch, still stood on the same spot, her little shadow by her side like a faithful hunchbacked dwarf. And although her mobile face continued to reveal all her hurrying thoughts, she kept opening and closing her mouth without making a sound.

Chantal's only ruse, the same as that of a Chevance, was her shattering simplicity. While a weak man or an impostor is always more complicated than the problem he is trying to solve, and thinking to encompass his adversary, merely keeps prowling interminably around himself, the heroic nature will throw itself into the heart of the danger to turn it to its own use, just as captured artillery is turned about and aimed at the backs of the fleeing enemy. Quickly she went up to Madame de Clergerie and putting her hand on the old lady's shoulder caught and held with her own those terrible expressionless eyes, always full of restless shadows.

"I am not afraid of you, Granny," she said. "I am not afraid of you, and why should you be afraid of me? No matter how uselessly unhappy you make me, you will never reduce me to despair, even today, even at this hour, because I will always find enough strength to forgive you. Oh, you are not as crazy as you like to pretend, nor as mean either. There is something, I don't know what, that is too heavy for you to bear, that weighs on your poor soul. Isn't it true? Something that is suffocating you, that you can't possibly keep any longer, but that no one is generous enough to accept from you, that no one seems to understand . . . And here you bring it to me just at a moment of my life when I have barely enough courage left for myself alone, you come to cling to a miserable little boat that is adrift. Where are we going, both of us?"

This seemed to throw the old lady into a state of extreme agitation at first, but she said nothing. Then all the thousand wrinkles of her cheeks seemed to deepen, and their inextricable network joined the furrows along each side of her mouth, while a dim light began to appear in the back of her dormant eyes. And, suddenly, her two dry little hands shot out like bullets, so quickly that Chantal had hardly time to turn her face aside to avoid them, while the slight old body stiffened with the immense effort.

"Let me go, Chantal!" she begged. "Let me go! I know you, darling. Would you like me to give you a present? What would you like? I have absolutely nothing to give, that is the trouble. Nothing to give, nothing more to give, my dear . . . No one knows what that means."

In her emotion she had loosened the knitted shawl and was holding on to it at the level of her knees, the end trailing in the grass at her feet. No one could have told from what depths of consciousness those plain and simple words had burst, nor even the source of that sentiment now transforming her worn old face, as though it had been emptied from within by that most consuming passion of old age—sterile regret.

For how many days, years, centuries had she, like so many survivors of another age lost in the midst of a new world as strange as Sirius or Orion and slowly pushed out of the universe of the living by mortal pity, accomplice of their useless lies, been waiting for the liberating, the living word? Evidently the tone, the accent of Chantal's voice had first struck her heart long before her pitiful slow understanding grasped the meaning of the words. But she had immediately recognized that sort of truth which had formerly been so hateful to her pride and which she groped for greedily now, feeling suddenly in her very bones a need for it.

For a long time Chantal looked down into the face turned toward her, surrendered to her gaze, completely at her mercy. The very violence of her agitation gave Chantal the illusion of an absolute inner calm, a profound, supernatural peace. The events of the morning, little by little, lost their meaning like a phrase heard in one's dream and that one discovers in one's memory at dawn, lifeless, colorless, like a dead bird. The idea that this tiny creature, lost with her in the heat and the light of a summer day, had once been her mother's enemy and rival seemed to her fantastic. A moment ago, without the least anger, she had avoided the old hands aimed at her, as one brushes aside a buzzing fly or a blade of grass. Now she felt like proffering her cheeks, she wanted to receive the blow full in the face. Then she would go back to the house over there beyond the trees, so foreign to her now, and would say to them all: "Strike me. I deserve it. I have never been one of you. Through ignorance I pretended to belong to you, through ignorance or cowardice. You have nothing to give me, I have nothing that you could use . . . What a foolish dream—the idea of exchanging anything at all with you! I can neither love you nor hate you. But you can, at least, destroy me. Deliver me from all of you!"

"Don't look at me like that!" said the old lady and in the silence her voice took on an extraordinary distinctness. "You look just like a martyr and I can't stand martyrs, my poor child. Obviously, obviously" . . . She took two short steps toward Chantal stiffly, as though shackled. ". . . Obviously, we must, you see, be fair (Chantal felt the sour breath on her neck). . . . I admit I was wrong that Sunday—yes,—I should have closed the door, your mother heard every word . . . Anyway I did it on purpose; you feel nasty like that sometimes; anger seems to melt in your mouth and run down into your heart . . . I'm no worse than anybody else but I felt like throwing the thermometer out of the window . . . a hundred . . . a hundred and one . . . on and on . . . it was enough to drive a body crazy! And your father as yellow as a lemon with his liver and his kidneys and I don't know what all!"

She came a step nearer and the look she raised to her granddaughter was veiled again.

"Do you think she really cried so much? Do you think so too? Are you sure? I kept my ears open while I folded my sheets, I was always listening. She gave great big sobs. But, of course, I was on the second floor in the linen room. Her window was wide open and sound rises . . . What do you think, eh? When you're so old, you imagine things, you make up things. Anyway, poor little thing, she died ten days later. So it wouldn't have done her any good even if I'd kept quiet."

The loosened shawl slipped off completely now and the comical tortured face appeared in the full glare of the pitiless light like the menace of night itself. It made Chantal's heart stop beating. But again the intrepid girl who had always refused to deceive herself, did not give ground, defied the shadowy dreams that she felt rising from the depths of her consciousness like bubbles in the mud. Anguish with its sightless face tore at her heartstrings but could not shake her courage nor humble that touch of mocking pride which was the flower of her young wisdom. "Am I going to run away from my own grandmother?" she thought, "I am ridiculous. She disliked my mother and what of it? Haven't I always known it? Have I discovered anything new? I was mad to come out here to these crumbling old walls, madder still to stay. I have done nothing but silly things all morning one after the other! . . ." But it was a voice lost in the storm.

For she was still unable to take her eyes from that hostile face assailed by the full power of the sunlight and stripped even of that secret immaterial shadow that is like the softening cloak of old age. The passions that had modeled it, now petrified, still survived in it, as those polished skulls are the sinister reverse of faces vanished centuries ago. She could read in all those carved reliefs and hollows, as on a funeral stele, the whole history of her race, the mark of ancestors hardened in the formless wax of time. That double furrow along the cheek belonged to Uncle Antoine—his pinched sarcastic laugh with which he used to greet the too prodigal farmer or poachers or a pregnant servant girl; that provocative curve of the chin, the heaviness of the too low-swung jaw—that was great-grandfather Ferdinand who lived to be a hundred and who had carried a cow on his head at the Saint Guénolé fair. And there the severe forehead of the Clergeries, her father's thick neck, the receding line above the eyebrows which gave the little man's expression something unhealthy and equivocal . . . And here! . . . Oh, God! That little line, so young, so childish, ending on each cheek in an imperceptible dimple that came and went with every changing emotion either of pleasure or pain.

In a flash she remembered her own face in a bad little photograph which she had slipped into her prayer-book, because she had been told that her mother was always pressing it to her lips so that she felt it must bear some trace of those kisses still. "Your mother adored your dimples," Monsieur de Clergerie had solemnly told her. "Why, she even asked Bourdelle, one evening, to take an impression of your cheeks! . . ." Her cheeks!

"*I have nothing,*" Abbé Chevance always liked to say. "*It took me thirty years to discover that I have nothing, absolutely nothing. What weighs on a man's heart is his dream . . .*"

No sign appeared in the sky, no miracle occurred. The thin line of smoke still rose through the trees melting instantaneously into the blue. The dry grass rustled softly, a pebble slipped from the top of the wall and splashed into the pond, and the frail butterfly flew over to the yellowed tip of the elderberry bush.

"Granny," said Chantal after a long silence. "We must go home. We must go home to God."

She picked up her grandmother's shawl and to get it out of her way knotted it around her waist.

"Don't be afraid," she said. "Now I am strong enough to carry you; I wish you were heavy, much heavier, as heavy as all the sins of the world. For, you see, I have just discovered something I have always known: we can no more escape from one another than we can escape from God. We have one thing in common, only one, and that is sin." She bent over the wet forehead, brushing it lightly with her lips. The unresisting head rolled helplessly, trustfully, on her shoulder, the eyes closed. Chantal had already started for the house carrying preciously her lamentable prey hugged tightly to her breast. The ferocious sun burned her neck and hands, seemed to inhale all the air of her lungs, absorbed even her thoughts, but now she knew that no sun in the world could ever dry up her joy henceforth.

"Granny," she murmured, pausing to get her breath, "I seem to be carrying you, but it is you who are carrying me . . . Oh, Granny, don't ever let go of me again!"

And her eyes, haggard with sunlight and fatigue, were full of a calm defiance.

5

"HERE, give me my onions!" cried the angry cook. "You're no good for anything, any more. You might as well go to bed. Yes, go on to bed with you. What a house!"

"It isn't true, I'm not crying," said Francine wiping her red eyes with the back of her arm. "Peeling onions always makes my eyes water. Is that my fault?"

"Don't lie, little fool! You were sobbing. I heard you from the laundry. A body can't help feeling sorry for you. What you need is a couple of good smacks."

"I wouldn't mind, I wish I was dead, Madame Fernande. If I die I want to be cremated—burned, you know—bones and all. I've written a note that they'll find under the marble top of my chest of drawers. I even think I'll give it to you, seeing as how Monsieur Fiodor is always snooping into everything."

"Keep it, you little goose, I don't want to have anything to do with such things . . . It's those novels that have turned your head. You ought to do like me, I never read them. At your age a girl thinks enough about men without getting herself all excited by things made up in books. But you're as defenseless as a baby. And the Lord knows you're as depraved as they come, with those eyes of yours that look like melted lead. Gray eyes! They're not human."

"Depraved? It's unhappy you should say. Oh, it's because I'm unlucky. I haven't any line of chance in my hand, I am a child of misfortune. And as for showing Monsieur Fiodor—don't make me laugh! A man like that—as tender and shy as a woman and as ferocious as a kitten!"

"Ferocious! Fiddlesticks! I know where to find your ferocious men, right in your precious movies. It's like all your talk of cremation, lines of chance and the rest of it—just your silly fancy. A good thick soup at six o'clock in the morning, a wine tonic before your meals, and herb tea before you go to bed to purify the blood, that's the advice of a mother of a family. But what's the use wasting my breath. Who ever listened to advice? Experience is an invention of old people to madden young folk, without doing anybody any good. I can think myself lucky you don't laugh in my face!"

"I don't feel like laughing."

"Laugh just the same. They haven't invented anything better against the follies of love. Otherwise you may laugh too late, and God knows where that will lead you, to laugh too late, after your heart is broken! Right to the well and into it head first."

"Why not?" sighed Francine.

"Don't talk like that, you wicked girl! If you go on thinking about it all the time you'll end up by doing it. I've seen more sensible girls than you bitten by suicide, what they call an obsession, snapped up like flies . . . We weren't born with a silver spoon in our mouth, you and I! Someone ought to put you wise. Just remember this—society people don't destroy themselves half as much as the likes of us. They don't go beyond Ohs! and Ahs! and swoonings and hysterics, driving all the servants crazy and making the fortune of doctors like Professor La Pérouse. There's someone knows how to turn the master round his little finger! But a chambermaid can't afford to have millionaire blues!"

"Can't afford it! That's where you're wrong! You can think what you please about me but I'm not so ignorant as I seem. I can't express myself, that's all. And anyway love makes everyone tongue-tied more or less. Besides, what they say about love in books is a joke. Love, Madame Fernande, is hard, it hasn't any pity, it grins at everything—like a death's head! I don't even care how I look any more. I haven't any vanity, a new dress makes me sick. You don't want to be loved for your clothes! In the beginning of course it's different. You like to show off a new coat or anything, a hat, a bit of ribbon, a pretty slipper with buckles, and you laugh at everything and say a lot of silly nonsense. You think love is something wonderful. That's why we're caught by it. We're taken in by the blarney, the smooth manners. But when the fish is caught, Madame Fernande,—goodby! Love shows itself for what it is—as bare as the palm of your hand, as bare as a worm!"

In amazement the cook let her huge arms fall on the table and when the girl stopped talking she gave herself a shake like a swimmer seized by a chill.

"You give me the creeps, Francine," she said, "I think you're crazy. There's a wind of madness in this house of Satan! The worst of it is I don't think you're fooling, I believe you're speaking God's truth. You certainly gave me a turn!"

She sniffled audibly and wiped her eyes. But back of the tears shone primitive female curiosity, stronger than any compassion.

"I'll get you out of this, dearie, I'll not let that filthy Russian gobble you up, that devil! Whatever has he done to you? Such ideas as he's put into your pretty head. When I think what a flibbertigibbet you were only last year, stealing my sugar and my chocolate and singing from morning to night! But, by the blessed saints, I'll not desert you, you can count on me, the police ought to be told. Tell me the truth now. He's threatened you, hasn't he, the monster?"

"Threatened me, me! Just say that again, you big sack of sawdust! Hypocrite! He never threatened anybody. He's unhappy, that's all. You can't imagine how unhappy he is—it makes you sick at your stomach really, it makes you feel faint! . . . and when he yawns the way he does, you'd think he was a king or a god. He tells about how it is in his country—the white sky, the white earth with little white birches, log cabins, frozen lakes, a big red sun and wolves . . . Then he talks about death so sweetly, kind of affectionately, and he admits that he doesn't love me, that he never can love me. Poor ducky!"

"Imbecile! Triple imbecile! *His country!* How she says it! What a voice! And *unhappy!* Yes, he looks it, doesn't he, when he plays poker until two o'clock in the morning. He dresses like a prince, he smokes gold-tipped cigarettes that smell of pepper and lavender. You should talk about unhappy people, you! Imbecile! And your own father, when your mother died, ruining his lungs blowing glass to bring up the six of you! And what's the idea of adoring this Russian beggar on your knees now, when not ten minutes ago you were calling him a crook, a ferocious, inhuman monster. I don't know what all!"

"Madame Fernande, I am sorry I insulted you, you must excuse me, it's my nerves. Only you really shouldn't be so unfair. I was too, at first. I wish I could make you understand, but I can't find the words . . . I'm not to be pitied as much as you think. I'm not really to be pitied at all. He doesn't love me—so what? I can't blame him for that. He's too unhappy and I have to be unhappy with him—because of him. That makes me his equal, don't you see? He said so himself! I don't give a damn about anything else. I don't want to be a trouble to anybody, I'll die like a fly. Naturally, that seems sad to you, it gives you the chills to listen to me. But me, I like that chill, it rests me—I'm so sick and tired of everything. Evening too is sad, Madame Fernande. Yet after the sun has roasted you all day and made the eyes pop out of your head, you're glad to see the darkness fall and the great night moths appear!"

"Good Lord! The darkness fall and the great night moths appear! I'd swear it was him talking. She recites her lesson by heart, poor innocent! And he'll lead her calmly to the bottom of the river, warbling his fine, empty phrases. That's what he wants, idiot that you are! Yes, he only wants your money. Don't lie—he's already got more than a thousand francs out of you."

"And what if he has? That's nothing to what I'll do, Madame Fernande. I am going to make a will and leave everything to him."

"All right, all right! Have it your own way. But now let me tell you, I've my work to do . . . I can't live on my income. Go and hang yourself somewhere else because, on my part, I'm not going to put up with you another minute. Does Monsieur de Clergerie pay you to mope around all day long, or to recite horrors in that sanctimonious, first-communion voice? I'll have him throw you out of the house, that's what I'll do, yes, and for your own good too! Back in Paris, you'll see whether your Russian comes running after you. Not much, he won't! And what's more I've got to see him and not later than this very minute about that keg of olive oil . . . I want to have some words with him—they've been burning my tongue for a long time. If you'd rather not call him, I'll send François."

"François is at the farm mending the washing machine. And why shouldn't I call Monsieur Fiodor myself? The idea! Do you think I'm ashamed? But you'll see what kind of a man he is, Madame Fernande. He'll turn you inside out like a glove, the darling!"

"Oh, have it your own way!" said the outraged cook. "And tell him to bring the keg on the gardener's wheelbarrow like other people, instead of playing Hercules. He very nearly dropped the barrel of port on my foot—one hundred *litres!*"

She took up her knife again with dignity. As the daughter of a village blacksmith who also kept a cabaret where the young people danced every Sunday, she considered herself quite an expert in matters of the heart. She had been accustomed all her life to that frank Norman joviality which never dreams of trying to hide from the servants—or even the neighbors—an honest debauch provided it is calculated with hereditary prudence, according to a man's fortune and station in life. She began to find unbearable the air of this house full of secrets, shunned by all the hunting squires of the neighborhood and the fat village priests, and which was so different from the other *châteaux* where she had worked—a house frequented by doctors, clergymen, historians, and dubious journalists, austere to the point of dreariness and eaten up, as she felt, by secret grudges and vices . . . Above all she despised the master's poor health, all his remedies and treatments, the childish squeamishness of his stomach, and all his other manias that she found womanish and degrading in a man. As a girl, when she had helped out as an "extra" at the *château,* she had known the young Madame de Clergerie who was then dying, and had afterwards discreetly transferred to Mademoiselle Chantal a sort of devout pity that was not without a certain delicacy and insight. His daughter's predilection for this motherly soul (he loathed fat people) shocked de Clergerie. "She's always sweaty," he would say. "It makes me sick to look at her." And he was never to know that in the tragic solitude in which this mysterious little girl was to make the supreme effort of her life, give up life itself, her only help and comfort would come from this homely solicitude. "She isn't very clever nor very devout," Chantal had replied, "and she certainly empties the whole salt cellar into the stories she tells me. But I love her because she never lies."

"I sent word that you were to use the wheelbarrow, Monsieur Fiodor. The laundry door's so low . . . I suppose you've scraped the casing again."

"What's the difference?" He set down the keg in its usual place and turned his sad impassive face toward Madame Fernande. "What's the difference, really? After all, this isn't my job. I am just trying to please you, to be helpful. I think you might let me do it in my own way, as the fancy moves me, even if I happen to scratch a bit of oak? It is a thing women can never understand—a man feels like trying out his muscles sometimes."

"Naturally, you're always in the right!" the cook cried testily, and it amused him to notice the impatience, curiosity and vexation her voice betrayed. "A body can't say a word but you come out with a torrent of words!"

"We Russians are like that," he said. "We're garrulous. Oh but I can talk like a Frenchman if I want to—even more curtly. The trouble with you, Madame Fernande, is that you *think* evil thoughts, much too evil . . . one shouldn't . . . one should unburden one's heart . . . I too have a word to say about Mademoiselle Francine."

"So, you've been listening at keyholes. Oh, don't mind me!" She was furious and disappointed. "What do I care? I am sick and tired of your airs! The mother of a family isn't afraid to tell you straight to your face what she thinks. This is no place for you, Monsieur Fiodor, in this reputable house, with these respectable people. There may be foolishness here, I don't say there isn't, but there's no evil. But you are really evil. You've driven Francine crazy on purpose, just out of depravity . . . you're as crafty as a monkey. She'll end up by killing herself and it's you who will have murdered her . . . Men have gone to the guillotine for less."

She expected an angry retort or perhaps a burst of laughter, some sign of defiance. On the contrary, the Russian listened to her in silence, motionless, and as pale as death.

"Is it possible?" he cried all at once in his melodious voice. "Look, Madame Fernande!" He tore open his shirt with a violent gesture, showing five deep scars on his smooth bare skin. "You see this breast?" he said. "Those are the marks of bullets. Yes, at Vrosky in front of the schoolhouse I was shot five times—I could almost have touched the muzzles of the five guns with my hand—and the snow was red with blood. They had made a fire with the school benches and the blackboard and were burning all our things, our papers and our pitiful trousers that we had mended with hemp and a pointed stick . . . I watched the dirty smoke rising into the sky. What man has ever seen his end so near, met it face to face? Well, Madame Fernande, by that memory, more sacred to me than any woman, more sacred even than my mother, I swear (and he made the sign of the cross on his lips) I did not mean her any harm. I acted thoughtlessly, stupidly . . . I wanted the girl to be my friend, a comrade. Is that a crime? She used to be so simple, fresh, and rustic—she positively smelt of hay. I would willingly have kissed her like a little brother. But now what can I do? She has denied her nature. She has taken up with ancient falsehood. Tell me then, which one of us has changed?"

"Oh," she said, "you know how to talk, all right. You're a crafty creature, but I know your tricks. Admit now that for weeks you were mooning around the girl, always whispering in her ear . . . She was like a poor little scared bird, and fascinated too, you could have held her in the palm of your hand. And then you taught her to swear in Russian, and to smoke, and to drink ether . . . disgusting!"

"What was I supposed to do? Make fun of her, be rude to her? You don't seem to understand, Madame Fernande." The expression in his eyes was suddenly so vacant it made the cook catch her breath in surprise and disgust. "No, you don't know what unhappiness is. That girl knows. You cry over your dead, over a lost lawsuit—that isn't unhappiness. To forswear Christ, to blaspheme isn't unhappiness. Unhappiness is as calm and solemn as a king on his throne, silent as a shroud. As for despair! Ah, it bestows upon us an empire equal to God's!"

"Is that the way you talk to a mere child, you humbug?"

"Madame Fernande," said the Russian, looking at her with that humble innocent smile of his, "you are wrong. It is easy for a woman to understand unhappiness. Yes, in every woman you will find a spring of sadness. It's like looking for water underground. But Francine, you see, has dried up hers all at once. Now all she can do is to cry, and get drunk, and open my letters, or drink out of my glass as soon as I turn away to light a cigarette. It's all too childish."

"And if she killed herself? I suppose that would be childish too! You devil!"

"Enough!" The chauffeur's face became suddenly serious. "I earn my living honestly, I do my work, and I will not permit you to insult me. I can never hope to make you understand me, Madame Fernande. I have done many reckless things in my life . . . unbelievable things . . . but never anything as reckless as entering this house."

"What are you talking about? This house?"

Monsieur Fiodor turned pale and kept pressing his hands together nervously.

"You know very well what I mean, Madame Fernande. That, at least, you understand plainly enough. In this house falsehood is more tenacious than elsewhere, it scatters its seed over everything, it will finally wear away the stones. The old lady is its offspring. She is like a mushroom growing between the roots of a tree at dusk . . . Not that she has committed any crime, I suppose; but her soul is in her trousseau of keys—the miser mother! And as for him . . . who has ever heard him laugh—a real man's laugh? With his moth-eaten beard, his flabby hands, that grayish skin of his neck, his breath! You must excuse me, Madame Fernande, but I really believe he has been dead for a long time."

"Good heavens!"

"And then his friends . . . the intimate friends, as you say in French. Christ! In Paris they amused me at first. But here I loathe them. Bishop Espelette is just like any lady professor at the Ostrov Institute for Young Ladies. I am sure his soul is a little flute. How his hands, his eyes, fawn on people, how he wants to please! He plays with Dr. La Pérouse, with the journalist, with the Jew, with all of them . . . They are like mournful children playing in the ashes on a winter day. They don't know what they want. They all, of course, want social position, a situation, fame, wealth, but once they succeed in getting a fine place for themselves, they discover it's too big for them and humbly long for something lowlier. Yes, Madame Fernande, nobody here has the courage of good or evil. Satan himself would appear as nothing but a trail of dust on the wall."

His long slanting eyes sparkled with pleasure; he lighted a cigarette.

"And now, Madame Fernande, I think we've talked enough. Don't you? Anyway I must go and fill my tank. I have to do a hundred miles before seven o'clock."

"Oh, just wait one second!" the cook begged almost humbly. "You see, I've had masters who couldn't hold a candle to these for manners, education, fortune and everything. And yet, on my word of honor, I've never felt so queer and uneasy before in my life. I have nightmares. I have to light my candle in the middle of the night. I even get the shakes, and that hasn't happened to me since my daughter died. Take the old lady, she may be cracked, that's true. But I can't get used to hearing her called old vixen to her face—and you don't even bother to lower your voices. I don't say anything—but believe me, I feel like crawling into a dark hole . . . And I'm sure she understands—only she isn't sure. Otherwise she'd scratch your eyes out, the wicked old thing! And then the master, why, he has a perfect horror of young people, everybody knows it. His wife died of boredom. He positively shrivels up people's hearts. Now, Monsieur Fiodor, without mentioning Francine, and not wishing to poke my nose into your affairs, I must say that this is no place for you. No, really, it isn't healthy for you here."

"Perhaps," said the Russian softly. "But it's too late now, Madame Fernande. I have to see the end of this adventure, you know that. These people aren't any better or worse than people anywhere—they are just mediocre, ridiculous, vile—but the air they breathe here is enough to make them blacker than demons. I too, I've lost my meaning, I am like a word in a forgotten tongue. Alas, Madame Fernande, evil is not the secret of this house—no—the secret of this house is Grace. Our lost souls lap it up like water and we find it tasteless, savorless, although it may well be the fire that is to consume us eternally . . . What can we do? We are all struggling in vain; we are caught in a net that is dragging us all pell-mell, somewhere we don't want to go. You must excuse my speaking like this . . . I seem to you crazy, delirious, drunk . . ."

"Not at all," the cook answered quickly. "You may be clever, but there's not much you can teach an old daughter of the Avre Valley. I know what you've been driving at, Monsieur Fiodor. I see your idea as clear as a carp lying at the bottom of a pond. Bah! You could say a lot more if you wanted to, I can tell by your eyes . . . An ordinary man when there's something he's keeping back—his eyes shine. Yours go to sleep. There's no mistaking!"

"And I know what you're thinking too," cried the chauffeur growing more and more excited. "What do we care about Francine, eh, Madame Fernande! The girl is nothing to us, is she? It's nearly two weeks now—I could tell you the exact hour—you thought you'd caught me, didn't you? . . . It was the day the old lady was lost . . . Monsieur de Clergerie was scolding and shaking his head, he's never seemed smaller and meaner. He smelled like a rat. And what heat! The mastic was running down the window panes in the sun porch . . . Why are you blushing, Madame Fernande?"

"And why should I be blushing? What insolence!"

Suddenly the Russian's eyes were emptied of all light.

"Because you think that I am Mademoiselle Chantal's lover," he said without raising his voice, but so distinctly that the words rang in Fernande's ears like a shout. "You saw me coming out of her room. Although the shutters were closed I recognized your skirt down the hall through the darkness."

Madame Fernande was making a desperate effort not to answer him. Long after he had stopped speaking she seemed still to be listening, her two fat forearms leaning on the table, her face turned toward him, so intent that her coarse features took on a certain nobility.

"Aren't you ashamed of yourself?" he went on.

"We are full of bad dreams, you and I, they are in our conscience. She is too pure, Mademoiselle Chantal, she comes and goes, she breathes and lives with the light, beyond us, beyond our presence. And yet, unknown to her, she radiates light, she drags our black souls out of the shadows, and the old sins begin to stir, to yawn, to stretch and show their yellow claws . . . Tomorrow, day after tomorrow—who knows—some night, this very night, perhaps, they will be altogether wide awake. I have made a prediction, Madame Fernande—this house is vile, unhealthy—nevertheless, you are going to see astonishing things! Right now it is crumbling to dust."

SECOND PART

This part introduces a new personality, Abbé Cénabre, the main protagonist of an earlier novel by Georges Bernanos, L'Imposture. *As this novel is not available in translation, an explanatory notice seems necessary: Abbé Cénabre is a priest of powerful intellect who has lost his faith, without, however, leaving the Church or relinquishing his priesthood. The only person to whom he confided his secret and his deceit was Abbé Chevance, Chantal's father confessor. Cénabre believes that Abbé Chevance, in his dying hour, betrayed his secret to Chantal.*

1

MONSIEUR DE CLERGERIE was no better and no worse than other men, but any sort of greatness obliterated him, left nothing. His natural suspiciousness which his rivals mistook for the mark of his race, the Norman stamp, was really only the defense mechanism of a creature so weak that he would have been the slave of his admirations and antipathies, by turn or all together, if his nature had been capable of any such expansiveness. In short, what he asked of fame was not the glory, but only the benefits. Among the thousand benefits coveted by servile ambition, Clergerie sought only the smallest, and with his patient ingenuity had made use of them with such art, turning trifles into such desirable nothings that his competitors were furious at having disdained them. Unfortunately, no man can yield to the temptation of taking advantage of his own mediocrity, establish his life on the least noble part of his nature, without running the risk sooner or later, of being, as it were, morally reduced in rank with the consequent anguish of inner solitude—the counterfeit image of that spiritual exile which is the price genius pays for glory. As the author of the *History of Jansenism* approached the goal he had modestly contemplated since adolescence—a chair in the Academy—he saw the circle in which he had hoped to enclose his destiny, gradually shrinking. The multiplicity, the intricacy of his intrigues had reached a critical point beyond which each step became dangerous, each decision irreparable. He had exhausted his friendships, could no longer even take advantage of an enemy. He had been the servant of a small and apparently inoffensive ambition for which he had made his life a vacuum. Now the vacuum was sucking him in, he felt himself slipping into the void.

"What have they against us?" he complained one day to Monsignor Espelette who had known the same anxieties, for he had not dared present his candidature for the succession of the Duc de Listrac, and after the vacation could expect only the worst from the hostility of the editor of the *Revue Internationale.* "Yes, what can they have against us? We have committed no imprudence, we have acted for the best, we have given everyone his due. In short we have been indefatigable. Why are people deserting us then? Does an honest man have to make a noise in the world at least once in his life in order to provide for his old age? Alas, dear friend, no one any longer appreciates a discreet ambition that bides its time. I am even afraid that it is misunderstood. Hints today are useless. To solicit has no meaning any more, one is expected to put one's cards crudely on the table, show one's game!"

But the Bishop was reassuring:

"You must realize, my dear sir, that every existence has its critical phase, its dead center. This characteristic of nature can be found even in the lives of saints, even sainthood has its arid, desert stretches. You have really no cause to complain. The interest aroused by your coming marriage—such a well-assorted marriage—will awaken sympathy and make your position secure—which indeed has never really been compromised . . . In addition, the Baroness de Montanel brings you her personal influence, and something infinitely more precious, the experience of a woman of the world."

The last words were received in silence. Monsieur de Clergerie had not, apparently, been listening.

"What a mournful summer!" he remarked. "I would never have believed that perfect weather could be so monotonous in the end—and all these thunderstorms!"

From morning till night, in spite of the closed shutters, the faint crackling of the gravel under the torrid sun could be heard, and when night fell, the imperceptible breeze that began to stir, smelled of fever and stables. All the forces of the day seemed to be decaying in the air like the pith of roots and leaves at the bottom of stagnant water. In the pastures, along the hedges still hot from the sun, the Norman bulls with their short necks, who had been drowsing all day, slowly lifted their crinkly heads and shivered with pleasure from their withers to their rumps, ferociously breathing in the heavy air and wrinkling their black muzzles.

"I fear that this weather is very bad for my nerves," Monsieur de Clergerie would confide to his guests every evening when the lights were turned on.

This was the hour he both longed for and dreaded. For age had not cured him of his old nocturnal terrors. In a deserted apartment at midnight he became the sickly little boy again, looked sideways at the closed doors, cowered at the slightest sound or else, his cheek in the hollow of his pillow, listened to the pulse of his temporal artery beating, reckoned the possible fibrotic changes of the tissues, the weakening of the heart, a lesion. He would get out of bed, open the window and gaze out across the shadowy park feeling his own hot animal breath blown back against his face. One night he had seen, standing motionless by the wall in the moonlight, the tall figure of Abbé Cénabre monstrously prolonged by his shadow, and his surprise kept him awake until dawn.

His disillusionment was moreover profound, and a real menace to his health. It had diverse causes, some of them hidden and incommunicable. This year he had fled Paris as early as June, worn out with fatigue, sick over his last failure at the Academy. The official announcement of his coming marriage had started tongues wagging and aroused the mirth of orthodox drawing rooms, whose echo reaching him had sent a chill down his spine. Yet, for months he had been secretly calculating his chances, weighing advantages and risks, resigning himself in advance to the inevitable humiliations, because he felt confident that he would be able to overcome irony and slander with patience and effacement. And then suddenly he discovered that a wife is not at all the same thing as a vigilant friend and ally. As the time for his marriage gradually approached he had become conscious of the physical existence of Baroness de Montanel, and he could no longer kiss her little dimpled hand without a feeling of boredom and distaste.

Never had the familiar house to which he was attached by a timid respect and by life-long habits stronger than love, seemed less made for real security, for peace. The past still seemed to dwell there, but only as a rotting corpse. The historian felt its obscure menace. He could be seen skirting the walls, an expression of uncalled-for gravity making his face look prematurely worn. "The master isn't yellow any more, he's green!" was Fernande's comment. The first days had been particularly intolerable among all the trunks and packing-cases, in the odor of musty chintz, and surrounded by watchful, pitying and perfidious servants. In vain he had them throw open the windows; the wind could moan through all the corridors, the attic resound with the cracking of old woodwork, but the immense dwelling would not be aroused from its slumber, would not come to life. Wrapped up in itself it seemed to be defying the precocious summer and the torrid sky. "I go from a cellar into an oven," de Clergerie wrote at the time to his doctor, La Pérouse, who had been nursing his phobias for twenty years, and who had at last been persuaded to visit him at Laigneville to try a new treatment for anxiety neurosis which the eminent psychiatrist intended soon to present to his colleagues.

For it was a strange thing that for the last three months Monsieur de Clergerie, as though urged on by a mysterious presentiment, had thought of nothing but filling up his empty house. In his haste to gather around him all the benevolent friends he could find, welcoming them avidly one day only to abandon them the next, he was like the dying man who draws toward him an invisible presence that he clasps like a cloak to his breast. People at first laughed at this curious vagary. Soon, however, the laughers fell silent. The world likes to understand, or, at least, it likes to think it understands.

In reality, what was slowly descending over the poor man like an icy November fog, like oblivion over the dead, was boredom. He was bored. In spite of all his pains, his economy of himself, and his marvelous dexterity, he would never succeed in keeping up to the end, to the final obsequies, the laborious forgery of his reputation.

But his life had another secret, another element of death. The strange vacuum where all the toil of years was being lost, grew steadily, and now the very earth seemed to be giving way under his feet. "Chantal has disappointed me," he confided to Monsignor Espelette. "I had expected more of her. I am at a loss to understand."

"Dear friend," the prelate objected, "I am afraid since the death of Abbé Chevance you are the victim of an obsession. What did you expect of Mademoiselle Chantal? What is it you have against the holy priest whose simplicity was, on the contrary, a great lesson to all of us? In spite of certain inoffensive manias which I notice quite often among the best of my seminarists—those, at least, of humble origin—he was a wise man who put his trust in Providence. Certainly discretion cannot be called cowardly. What responsibilities we assume, whose burden more circumspect men know how to avoid! There is no doubt, I think, that your daughter has shown very evident signs of her religious vocation. However, God, it seems, has not yet spoken the final word to her young heart."

But Monsieur de Clergerie returned bitterly and with unconscious cruelty:

"Let's not indulge in formulas. Your Grace knows very well how proud I was of Chantal! Only last year the Mother Superior of *Sainte Gudule,* where Chantal was brought up, again spoke of her in a way that would have rejoiced the heart of the most exigent father. Yes, there was a supernatural force for good in the child. I have seen how it affected serious men who are not in the habit of giving way to impulse, nor of according their admiration lightly. In the little circle of the Baroness Mellac—who was good enough to invite Chantal to assist her in her splendid work, *The Social Foundling Home*—she captivated everyone; the ladies listened to her as to an oracle! I am not so devoid of certain scruples as people seem to think; I know how a delicate soul shrinks from flattery. I should have approved entirely if my daughter had simply kept away from her too indulgent elders, awaited more favorable circumstances to show her full worth. But that is not at all what has happened. Abbé Chevance seems to have imposed on the child the narrowest, the most commonplace rule of conduct, such as any confessor advocates for a school girl. I should have thought that so strong a character would in the end have broken such narrow bonds. Not at all. The dear child, to all appearances, is perfectly satisfied . . . But the watchful eye of a father is not deceived! It is stifling her. There are certain indications I have observed that are plain. Yes, in all her gestures, even in her laugh, which I must confess I can scarcely endure any longer, is the indubitable sign of a voluntary illusion, an innocent duplicity."

"If you will permit my saying so, there seems to me a good deal of fatherly complacency in your excessive solicitude," said Monsignor Espelette.

"That is what you all think!" Monsieur de Clergerie protested bitterly. "But why is it then that you share with me this strange uneasiness? Oh, but you do! Why deny it? You must admit that it is extraordinary, the place a young girl, apparently so simple, occupies here in this solitude, among experienced men. What is she hiding from us? What is she hiding from her best friends? . . . What strange hours are we living through!"

But the Bishop of Paumiers assured him that he was mistaken and that undoubtedly La Pérouse was really the cause of all the trouble.

"I fear he is sadly undermining your health by giving an exaggerated importance to every trifling nervous symptom, the price all intellectuals have to pay. He himself I have heard is far from well. God forbid that I should spread a rumor that may be only malicious slander. However, I have been told of certain, well . . . certain eccentricities . . ."

He blushed and waved his beautiful hand as though brushing away these indiscreet words. Ah, well, what did it matter? The next evening would be the same as the one before, just as melancholy, with the windows wide open to the August night that never slept. The deserted bridge table was still covered with books and newspapers. Around the single electric light bulb which drew only a tiny circle out of the darkness, a night moth fluttered, then flew away on its great, weary wings. Professor Abramovitch had left two weeks ago for Prague, and until next winter his high, nasal voice would no longer be heard reading Sanscrit texts, his finger riveted to his fat oriental chin. The Bishop of Paumiers had reserved rooms at the Hotel Sagittarius in Vichy and was preparing to leave for his annual cure. Even La Pérouse would be going soon to preside at the closing session of the *International Psychoanalytic Congress* at Bremen. And Monsieur de Clergerie was thinking with secret terror that he would be left alone in the company of Abbé Cénabre.

In truth, the celebrated author of *The Life of Tauler,* whose popularity with his readers was constantly growing, had succeeded in baffling his best friends. He too was slowly sinking into the shadows. Around certain exceptional individuals meant for great solitary passions, ambition and avarice, the most secret forms of deceit, the air quickly becomes stifling if their powerful reserves of force, instead of being slowly exhausted, either according to fortuitous circumstances or a rigorous plan, begin to decay. And so, ever since he had stopped pretending to himself, was no longer obliged to rectify each day, each minute, his own image as in a deforming mirror, had only to impose on the outer man the strict discipline of his life, the poor man had felt his emptiness growing which even the most arduous, almost demented labors, had not helped to fill; and there was no further need for him to nourish his imposture—it was in him like a dead fruit. The last volume of his *Florentine Mystics* had caused some surprise by its rigorous construction, an increased vigor, a certain headstrong tone, attaining at moments a sort of pathos whose mystery no one could fathom. And this time the work had not given Abbé Cénabre the least relief even for a moment. On the contrary, the effort had opened up his wound again. No matter how he might dissemble to the world in the future, to himself he had made the final admission; he could no longer continue the terrible game of fleeing and then pursuing, by turns, his truth, his own truth, in the darkness of his soul.

The few friends whom he was still willing to see, began by complaining, but in the end, so hard, compact, intolerable is the silence that envelops such a man, they felt more like hating him. He had, moreover, prolonged his stay in Germany three weeks, had then rented his apartment in the *Rue de Seine* and sold part of his library. On his return from Carlsbad everyone noticed how drawn his face had become, and the prominence of the bones and the muscles gave it a singular look of brutal, almost blind force. But more than anything else the voice had changed. It was now hoarse and weak, quickly exhausted. It was whispered that fatigue had at last got the better of this powerful nature, that he was suffering from severe laryngitis, probably tubercular. And as though to prove the truth of the gossip he had left Paris, bought a place near Draguignan, a little house with a red tile roof, hidden in the palms on the outskirts of a tiny village. With the first fine days of spring he would go to a dusty hillside and sit there in the sun until nightfall. An old woman kept house for him and slept in an adjoining shed. "*Sick,* the poor, dear man?" she would exclaim. "What nonsense—I've never even heard him cough!" The nearest church was a mile away along an impossible little path. He had never been seen there.

It was from that distant spot that several pressing

letters from de Clergerie had finally brought Abbé Cénabre to Normandy. The historian had written him of his coming marriage, and not able to hide his growing distress, had complained bitterly of his complete solitude, his mother being now in her second childhood and his daughter, ever since the death of Abbé Chevance, lost in a sort of daze. And he had very adroitly added that the long absence of Cénabre had left the door open to slander, and that it became expedient for him, if not to return to Paris, at least to be near by. Moreover, it looked as though the summer would be unusually hot and no one would understand his staying longer in the south.

Alas! After the first look exchanged between the two men, de Clergerie knew that his undertaking would be a failure, and almost regretted his imprudence. In a few hours Cénabre had succeeded in discouraging even the inexhaustible good humor of Mgr. Espelette. He never left his room, remained silent all through meals (he was on a severe diet), and complained of insomnia. He would walk around and around the central green every night, enraging the psychiatrist who was kept awake by the crunching of the gravel. Only once had he emerged from this taciturnity to question Chantal avidly on the death of Abbé Chevance, and after a brief colloquy, as though disappointed, had retired once more into silence.

Since then Monsieur de Clergerie through a sort of timidity he would have been hard put to explain, scarcely dared mention his daughter's name in front of the priest. In this lonely house, in this unbearably bright, oppressive summer, in the midst of these watchful men, Chantal's soft voice, so pure and unaffected, her gay laugh overheard by chance, resounded almost painfully, seemed unnatural. Moreover, the historian's apprehensions, his naïve confidence, to each one of his guests in turn, certainly did nothing to dissipate the uneasiness. It was on the contrary increasing daily without their realizing it, taking on the proportion of a premonition, an ominous sign. The invisible net was gathering around its lovely victim.

2

"FOR me, heat is fatal," Monsieur de Clergerie admitted sadly.

Almost invisible in his deep leatherette armchair, he waved one hand languidly back and forth, while the other dabbed at his bare thigh with a bit of cotton soaked in ether. Through the closed shutters a ray of sunlight fell on Dr. La Pérouse's shoulders as he wiped the thin platinum needle with priestly solemnity. An absurd sadness hung in the air.

"Absolutely fatal, isn't it?" persisted Monsieur de Clergerie.

The illustrious psychiatrist turned slowly toward him a triangular face with suspiciously shiny cheekbones.

"Fatal is a very big word, my friend," he said. "A slight infection at the most, I would say. You should not complain! Slight infections give us immunity from more dangerous ones by facilitating the multiplication of those precious antibodies. Health is only an illusion. This term introduces into our hypotheses the notion of equilibrium, of beauty. Whereas, I believe, a biologist or a doctor who proceeds on the belief that there exists a sort of universal harmony will commit nothing but blunders. In reality life has neither method nor principles, nothing but a disgusting obstinacy. Look at all it destroys for the meagerest results!"

He raised his arms and began kneading an imaginary substance, soft and sticky, while his mouth, whose slight deviation was already noticeable, became horribly distorted. Monsieur de Clergerie gave an unconvincing laugh.

"Oh come, doctor! Really, my dear friend, when so many wretches bless your name! Why should you slander yourself? What bitter jesting."

But La Pérouse continued kneading his invisible mud.

"I am one of the chaste," he went on in the same soft dreamy voice. "I am one of the chaste like most hard workers, such as Balzac and Zola. Desire poisons the blood of most men. What do you expect? You can look at life any way you please, from any angle or upside down, it is always the same pile of filth!"

He stopped abruptly, reddened, and hastily thrust his hands in his pockets to hide, no doubt, the slight trembling of his fingers, the tragic sign that for the last few months had not escaped the notice of his interns.

"I can't understand, no, I fail to understand!" Monsieur de Clergerie kept repeating plaintively.

He realized obscurely that this extravagant and

powerful nature, which had exerted such an ascendancy over him, was failing day by day, that there was now no remedy. But he was afraid openly to disown him yet, this salutary wizard, this master of anxieties and obsessions, to whom he had entrusted his soul. The doctor's frenzied, maniacal paradoxes, his contradictions, fierce and childish by turn, his obscene insults, and even his tortured cries, were they not like the scattered wreck of those ten volumes of irreproachable clinical observations and generalizations, bold enough to have held for a moment the attention of wise men? His entire work with its costly and deceptive bibliographic arsenal, his tables, his outlines, his statistics, had probably all had their source in the ruminations of a timid and dreamy adolescent, incapable of overcoming the terrors, desires, and disgusts of puberty. Pitiful contradictions, paradoxes more pitiful now that the expiring will could no longer control them and delivered them over, just as they were, to the malicious curiosity of his students and rivals. . . .

And, after all, among his pitiless colleagues who joked among themselves over the latest pronouncement of the fallen master, which one of them would have been capable of making a diagnosis, of predicting the fatal moment when the powerful, and at the same time puerile imagination, accelerating its rhythm, would begin to poison the mind instead of nourishing it?

"Ah, . . . you don't understand?" cried La Pérouse as though in the greatest astonishment.

He sat up straight, his arms still resting on the arms of the chair, visibly making an effort to control himself, impassible and with that imperious tilt of the chin which had restored courage to so many cowards. And on his set face only a sort of shadow moved on his right cheek, the imperceptible twitching of a rebellious nerve, like a wrinkle on the surface of the water.

"You are a noble but disillusioned soul!" protested de Clergerie in desperation.

"No . . . pardon . . . I am raving," said La Pérouse after a moment. "Yes, I am certainly raving . . . It is the weather . . . the barometer at 30.70! Really," he continued with sinister seriousness, "it is unbearable!"

And as though the sound of his voice had come to him only gradually out of someone else's mouth, he listened curiously, gave a little start and grew pale. Then little by little his face resumed its soft, dreamy, almost vacant expression which contrasted strangely with its rather brutal modeling, the reliefs and hollows, the grain of the skin, roughened by sun or rain, the open air, the seasons, in which only after some time one noticed the tell-tale puffiness characteristic of his malady. Again silence fell . . .

Monsieur de Clergerie coughed, expectorated, and weary of argument, began carefully wiping his glasses.

"I am so surprised, so amazed," he said. "I have been wanting to talk to you about something all morning, a serious affair, very serious, in short, what our forefathers used to call a family affair—never unimportant, naturally!"

He stole a stealthy look at La Pérouse and then almost immediately lowered his anxious eyes.

"Well then—I had to accustom myself gradually to the idea of my coming marriage . . . So far I have managed very well . . . I've been very careful . . . Oh! my dear friend, you are right! Lacking volition, a certain prudence, a constant watchfulness will attenuate marvelously any shock. People think I am more excitable when, on the contrary, I am really only taking the edge off my terrible sensibility that has made me suffer so . . . For, following your advice, I make a point of dissipating in gestures and attitudes, any feelings that might threaten my equanimity. Even my daughter has been misled . . . I am sorry to worry her . . . Why do you frown like that?"

"I should prefer not to hear you speak of Mademoiselle Chantal, your daughter!" he replied calmly and began pacing up and down the room. "Medically, I know nothing about her, and I do not wish to know anything. I could only have wished that, because of a certain heredity, you had in the past consulted Baour, or perhaps Duriage . . . at the critical period, the formative period. The opportunity has passed, let us say no more about it."

"Then you think . . . you fear . . . you think there is reason to fear?" Clergerie, already overwhelmed, questioned miserably. "Fear what?"

He stuttered and stammered, unable to stop himself, as though the keenly attentive glance of the master fixed upon him had torn this pitiful avowal from him. For this was indeed that formerly honored master, the happy rival of the aging Charcot, the vulgar but powerful forcer of secrets, the cruel prop of failing energies, shepherd of a wild-eyed flock, who now with his head bent slightly to one side, transfigured by a pitiless, unquenchable, furious curiosity as though by an eternal youth, was gently urging him to continue . . .

But even before Clergerie could reply, La Pérouse in that hard, that famous voice of his, whose vulgarity could never succeed in dishonoring the imperious tone, flung over his shoulder:

"Let us speak frankly as usual. You are being stopped by a straw. In truth you are afraid of something without knowing what, and so this obscure indefinable anxiety has finally settled on your daughter, and you complain of not knowing her opinion on the subject of your marriage which you gratuitously suppose to be unfavorable. But isn't there something else? And isn't it my job to bring it, that other thing, into your field of consciousness by means of the simplest, the very simplest possible interpretation. You will observe that I do not say the most rational. Oh! I am not going to show you anything very terrifying, I only ask of you sincerity and a cool head . . . Well then, dear friend, here it is, you have lost faith in your daughter, that is the sore spot I must put my finger on. Does it hurt? I would not have to be a doctor to tell you this . . . Any witness with a little common sense would have made the same observation."

Cruel as this brutal incision of the lancet was to the unfortunate Clergerie, for the moment he only felt the delicious remission of shame which follows confession, and tears of joy came to his eyes at having been delivered of a secret that a will stronger than his own had torn out of his consciousness. He spoke Chantal's name with a real fervor.

"Lost faith in Chantal? Ah, no, my friend, really . . . But in what sense exactly do you mean?"

"Oh, quite ingenuously," La Pérouse replied, absently watching his patient with an air of boredom, already sure of the outcome of this unequal battle. "There are few fathers in the world who have not had the same experience sooner or later. Parents always learn too late that children have a life of their own which is closed to them. Even if they would like to, our children themselves can do nothing about it."

"No, I have not lost faith in her!" Monsieur de Clergerie repeated. "In no sense. The very idea is absurd. All I could admit—oh, only for the sake of the most scrupulous sincerity, is that for the last few weeks I have begun to feel a vague realization of certain obligations . . . certain duties which I have, to a certain extent, neglected until now . . . quite unconsciously . . . Yes, I have perhaps unduly counted on her precocious wisdom, her experience, her sense of moderation, of measure . . . Perhaps my daughter is less well armed than I had supposed against the enthusiasms, the illusions of her wonderfully generous heart."

"Just what I told you," replied La Pérouse calmly. "You have certainly a very suspicious nature. In the beginning one merely indulges in harmless speculations, then one begins to take pleasure in them and, in no time, imperceptibly, one becomes a real paranoiac. It is perfectly commonplace."

"Oh, but . . . but really . . ." protested the historian weakly. "I too have my rights, my duties . . . I cannot be wholly indifferent . . ."

"Let me add a few words," continued the psychiatrist, "we must reach a conclusion. You have never found either in your daughter, nor formerly in your wife, that complementary being, whom we all hope to find—the privileged witness of our lives, just inferior enough to us to safeguard our pride, whom we may indulge with impunity and before whom we need never blush. Well, at your age all the disappointments and humiliations of the past have a tendency to reappear on the threshold of consciousness, like those chronic wounds that begin to suppurate every year at the autumnal equinox. It becomes more and more evident that the image of your daughter is being superimposed in your mind on that of the late Madame de Clergerie. That is dangerous, very dangerous. It is not easy to get rid of the dead. The dead are persistent . . . Of course I am joking, you understand. It is we, ourselves, who resuscitate the dead. The dead are our old sins. Come now, a little courage; don't try to dodge, to get around that humiliating feeling of another person's superiority. Face it without blushing. Admit even that it has prompted your conduct. Your wife, your daughter are not superior to you: our moral nature depends only on our glands. However, the poetic sense which gives the moral tone to our acts is, to some extent, lacking in you. Let us conclude. You have not forgotten our little conventions? I do not deny the benefits of confession that the Catholic Church offers the faithful! You are free to make use of it; it is dangerous only for a very limited number of patients . . . You know, however, that our conception, the conception of psychiatrists, is very different . . . We undertake to clean out, not only the conscious, but the unconscious as well—a much harder operation. Once again, do not be terrified at having to admit plainly, cynically, the intentions that ten minutes ago would have seemed to you infamous. Very well, then! You are going to repeat after me word for word, in a loud voice, emphasizing each syllable . . ."

"No! Oh no, Oh no!" cried Monsieur de Clergerie. "I don't mistake your intentions, dear friend, nor deny the efficacy of your methods—they have helped me, I admit. But this remedy is really Spartan . . . Spartan . . . Spartan . . ."

He repeated the word three times like a powerful exorcism. With his remaining strength he hurled it at his persecutor:

"You know that I do not refuse . . . ordinarily . . . to unbare . . . when you demand it—even to the point of making myself ridiculous—odious sentiments, those involuntary, spontaneous sentiments that a respectable man avoids thinking about or examining too closely. But it seems to me that your investigation—even your solicitude should not go beyond the threshold, the sacred threshold . . . that is, I mean, the threshold of the home. Don't you think so? I beg you to consider . . ."

"Enough!" interrupted La Pérouse coldly, but the laconic adverb was uttered in such a way as to make one think of the brutal but salutary intervention of a surgeon's knife. "We always lose so much time. Just talk to me as though I were a wall. Why do you care, since we are responsible, all of us, only for our conscious thoughts—we have no control over the unconscious. And besides, you may be sure, it's nothing to what I've heard before!"

"You, . . . you really go too far," Monsieur de Clergerie moaned. "You are taking advantage of a physical depression . . . My . . . fatigue . . ."

"An excellent symptom!" La Pérouse almost laughed with satisfaction. "Your distress is the proof that I have guessed right . . . We are loosening roots that are devilishly tenacious and deep down . . . Ah, dear friend, we are well repaid for our pains when we can drag out into the light . . ."

He pursed his lips, and avidly breathed in the air through his tightly closed teeth.

"What a nightmare!" groaned Clergerie. "What vulgarity! What are you after? Where is this leading?"

But it is doubtful whether La Pérouse heard him, and probable, moreover, that this miserable wail did not get beyond the rampart of books and sheets of white paper. Until now the illustrious professor had never tried to profit by an advantage gained over his frail victim. This time he seemed to lose for a moment all restraint, all control over his dangerous diversion.

"Yes, yes, of course, I understand your repugnance," he said. "But for heaven's sake don't get childish! Let's be calm, serious. Psychic life is still life,—that is to say, a cunning detestable manoeuvre against the purity, the majesty of death. We can dream all we like of coldness, of whiteness . . . better still, of the unpolluted sidereal night, blackness—absolute, empty, sterile . . . Alas! the interstellar spaces themselves are fecundated, cold light transports the germ from one sky to another, rocks it to the absurd rhythm of five hundred million vibrations per second without killing it! Nothing can get the better of the abject life secretion, neither heat nor cold. Even a God wouldn't be able to cauterize at a stroke all the points of suppuration. The inestimable price that I set on . . ."

With the palm of his hand he kept gently tapping and stroking the window pane.

"Well, well . . . I was working myself up into quite a state," he said. "What the devil do you care? Remember just one thing—this little outrage to your feelings I demand of you, has only one aim. There is nothing worse than an obsession that disguises itself as a religious or moral scruple. I shall prove to you that yours is open to suspicion, then force you, in my presence, to admit it! In this way fixing your disappointment and shame as a photographer fixes a fugitive image on a sensitive plate by washing it in an appropriate bath."

He strode across the room, vigorously beating out each syllable with his right arm. Turning abruptly he stopped suddenly in front of his singular patient. Clergerie was weeping. Behind his spread-out fingers he showed a face shining with a mixture of tears and sweat like a sort of froth.

"I am mad," he stammered, "mad . . . I am a pitiful madman . . . hereditary neurosis . . . afraid of suffering . . . But all the same! . . . To play this horrible game . . . to abdicate . . . to abdicate my dignity . . . Have I the right?"

But on hearing the word madman, the extraordinary psychiatrist had thrown back his head with a furious jerk of his shoulders:

"Mad? Mad, you say? . . . What kind of a joke is this? Mad?" (Instantaneously his neck and forehead grew purple). "I have the greatest consideration for my patients. Nevertheless I cannot tolerate—you understand—I cannot tolerate their loss of respect. What are we coming to! And allow me to point out, sir, that I have not even the alternative of depriving you of my services. No, my dear sir! I cannot hand you over to one of my colleagues at this point, in the state you are in, right in the middle of a treatment, just as we are beginning to establish the psychogenesis of your neurosis. To take advantage of this professional scruple is the act of a coward, yes my dear sir, of a coward . . . Exactly."

"Please, please . . . ," implored de Clergerie . . . "you have always given me a little time . . . very considerately . . . humanely. Believe me I understand perfectly—it is nothing but a kind of ritual—unimportant—an ingenious ritual . . . that is, a simple formality . . . nevertheless . . ."

"Oh, all right then, go to the devil! The entire responsibility of what happens is on your own head. One does not, let me tell you, suddenly give up a treatment just at the moment of transference. I consider it my duty to tell you that your sort of neurosis can constitute the precipitating point, or the preparatory stage of a real psychoneurosis. It is not at all unusual to see an anxious individual develop hysteria, and become an obsessive hypochondriac."

"Really, dear friend . . . you can't make me believe that the least resistance to one of your suggestions will necessarily have such alarming consequences. I am afraid you have taken too tragically those vague worries that every father experiences . . . Perhaps I have spoken hastily, imprudently? . . . You are complicating the discussion terribly. . . ." He concluded with a painful smile.

La Pérouse had hastily hidden his hands behind his back and now roared at de Clergerie:

"You asked my advice, didn't you, on the particular case of your daughter, of Mademoiselle Chantal?"

"Of course . . . I don't deny it."

"Well, all right then, we agree. I hope to do no more than to enlighten you. I shall proceed with the greatest caution, I suggest no treatment. What is there to treat? The young woman seems perfectly normal. She is very pious, you say? What of it? I make no distinction between religious introversion and any other kind of sublimation. We do not consider the introvert in any respect a neurotic, but simply mentally unstable. It is indispensable simply that we should be in agreement and act accordingly . . . Why should I not admit that the case interests me? I just missed Abbé Chevance by a hair, by a breath. Madame d'Arpenans was to introduce me at your friend Tissier's. He was at that time—what's the name—assistant priest, parish priest?—no matter—at *Notre-Dame des Victoires*. My colleague Dubois-Danjoux insists that only hysterical cooks were to be seen going in and out of his confessional, whence his nickname, which I had never understood before—'confessor of Biddies' . . . A perfectly delightful crank—a sort of saint!"

"I deplore his loss," said Monsieur de Clergerie gravely, taking courage again now that the attention of his salutary tormentor was turned to other matters. "I myself heard him regret in front of a large gathering, the indiscretion of his penitents."

"Did he really? Are you sure?" cried Dr. La Pérouse with extraordinary interest.

The gleam died out of his eyes almost immediately and he began to nod his head, weirdly pursing his lips so that not only his teeth but his gums as well were visible.

"I am often accused of being a coarse, brutal materialist. What a foolish mistake! I have spent my life looking for undefiled springs, and I seem to sense them throughout the world, men who . . . What can we learn from our patients, will you tell me? Almost nothing. All our results are distorted. Nine times out of ten the simulation is perfectly plain, and yet with all our minute questioning we fail to circumvent the lie."

"My very dear friend," said the historian, perhaps unconsciously speaking more gravely and pompously than ever, "I am not a perfect father, but I am not completely blind either. Even if you have unjustly and cruelly challenged my modest intentions, I am grateful to you. The struggle that has been going on in me for weeks cannot continue. My reason, my health, even our daily bread, as well as my advantageous marriage are being compromised. I am very happy therefore to delegate a portion of my paternal rights to you. Remember only that my daughter is sincerity itself. You are going to find yourself (if I may use the expression) confronted by the most delicate, the most discriminating conscience. . . . Oh, I truly admire your respect for religion. I do not, believer that I am proud to say I am, I do not underestimate the services that scholars like you have rendered Catholicism—progressive, modernized Catholicism! Today, psychoanalysis—a moderated psychoanalysis, yesterday, the pragmatism of William James and the anti-intellectualism of Bergson . . . and why not? . . . in short, a certain idealism reconciles all creeds! But one can never be too careful in dealing with an excessively fragile sensibility . . . You are a psychiatrist, sometimes you are prompted to consult a colleague, a specialist of the lungs, the liver, the heart . . . So you will understand, I have asked Abbé Cénabre to carry on a little investigation on his part—in his own way . . . My tranquillity will be assured if you consent to . . . if you would make use of his experience. He is one of the masters of the spiritual life. On the other hand as a scholar, a savant, his loyalty . . ."

Again the psychiatrist's neck and forehead became suddenly brick red.

"Your Cénabre," he fairly choked, "your Cénabre! . . . But what are you talking about? Cénabre! You want me, in my position, at my age . . ."

He no longer thought of hiding his hands now trembling under the nose of his poor patient, terrified by this explosion of incomprehensible fury.

"My Cénabre! Come, come, my dear friend . . . Abbé Cénabre . . ."

"I refuse to share with anyone whomsoever the responsibility of a treatment," said La Pérouse apparently a little calmer although he spoke in a monotone that was almost unbearable. "You must understand my little burst of temper. You have confided your daughter to me. Henceforth she is sacred. Yes, dear Sir, no one shall touch a hair of that young woman's head without my permission, without my supervision. I stake my reputation, Sir, on this enterprise . . . Your Cénabre! . . ."

He started toward the door but his miserable victim had already intercepted him.

"I beg of you, please," he said, "we can be heard . . . How could I have known! What is it . . . What is wrong? Never mind, you will explain later. People in the library . . . a step away. Only think . . . This partition is no better than paper!" He kept striking the wall with his elbow in despair.

"I have nothing against him," continued La Pérouse without lowering his voice. "You do not seem to appreciate what an utterly intimate operation such an inquiry as I am undertaking is! The least tactical error and we are in danger of making fools of ourselves, of becoming odious. To follow all the ramifications of complexes so fine, so subtle, so fragile, to take apart, piece by piece, the ingenious system compensating for libidinous impulses, to find the intangible fixation, the tempo of a delayed or too precocious development, what a cool head it demands! What purity of intention! Yes, what purity! The genius of both sexes together—that's what's needed; the power of the one, the modesty, the delicacy of the other—a kind of androgynous state, my dream!—And you ask me to accept the collaboration—what am I saying—the supervision of a man who sweats virility through every pore . . ."

He turned pale with disgust.

"Doctor, I must insist . . ." began Clergerie.

Astonishment and anger as well as the terror of being overheard, gave an unpleasant insistence to the poor man's ordinarily humble and furtive glance. La Pérouse burst out laughing.

"Why didn't I ever think of it before? . . . Laborious and austere . . . of course . . . Austere, that's easy enough to say! But first of all we mustn't confuse austerity with one of those forms of melancholy we all know so well, my friend, that is, the premonition of spinal paralysis. Ah, Ah!"

"I must insist that you pull yourself together, La Pérouse . . . how dare you speak like that about a master . . . an exemplary master . . . whose private life is above suspicion! Naturally! Now please . . . one more word! I feel it my duty to repeat . . . But where the devil are you going? What are you going to do? But this is a real provocation . . ."

The rest was lost in a blurred murmur for the psychiatrist, who had closed the door. The last he saw of his patient was a stupefied, gaping mouth and, in the tumult of his thoughts, he had a vague feeling of having committed a blunder, was conscious of that pinched sensation in the pit of his stomach that a distracted person always feels when something foreign to his dream vaguely intervenes. But the assemblage of half delirious images, provoked by his fury and disappointment a moment ago, were still too real to yield all at once to the testimony of his senses. By this almost imperceptible delay, this break in the inner rhythm, might have been measured the progress of his insanity. For long before the mind, finally petrified, is fixed forever in a monstrous immobility, a truly mineral immobility, and which is such a cruel contrast to the vain agitation of the body, images have a singular viscosity, stick together and seem to pass with difficulty from the field of consciousness, leaving a bright trail behind. Nevertheless, this time his gesture still was quicker than his mind, with the result that his attitude was really that of someone who has absentmindedly opened the wrong door—finding himself in the half-light of the library with its closed shutters when he had thought to have come out into the garden. Only his voice might perhaps have betrayed him.

"You must really excuse me," he said. "Where is my head?"

"On your shoulders, my dear sir," replied Abbé Cénabre. "You will pardon a harmless joke. If we are to believe some of the fellow-citizens of the governor Pescennius—the first Bishop of Paris and his companions, Rustique and Eleuthère, could not have said as much."

And his words were immediately followed by that curious laugh, which Lagarrigue had compared to the rolling of a little Soudanese bark drum and which seemed to burst, all at once, out of that immense chest. It almost succeeded in discountenancing the doctor.

But La Pérouse was not the man to give ground. Better even than the coolness of a courtier whom nothing can fluster, he had the imperturbable offensiveness of the master of many shameful or lamentable secrets, who is trained to force with a few pitiless words, as with a battering ram, souls surrendered in advance, which it would be hazardous to spare.

"My voice is too high and distinct," he said with savage frankness, "and you made a mistake to listen. In the matter of certain syndromes of a rather special character, a priest is always a little secretive. The old empirical morality was wrong in considering the hypersexual as the dangerous man, the man of violence. One should remember that revolutions have always been made by eunuchs—Jean-Jacques Rousseau, Robespierre, Cromwell were all cold propositions!"

Without haste, Abbé Cénabre laid down the book he had been holding in his hand, and his head and shoulders disappeared in shadow as he raised himself from his chair. A thin ray of sunlight played on his modest watch chain.

"I gather," he said, "that you are anxious to avoid a misunderstanding that might arise from an excess of frankness on your part. But, rest assured, I don't understand a single word of what I have just heard. What have I to do with Jean-Jacques Rousseau, Robespierre or Cromwell? Doctors' jargon, I suppose.

Besides you have no reason to worry—in this house it is impossible to hear conversations from one room to another. You can readily prove this to be true if you like."

He quietly resumed his seat. The light now touched his thick and only slightly gray hair. La Pérouse was struck by the inexorable sadness of those bright watchful eyes. The insolent reply he had prepared died on his lips. He merely shrugged his shoulders, made a vague gesture of doubt or impotence, turned and re-entered the study, which he crossed without turning his head. Clergerie looked up from behind his rampart of in-quartos, but his uncertain and painful little smile was addressed to a banging door.

3

THE sunlight slipped down from the zenith in large slanting sheets, flowing over the high white stones to surge in multicolored waves at the four corners of the lawn—yellow and purple over the dahlias, pink and white over the carnations—lost finally in the darkened green of the borders. But that, one might say, was only the leitmotif of the symphony woven into the close web of the orchestra. The immense sheet of light had already been broken up against some translucid reef in the air, and the invisible wind playfully scattered the foam to the most inaccessible places—to the middle of the shady slope, the farthest leaf of a lilac bush, to the extreme tip of the black pine tree. It was not so much like the vast universal conflagration of day as an insidious fire over the dry hillside, the quick undulating flame running from one twig to another, like a tiny scarlet tongue. For at certain hours of the day in unusually hot summers, nature instead of relaxing, stretching out under the caress of the sun, seems on the contrary to shrink silently, timidly into herself, with the motionless, stupid resignation of an animal when it feels the mortal bite of its enemy's teeth sinking into its flesh. And indeed that stiff rain of heat pouring out of the mournful sky, that shower of white-hot arrows, the infinite suction of the sun, made one think of vicious bites, millions upon millions of bites, a gigantic gnawing.

Monsieur Fiodor, his long legs sheathed in leather gaiters, his sleeves rolled up above his elbows, was washing the car. He did not bother to turn his head.

"Look out," he said between his teeth. "The idiot is at the pump."

He stepped back, and seizing the bucket, swung it gently, without the least effort, as though it had been a truss of hay.

"Look out below!" he shouted, showing his white teeth.

The water splashed against the wall ten yards away.

"What idiot?" asked La Pérouse. "What pump?"

"You're an infant! That was a joke . . . I hate to have people sneaking up on me like that. You see . . ."

He threw down the bucket on a pile of oily rags behind him, and reached up for his coat hanging on the wall.

"A disgusting mess, eh?" he said. "Friend, that reminds me of my youth. My grandmother's house didn't have any windows either, only an enormous door, studded with nails, made to resist hatchet and cannon ball, with a niche for the icon. But imagine, after my father's death she broke the icon and spat upon it, the old Jewess! And rags on the ground too—what a collection of rags! Five thousand, ten thousand, twenty thousand roubles worth of rags perhaps . . . worm-eaten tatters, greasy rotting cloths, and underneath, friend, the most magnificent Turkish or Persian gold braid, beautiful Caucasian embroideries hardly tarnished at all, priceless dalmatics, high Byzantine head-dresses of cloth of gold . . . Day and night she crouched there on her riches like an old brooding hen, and her little black hands were marvelously clever at tearing in pieces those little salted fishes that she would push into my mouth with her dirty thumb."

"I would be willing to swear that there isn't a word of truth in what you have just told me," said La Pérouse. "No matter . . . I want to ask you something."

"Not a word of truth?" replied the Russian, insolently . . . "But where are my wits? A nobleman here, a Jew there, yesterday a Cossack, a prince, a governor, a general, tomorrow something else, even the wife of a pope would lose the thread of so many lies . . . Do you remember, little father, the day the Artiguenave woman sent for you, thinking I had killed myself. 'Oh save him, Doctor, you are a great master, such an illustrious professor, save him! I admit . . . he is my lover. I would give half of my fortune to save him. Cure him! He must talk to you honestly, he must. If he lies it is not his fault, he has lost all taste for life, even for himself.' And she was right, I had."

He took a cigarette out of his pocket, opened it, blew away the thin paper, rolled the blond tobacco between his palms, picked it up with his finger tips and put it carefully under his tongue.

"I'm listening," he said finally. "What do you want of me this time?"

La Pérouse gave that quick movement of his neck and shoulders that betrayed either anger or embarrassment, and said in the tone he would have used to persuade a stubborn child:

"What is the matter with you all, you and the others? I swear that girl is driving you crazy. Nobody ever noticed her before, she didn't take up any more room than a dog or a canary . . . At present five maniacs watching, watching with absurd anxiety her slightest movement, hanging on every word of a little school girl who probably has nothing more serious to worry about than her soups and her sauces. Frankly, they act as though they were frightened . . ."

"Me? I don't give a damn!" interrupted Fiodor.

"That's what one says," returned La Pérouse . . . "Bah! I know my weakness. I always like garrulous people, I like to listen to stories, I adore gossip. And then besides you are subtle, shrewd, a real fox . . . Never mind! What's the use of arguing? There are queer little girls all over, the species isn't rare. And I may as well tell you that what you mentioned, although curious, very curious, has nothing new in it for me."

"And I, let me repeat," said the chauffeur, "I don't give a damn! I have seen strange, unbelievable things —that's enough. Why do they have to be new? . . .

Now, tell me. Am I to have the powder today or not?"

"You are all alike," declared La Pérouse unruffled. "You have to have a supply on hand, a regular stock. After that you waste the drug, you share it with your pals—just for fun, like children . . . Very well, will five grams do?"

"Too much!" said the Russian carelessly. "Two grams will be enough, thanks. That'll make my day."

Although the look in the Russian's eye was gone in a flash, it did not escape the even keener eye of the old master of secrets.

"I've caught you, my boy," he said with his terrible boyish laugh. "You are right, two grams are enough. Do you think me so stupid? I agree with your Artiguenave woman, I think you want to kill yourself. Don't be annoyed, you've a clever tongue in your head, but of all the obsessions that of suicide is the easiest to spot . . . you're as wily as a woman or a savage, but in spite of yourself each one of your muscles gives your secret away without your knowing it. Yes, you repeat the same gestures a hundred times a day. You don't fool anybody. One would have to be blind."

"Brute!" murmured Fiodor between his teeth.

"Besides, I really have no faith in the suicide of men like you," the doctor continued with a paternal air. "You are too intelligent, too curious; the tiniest obstacle stops you, holds you back just long enough; the morbid fantasy can't become crystallized . . . Otherwise you would have been dead two years ago. What a time you gave us, my boy, what pretty scenes!

But I know you! You're much too depraved to kill yourself."

But Monsieur Fiodor had regained his serenity.

"Let's speak of serious things," he said. "Do you know why I am here, at this hour? With the big sponge, this blue smock, the buckets? They mean nothing—I'm putting on an act. I washed the car yesterday. But you see she will be coming back this way, I'll see her go by, in just a minute, coming home from mass . . . Only last Friday . . . Imagine—I rush out of the garage like a demon, it was as though I were jumping again with my horse into the river from the Grodno bridge, drunk—as I used to. The air whistled through my nose, I couldn't breathe . . . Ah, who watches over her? . . . How does it happen that to approach her, to speak to her, I have to make such an effort, grit my teeth? And she throws me a look of terror, of scorn, of pity—I don't know what . . . Then I am drowned in shame, brother, it courses through my veins, all the roots of my flesh are revived, refreshed. What difference does it make whether these things are new or not? For me, they are new, they are the only new things I have ever seen."

"That'll do!" said La Pérouse brutally. "Forget it, Fiodor, won't you? There are no miracles here, you know, no miracles except the phantasmagoria of a Russian brain congealed by ether. . . . What's more, the father begins to be worried, the servants are gossiping, and thanks to you, Francine appeared the other day saturated with morphine. I had to send her to bed. She was a sight. A pretty spectacle, three hundred kilometers from Paris in the midst of this bucolic setting! You have to start fires everywhere, it's your nature; you belong to the race of men who play with matches. . . . But I forbid you to talk about the young girl; ill or not, she has been entrusted to my care; I shall question her if the case interests me. You won't have to watch through keyholes any longer. . . . Why do you look at me like that?"

"I am looking at you, it is true," said the chauffeur. "I am enjoying looking at you." Like a cat he had climbed onto a pyramid of gasoline cans. His elbows on his knees, his chin in his hands, he sat watching La Pérouse intently, and it was as though a light was being turned on and off in his eyes. "Formerly," he continued, "after we had spent the night together at poor little prince Vassilof's place, with Couprine, Dorolenko and that bus driver, Alexis . . . Alexis Semcneioff —you remember his long dressing gown designed by Drécoll, and the tube-roses and lilies in his gray hair —the next day I would get away from the Renault factory to go and listen to you in the big amphitheatre of the *École de Médecine* among all the professors; and it tickled me that I knew you better than any of them did—for I never liked you. No, I never liked you. There's a streak of weakness in you, friend. Are you one of us or not? Nobody knows. Perhaps we were just animals for you to play with! The curiosity of savants is strange and puerile. Perhaps you could only lie to animals of our species?"

He spat out his tobacco in front of La Pérouse in a jet of amber saliva.

"I don't want to offend you," he continued scornfully, "but I think I should add that before troubling yourself about me and my suicide, you would do well to give an ear to what is being said about you everywhere, even in the kitchen. . . . Yesterday, that idiot, François, was imitating your voice and your gestures for us. It seems that you can't pick up a glass any more without letting it drop, your hands tremble. The idea of boasting of being able to go among madmen with impunity, classifying them, finding a place for each one in the show window, with his label and number —rot! *The bear rejoices when the hunter falls on his own sword,* our old Pushkin said. Ah! Ah! . . ."

"You talk like a fool, Fiodor," replied La Pérouse without moving a muscle of his pale face. "Gossip doesn't mean a thing to me."

He breathed heavily, pressing his lips together.

"Look, does my hand tremble, imbecile!"

He stuck his great hand under the Russian's nose, slowly flexing his fingers.

"Eh? Is it trembling?"

They both burst out laughing.

"Possibly," murmured Fiodor who had just come down off his perch, "you should not tire yourself, friend, you are pale, . . . Yes, you are damn pale," he continued in a low voice. "Be careful. You'd better let her alone, God's saint, whom angels visit. What

$3.00

GEORGES BERNANOS

JOY

A Novel

Translated by Louise Varèse

In JOY, another of Bernanos studies of holiness, the protagonist is a young girl, set against a background of sterility and corruption. The novel was greeted with a rare unanimity of praise as an outstanding book:

NEW YORK TIMES BOOK REVIEW: "Bernanos is perhaps the only modern author who can succeed in translating the mystical experience of exalted religious visions into the language of literary art. Even the most critical and skeptical reader will find in Bernanos the same convincing authenticity of the inner life as in the writings of the medieval mystics."

CATHOLIC BOOK REVIEW: "Bernanos' achievement is stupendous. He has managed to create in fiction something like the real effort and passion of the soul. There is a reality about his work which stuns, shocks and in its own peculiar way edifies everyone who dares to read it. Here indeed is the answer to the demand of many readers for literature which goes beyond realism to reality itself."

CHRISTENDOM: "Bernanos is portraying a mysticism he no doubt understands and there is nothing spurious about his delineation of spiritual delicacy. The battle between sensuality and purity, between the evil of mediocrity and the understanding of the pure in heart, between earthiness and spiritual gallantry is joined in these dialogues. It is a real struggle and is portrayed with consummate skill."

good will it do? She's already made a poor wretch of me. . . ."

"Truce!" cried La Pérouse. "Because I made the mistake of questioning you once or twice, you think you are precious, indispensable. Poor imbecile! Even if you saw, really saw what you say, what are such trifles to phenomena I have observed and observe almost every day. But one madman like you is enough to turn any house upside down. I shall finally be forced to say a word to Clergerie. And why, by the way, did you refuse to consult Devambèze at his clinic? This is no place for you."

"Go right on talking," said the Russian bitingly, with greater insolence than ever. "I made a mistake, I admit. Nevertheless I should like to have seen the end of all this, the outcome."

"The outcome? That's simple, my boy. You'll be kicked out at the end of the summer. Luckily for you! Bourgeois tranquillity, a peaceful house, provincial morals and manners, nothing more is needed to kill you. . . . But the evenings at Moïse's place, staying up all night, music and the shiver of dawn in empty streets, that's your medicine, keeps your nerves in order, fits you like a glove . . . You see, men like you invent their lives day by day, they make them up as they go along like a book, they'd like to assign us all our parts. To hear you talk one would suppose that this corner of Normandy was the gathering place of a witches' sabbath. . . . Simpleton! Every family has its little secrets, we doctors know something about that! The reassuring part of it is that these secrets are so much alike. Like those little brick houses with their little gardens in workers' settlements—you'd be lost without the numbers. An excellent man tormented by scruples, an avaricious old lady in her dotage, a sentimental, visionary young girl, dubious friends. . . . My God! thanks to you, the backstairs is the only entertaining part of this house. And even that! In Paris, it would be nothing."

While the doctor was speaking, Monsieur Fiodor had been carefully brushing his jacket and boots.

"You can keep your powder, friend," he replied casually. "You can keep it. You'll not make me talk for two, or even five grams of poison. I can do without it. No! you'll learn nothing from me from now on. All your tricks won't help. Act as you think fit, on your own, any way you like. Why go on pussyfooting? You look like a big black cat. Yes, you look like . . ."

He jumped back suddenly, hitting against the double door of the garage which, turning smoothly on its hinges, swung wide open. The enormous car with its varnished sides and all its metal, sprang out of the darkness as though it had fallen from the sky into the light, in the midst of a burst of foam.

The cry they had just heard hung suspended in the air, too different, too distinct to be confused with the peaceful hum of the day. It hardly rose above the thousand familiar noises that are constantly rising and falling in a perpetual interchange, perhaps even according to a precise, unchanging rhythm which to the human ear is only confusion. (And yet who has not recognized, through the mist and the smell of mud and tar, some giant seaport merely by its powerful breathing, the prodigious beating of its heart—something indescribably terrible and childlike?) It rose no higher, but hung there suspended in the air. They looked at each other in silence for a moment, more surprised than alarmed, listening, their nerves so shaken by this unexpected, mysterious conclusion to their obscure dispute, out of the blue, out of empty space, that a sudden reassuring explanation would have made them burst out laughing. A second cry was already rising toward the first as though to join it in the same precise spot in space. But it apparently stopped half-way, seemed to end in a feeble, scarcely audible quaver, and almost at the same time they heard the crunching of the gravel under tired, tottering feet.

"The old lady has escaped again," said Fiodor. "That blessed Francine!"

The noise came to them from the other side, through the thin wall of bricks and tiles, and to see what was happening they had to go out hurriedly through one of the stable doors, skirt the wall of the dependencies, coming out beside the isolated right wing of the little château, lonely under the shade of the immense linden trees. The part of the park that lay before them did not extend beyond the adjoining lawns, ending at the left in a sudden dip of the ground, at the right in the last disheveled clumps of the shaded alley, which was Madame de Clergerie's favorite daily walk. A shadow glided along the freshly whitewashed wall now dazzling in the sunshine, and darker, but hardly denser than the shadow, a strange distinct little figure advancing with sudden mysterious starts and stops, like a dislocated marionette. They lost sight of her for a moment, saw her and lost her again with the windings of the path. Finally she came out twenty paces away with a last weak cry, shrill and hoarse at the same time, an old woman's cry, or a bird's.

"Don't move! Don't speak!" whispered La Pérouse in his companion's ear. "Let her recognize us gradually. Don't make a noise! . . . Poor Clergerie has only to appear now and what a fit!"

Exhausted, the mad woman had stopped, trying to keep her eyes, that were frightened and furious by turns, fixed on the two men, but no longer controlled by her dying will, they kept wandering. Her face was crimson but dry, and her trembling hands, as red as her cheeks, still gripped the heavy woolen skirt she had picked up when she began to run, showing heavy woolen stockings, deformed by knee-pads. For a second or two her head oscillated violently on her shoulders while she tried in vain to struggle against this terrible silence that stifled her anger, the voiceless emptiness into which those thoughts and images, assembled for a moment by the all-power of her hate, were disappearing. But the silence was too strong for her. For the last time she cried out from the depths of her distress to the two impassible witnesses, to the beloved house itself, as indifferent as the men. . . . The same fog she knew so well began slowly covering men and things, and they became more and more tenuous, without thickness or weight, like their own reflections in water. And giving up all hope of ever being able to impose her law on this world of phantoms that were forever gliding away, she said rapidly and in jerks, like a child reciting a lesson:

"The—girl—slapped—me! The g—irl sla—apped me . . . !"

She danced up and down in a tantrum, still holding her skirt with both hands, for now, to her impotent anger, was added the fear of these two strangers barring her path, standing there on the threshold of her house, witnesses of her shame.

"Don't move," said La Pérouse always in a whisper. "No! No! Don't call anyone. It is after all very likely that the girl really did strike her. . . . You can see the mark on her cheek. Wet a towel in the water barrel . . . a rag, your handkerchief, anything. . . . I am going to speak to her."

"Don't speak," said the voice of Mademoiselle de Clergerie behind him. "Above all don't try to cover her head! My God, Fiodor, go away. . . . I mean, go and warn Francine, she must be hiding somewhere near by. Tell her to keep out of sight! . . . Dr. La Pérouse, perhaps it would be better if you left me alone a moment . . . only a moment. . . . These fits are so hideous, so frightful! If only Papa doesn't suspect . . ."

"Granny," she continued softly, "poor Granny . . ."

Then quickly picking the mad woman up in her arms, and pressing her cool cheek against the miserable old mouth, she carried her gently toward the house.

"Please go ahead," she said to La Pérouse, panting a little. "Don't touch her yet, don't let her see you. . . . Go up that stairway in front of you. I shall take her to Fernande's room. No, no, she doesn't weigh a thing. . . ."

They laid her down on the cook's bed but twice she slipped from their hands without crying out, and with a moan that went from high to low, finishing in a sort of modulated sigh, sat crouching with her back against the wall, the sheets and blankets gathered around her, shivering with weariness and pleasure.

"Forgive me, Granny," said Chantal, "forgive me. . . . It is I who hurt you, don't you remember? I didn't do it on purpose, I couldn't hold you any longer, I lost my balance and we both fell down together."

The old lady hesitated, shrugged her shoulders, visibly perplexed, disconcerted by such an unexpected intervention, by the darkened room, the bare walls, the silence.

"Bah! Bah! The girl slapped me—yes, that bad girl!—she slapped me . . . There . . . There . . . right there."

She tapped her finger savagely on her cheek over and over again.

"Oh, no! Granny, really you must have been dreaming. Are you, then, always dreaming? You were frightened, a little frightened . . . you'll be all right in a moment . . . in just a moment. Look at me, Granny. Would I let anyone slap you, I, Chantal, your little granddaughter?"

"Swear it," said the wily old lady after a short silence. "Swear that nobody gave me a . . . that I wasn't slapped. I'll believe you, darling, you don't lie."

"Go on, don't be childish, swear!" said La Pérouse scarcely lowering his voice—(as he used to talk to his interns in front of patients, in a monotone, intelligible only to the initiated.) "Be careful, she'll try to get around you."

But the mad woman did not hear the reply and to the astonishment of the doctor, she continued:

"*You* wouldn't fool me, you are a good little girl. Put your hand under my neck, there, help me stretch out my legs; I must frighten you, I look like a witch. Hold me tight, my pretty. I'm thinking of our walk the other day, you remember you carried me in your arms. . . ."

She brought her two clenched fists slowly up under her chin. Then her eyes began to close, her features relaxed, and only in the bitter corners of her mouth suspicion still lingered. Dr. La Pérouse was already tiptoeing toward the door when Chantal's voice stopped him, stunned, on the threshold.

Until that moment he had only been aware of the ordinary rhythm and cadence of that voice, but suddenly he discovered an accent, a timbre, he could not have said exactly what, hardly perceptible in ordinary conversation. And at once it seemed to him that he had always known it; yet he could not have said whether Chantal had raised or lowered the tone, and the kind of start it had given him was not that of a pleasing surprise to the ear, a perfect consonance. What had unnerved him, for an instant, was the sort of augural sadness of the voice, a sadness not comparable to any other, because the subtlest observer could not have detected the least suggestion of rancor, the vexation of disappointed love which embitters all human sadness. A disinterested, supernatural sadness like the censure of angels. And at the same time so simple and so clear, with such a tremor of innocence and of suavity that it had pierced the secret, the intact part of his soul, so that he scarcely distinguished it from the delicious and excruciating anguish of his own heart.

"What's the use, Granny," she was saying. "You are not crazy, have you ever been, I wonder? But you are all crazy really. Yes, all of you, I believe. It would take centuries and centuries, it will take all the time God has at his disposal to teach you to be happy. Oh! you can look at me like that all you please, pretend astonishment—you understand me very well, my poor

Granny. Why should you pretend with me? I know everything, I know what you tried to hide from me the other day, absolutely everything, I am not so stupid. But what's the use? Here you are, exactly as you were twenty years ago, you fume and fret, you invent a thousand excuses, you refuse to yield, you hold your sad little life hugged to your breast with your keys . . . One would have to cut off both your arms before you would give it up . . . Only, you see, you are afraid of me—you may laugh if you like—as you were afraid of my mother, extraordinary enough, isn't it? And the worst of it is that you are all like that, you are all afraid of me! What have I done to you?"

She was still holding the mad woman's arm pressed to her breast; but suddenly with a movement so spontaneous, so unexpected that it caught La Pérouse unaware, she turned her sad thoughtful face toward him with an indefinable expression, a sort of quizzical despair:

"Yes, all of you. I know it now, I have finally understood. You are expecting something of me. But what? Nobody knows . . . I begin to guess what it is. . . . Even Papa is suddenly enormously interested in his daughter, just like that! I seem to be uttering oracles. I have asked myself, "Are they going mad?" Not at all. You are interested in me as Thisbe is interested in the larks! A lark doesn't amount to much, a tuft of feathers around a song, really pretty small game—it is just the miracle of their tininess, their lightness, and then they are not good for anything, a dessert, a fantasy . . . But be careful, I shall defend myself. . . . Is it my fault that you have lied so often to God? Am I so constituted that you had to give me your lies to keep? I refuse to bear them for you. . . . I have only my poor little trifle of a truth, my own truth; I am not going to give it to you, it wouldn't do you any good."

She leaned her forehead on the bed hiding her face in the covers, and La Pérouse saw by the shaking of her shoulders that she was crying.

"Mademoiselle Chantal," he said, "I am ashamed."

She raised her head quickly and, with one of those looks of intrepid sadness in which he seemed to read his fate, imposed silence. Then almost immediately she began speaking to her grandmother again in that tone of childlike entreaty:

"We are going to take you to your own room, Granny. You see, don't you, that you are in Fernande's room now? You must promise to be obedient until you have had a long night's sleep."

"Obedient?" asked the old lady thoughtfully. "Must I also obey Francine?"

"Don't think of Francine, you are not going to see her ever again! I promise you."

"I'll never see her again? That will be better. Neither Francine nor anyone. I must hide, I haven't any more strength, have I? And now keep this for yourself, my little girl! The workmen are coming back, and the buyer from Beaumesnil for the cider apples. . . . We'll settle the price in advance, by contract this time. . . . Tell them I'm not well."

"I shall say that you are old, Granny, very old. . . . Oh, that will not be news to anyone but you! . . . And even you! Because you're not so sure, really, that the buyer from Beaumesnil is coming today, nor the others either, for there are many, many others—how I should like to free you of all these people. . . . What will you do with these corpses? They all died that day we met out there in the sun, one morning, don't you remember? I carried you in my arms, it is true, light as a feather, as light as you will be in God's hands—an ant, a poor little ant. . . . An ant spends all its time filling its granary, and then goes off and dies alone, behind a little stone. . . . We ought to imitate them."

"Alone?" said the old lady with curiosity. "Really alone? Is it possible? Everything is always moving, murmuring . . . I am never alone."

Delicately she put her hand on Chantal's shoulder and said after a short silence, her eyes closed and with a profound sigh of concentration:

"Yet, when *you* speak I hear nothing else . . . I don't even want to defend myself any longer, my head feels better. Why, to be sure, I am old! But just the same I have more sense than they have. . . . You don't lie, my sweet. . . . A body can listen to you, can breathe; it's really refreshing. And of course you are right! At my age I should let things go. My hands can't hold anything any longer, I fret over trifles."

From under her eyelids she stole an indefinable

look at her granddaughter, both anxious and shrewd:

"What would you like me to give you? There is the set of emeralds that came from great-aunt Adoline . . . But what use would they be to you, you couldn't wear them. . . . You'd do better to choose something more substantial."

"Bah!" said Chantal, "don't worry . . . I know what I am going to ask you for. And after that you will be able to sleep, sleep tight, sleep as you have never slept before."

At that the old lady opened her eyes wide.

"Give me your keys, Granny, your beloved keys."

"My keys?"

"Yes, that's what I want you to give me, your keys. It is your keys that keep you from sleeping. Each one of them is a little demon, and each one of those little demons alone is heavier than a mountain. With such a weight, my poor Granny, even the angels, even if they tried all of them together, couldn't carry you to Paradise."

"My keys!" the old lady repeated growing pale. "What's all this talk about angels and demons? Just because of a harmless whim of mine! You're cunning, my little girl, but this time you're wrong. I have them here under my woolen shirt, here, you can feel them. . . . I like to hear them rattle—listen—click, clack, clickity clack and click and clack. . . . Ah, yes! It amuses me. What harm is there in that? Keys! Keys are nothing to me . . . !"

"Of course not, and so you will give them to me,

give them up. . . . You said a minute ago that at your age your fingers couldn't hold anything any longer—Oh, Granny, the dead have forgiven you long ago! It is you who are hanging on to the past. God grants you remorse but He doesn't want you to make a habit of it! Your keys are your bad habits."

The mad woman listened with extraordinary attention, marking each word with a slight nod of her head, and La Pérouse noticed a dawning concentration in those restless eyes.

"Nothing has ever been seen to equal it!" he muttered under his breath.

But although he had barely whispered, Madame de Clergerie was aware of a doubtful murmur. It took her a moment to recover, and the effort she made distorted her features again, and for a second appeared that expression of mingled shrewdness and distress.

"My keys! What! Do you think I take a miserable trousseau of keys for the Holy Sacrament? I would astonish you indeed, my dear, if I told you what I really . . ."

Chantal laid her head gently on the pillow.

"Not so much perhaps," she said, "you know very well that your keys won't open a single door or drawer in the house, you never use them, they are make-believe keys. Only you don't want us to think you know it. Yes, Granny, let me tell you—and don't be angry. . . . At your age, so close to God, even one little lie is too many! The soul is too weak. And, besides, there are all the other lies, lies of a life-time! . . .

They always leave something behind; old people are poisoned by them. Tear out this one at least, the others will come with it all together, like the bindweed around the currant bushes. . . . Then you will be reconciled with the living and the dead, I give you my word, I swear it. . . . You will be able to sleep in peace."

"You have guessed! I can't believe it!" cried the old lady in a voice that was trembling with joy. "You guess everything, it's wonderful. Yes, yes, I knew it . . . *They* are really not good for anything . . . I can even tell you the day they were put on my table in place of the real ones. They still smelled of rust, the man was scouring them with sand under my window the day before. . . . Never mind, take them, I give them to you. . . . Now that you know, what good are they to me? Anyway, I'm tired . . . Even my heart is asleep, my pretty. Now I can be just as tired as I please!"

A slight shiver passed over her shoulders. She was asleep.

"What do you think?" asked Chantal. "Wouldn't it be better to leave her here until evening? I know her, she will wake up for supper."

She may have tried to smile, but La Pérouse only saw her hollow cheeks, the lines around her eyes, her poor drooping mouth.

"Your grandmother, Mademoiselle Chantal, will not eat tonight. You have driven her too far, she can't stand any more."

"Nor I," said Chantal, "I can't stand any more."

She went over to the window, resting her forehead against the pane in silence, and he thought he saw her lips moving. To him the idea that she was praying was suddenly unendurable.

"Your method is ingenious," he said. (At the same time he watched for the start of her blond head at the abrupt burst of his voice). I find it rather cruel. Why take her rattle away? There's one for every age."

She turned quickly to face him.

"Really?" she said, "is that your opinion?" Her voice was anxious. "But no," she continued, "you only say that to hurt me, to make me angry. In what way is my method ingenious? My method! But I have no method, Doctor. I have been taught nothing, and I am quite incapable of inventing anything. Anybody would have acted the same. . . . I know my grandmother better than you do. She has loved life too well, that is the trouble, old age humiliates her, she won't give in, she grits her poor old teeth. It is true, her mind is no longer very certain, but with her shrewdness she knows how to take advantage of everything! She has constructed her story, lie by lie, like a bird its nest twig by twig, and you act as though you believed it, you refuse to free her. My God, it seems to me there are no more dangerous lies than the ones we commit against ourselves."

She ended almost in a whisper. Her hands, as she gently folded back the blanket, were trembling with impatience and fatigue. As she leaned over the bed her knees almost gave way, she had only just time to lean her elbow on the side of the bed to steady herself, but so quickly that La Pérouse hardly noticed. He seemed to read a challenge in her proud, sad eyes.

"Your turn will come, my dear young lady," he said. "Yes, the hour will come when you will search avidly among all the lies you scorn today, for a last miserable little one to help you live and die. I have seen young lives more insolent than yours surrender in the end . . . they surrendered body and soul."

"Is it possible," she said, looking at the psychiatrist with unspeakable surprise, "is it possible to surrender?"

He started to laugh, a laugh so vile, so ferocious, with such evident desire to humiliate her, that she turned crimson. Nothing could be heard but the quiet breathing of the old woman and the scratching of a branch against the window pane.

"Can't you understand?" she said. "To whom does one surrender? To whom does one surrender one's soul? I believe that one gives oneself or one refuses oneself, but does one surrender?"

Her voice grew fainter and fainter and was scarcely audible on the last word.

"Oh," cried La Pérouse, "an old physician's vocabulary is not very rich, you'll have to make allowances . . . *give yourself, refuse oneself,* those are, for me, meaningless expressions. I have never seen anyone refuse himself to what he loved, nor give himself to what he hated; man and his desire are one and the same. But I believe that everybody surrenders in the end, as soon as one's forces begin to fail and with them the desire of pleasing. And, since this discussion seems to interest you, I might add that the role of redresser of lies is, without doubt, more imposing than useful. Moreover it has been tried before, the method is well known. My former master, Durault de Séverac, considered simulation . . ."

"Oh, please!" cried Chantal. "I acted spontaneously, stupidly, without thinking. I should be very much embarrassed to come face to face with your illustrious professor. Seriously," she hastened to add, "please don't think that I am joking. I am truly ignorant, I don't mean half-way either, and that's how I am going to stay. For there is nothing worse than an amateur doctor, unless it's an amateur painter."

"Oh yes, there is," Dr. La Pérouse rejoined quickly, "there is the amateur of souls, the fanatic who assigns you a conscience in order to have the pleasure of moving in and of bringing his own furniture with him. . . . We all manage to get along with our own portion of truth and falsehood . . . I myself . . ."

"Why do you speak of yourself?" Chantal asked gently. "I am certainly incapable of forcing anybody's conscience. What have I done to you? Why are you defending yourself?"

"Pardon me, I am not defending myself! I simply refuse to be fooled. Yes, young lady, I am long past the age when I let myself be influenced by anybody who comes along, and after thirty years of remaking the souls of idiots out of the leavings of their old ones, I despise myself enough to have the right to spare myself certain useless and humiliating experiences. Let's be frank—at times I have watched you with a certain curiosity, with interest, and, shrewd as you are, you've known it all along; and either through indifference or through contempt, you have very deftly stimulated my curiosity without for a moment thinking of satisfying it. For you and your kind, curiosity like mine is simply vulgar and illbred! Today, this very morning, Clergerie questioned me about you . . . Oh, as one questions an old friend! After all, I've known you since you were a little girl with your hair down your back and baby hands, unbelievable, little, white tapering hands!"

She came toward him, her head held high, almost haughtily, and in her golden eyes that mocking gleam that lent such a unique, such a heartbreaking expression to her tired and so sadly resigned face.

"Papa questioned you?" she said. "Really! There's nothing I'll have escaped! What does he object to? My life is one of the least extraordinary imaginable, I want it to be like that, I pull it down as low as possible, and, with the excuse that my poor mother had a horror of housekeeping, I shall end by spending the best part of my time in the kitchen. What more do you want? What does everybody think that I am hiding? A secret, a real secret, but that is a luxury! I haven't the time. . . . Besides, you must admit that Papa is extraordinary. For the last two years he has hardly been aware of my existence, and now suddenly he goes to the other extreme—he counts all my steps, he questions you, decides that I should be examined by a psychiatrist. Even you, oh please don't interrupt me, there's no use waking my grandmother . . . I am not such an idiot, I see you drawing the circle closer and closer around my modest person, I shan't escape you any longer . . . so much the worse for you . . . Sometimes it happens, when hunters think they have hemmed in a magnificent male pheasant in the high yellow clover—it is only a gray female that flies off. You have no idea how terribly gray I am . . ."

"So what?" put in La Pérouse coarsely.

"So," she replied, "you will simply be forced to invent a fine story to console yourselves—that is what legends are for. Today you are still trying to surprise some characteristic trait, no matter what, which will make it possible for you to classify me. I can see you setting your poor little innocent traps with the candor of the worthy entomologist who, twenty times in succession, turns an unhappy beetle over on its back. You want to know where I came from, where I am going . . . I am left at liberty, but all the exits are watched; you'll surely catch me! The temporal gateway is under your guard, and if I should want to escape into paradise, Abbé Cénabre keeps watch at the gateway of the spiritual world. . . . After all, what if I prefer staying right here, not going anywhere? I was born to live from day to day, like an old crow preening his feathers in the snow, waiting for the spring.

Yes, an old crow! Don't think I am so young . . . you'd probably lose your head sooner than I; I am rarely thrown off balance, I belong to a very common species of individuals—very tough and old before their time, who always make the best of things. And then, you see, I must tell you—there is something else you seem to have forgotten—you are really astonishing! For after all I observe you, too! If only thinking could give you all a little discretion from time to time, a little prudence! You would be less apt to hurt me uselessly."

"Who has hurt you uselessly? Why?"

She hesitated, shrugged her shoulders, and the mocking light seemed to fade, to retreat into the depths of her sad tender eyes.

"You would be afraid of being ridiculous," she said following the train of her thoughts. "Yes, you would blush to bring confusion into my life on any pretext, even on that of friendship for me. . . . There are so few things in my life, you understand! It is like a student's room,—the bed, the table, the two chairs,—I can keep it neat and clean. . . . What right has anyone to make it into a jumble shop, one of those curiosity shops that I detest? Well, I am going to close my door, that's all. . . . Everybody has to say his name, his real name, show his face. . . . From now on not everybody who knocks will be admitted."

"You would have been wise to take such an elementary precaution sooner," said La Pérouse, "and because of others besides myself."

He had launched his insult coldly, deliberately, with a contained and lucid rage. And yet, in the same fraction of a second he felt a very different kind of anger rising in him out of his very entrails, a sort of furious panic which was like a revolt against death.

She looked at him for a long time in unutterable surprise but he was unable to detect the least sign of fear or embarrassment. She did not even blush, the curve of her lips never altered, her alert, delicate face remained motionless except for the quivering shadow of her gold-tipped lashes. Finally she said:

"Doctor La Pérouse, you have spoken too late. Yes, it is now too late, you cannot offend me. But if you know my poor secret, what more do you want? Surely you know enough."

"No," he said, "Fiodor is a crazy fool. What does it matter what he has seen or has not seen? It is from you, from your own lips, that I shall learn if he has lied."

He had brought his face so close to hers that it almost touched her cheek. He was grinning like a maniac or like a man who has suffered a fundamental deception that has attacked the very roots of his life. She saw his eyes moving gradually as though two thin crystal blades, only slightly blurred, had slowly slipped one over the other.

"Listen," he said. "I have been a doctor, it is true, but no longer. Tomorrow I shall be nothing at all. . . . Yes, you will still be just as young and strong and fresh, with that odor, that perfume of wild blackberries about you, while I shall hear the rain falling drop by drop on my grave, on my coffin, the continual settling of the earth, and many, many feet down under limestone and clay, the noise of a little spring running along, rising, hurrying toward the light, leaping like a little beast from one mossy stone to another onto the grass. . . . What do you care for science and learned men—as a matter of fact I have never been one of them; I wish they were all dead. I have never really loved anything . . . Whom would I have loved? I have spent my life looking at myself in the faces of my daft patients as in a mirror. I know the particular, unchanging meaning of each one of my grimaces. I can no longer make myself laugh or weep. . . . But I'll still show them, my child. Formerly, just a look, a single assault of my eyes would annihilate any persecution mania or obsession, like a blow in the solar plexus! The students would actually see the thing coming out of the patient's mouth, they would poke each other with their elbows, and they didn't feel like joking any longer I assure you. Those are the good moments of life. In short, I think I am a competent judge of a person's state of health! So then, when you said to your grandmother a little while ago, 'The ant fills its granary and then goes off to die behind a little stone'—something like that—I thought, she has been playing with Fiodor, she has been making fun of us. Come now, confess, you were making a fool of the Russian, weren't you?"

"Oh, Dr. La Pérouse, have you made a wager, all

of you, to drive me to despair! After all! I tried to be patient, to wait, to hide for a few weeks, for a few miserable weeks a . . . a . . . well, an indisposition . . . I am not the only one, you know! You remember, Marie de Saint-André—you took care of her? She used to walk in her sleep at school. She would go along the roofs, and then afterwards remain for an hour, two hours without moving—in a faint, I don't know what, as stiff as a board. And here everything comes crashing about my ears just because a veritable Russian-Ballet personage has taken it into his head to follow me about the way one follows a lion tamer, hoping the lion will eat him! For, after all, I'm not more prudish than most girls, but there are moments when stouter ones than I would be thrown off balance, lose their heads—when I begin to envy girls who can run to their mamas with such unpleasant confidences. . . . But imagine telling a story like mine to a father like mine! . . . And, even granting I have been somewhat vacillating, a little cowardly, haven't I been sufficiently punished? Moreover do I owe you the truth? Am I accountable for you to God?"

"It's not that," said La Pérouse. "But, of course, I could hardly expect you to understand, to have any conception of what the last illusion of a condemned man can be! I believed in you. The word love has no longer any meaning for me, but what I felt can be expressed in no other language: I believed in you. Even today, even at this instant, I search your face in vain for the least mark, or sign, the imperceptible stigma of the past! For you, O wonder, there is no past! When one has scrutinized as many physiognomies as I have, that from a distance seem to be alive but are in reality only grimaces congealed for centuries by some hereditary taint, what a surprise suddenly to discover a human being, the most humble of human beings, who is at least in profound accord with herself, free and intact! You were that being. I knew you like that. I have never seen anything like it, never . . . you were . . . you were . . ."

"I know what I was," she said with a pathetic trembling of her lips and her eyes grew darker. "I have understood at last. . . . It is really true, then! What am I to expect! In twenty years perhaps I shall be one of those poor wretches one meets in your waiting room! Do you remember Mrs. Ascott and that poor Hélène Walsh, or worse still, one of those hideous bigots who were the despair of Abbé Chevance: 'They are, I must say, terrible bores! . . .' he would sigh . . . Oh, God!"

For a moment her eyes questioned him with a miserable smile that unconsciously implored him. It was her only moment of weakness.

"And after all!" she went on, shaking her head as she used to when, on the broad flat highway between Dombreville and Trévières, speeding her car, she would lean her head far out to hear the rush of air pounding in her ears. "We too, Dr. La Pérouse, we too must give up our keys."

He looked at her stupefied, stammering:

"I didn't say anything of the sort . . . You—you are . . ."

"Oh, I really wouldn't bother about that," she said. "It is of no importance to know who I am; definitions are always misleading . . . Yes, I should have liked an uneventful life, as transparent as possible, and in the end to be a little old lady with pink cheeks laughing to herself from morning to night, pink as a rose, who would die just as naturally as she put her stockings in the fireplace on Christmas Eve. But instead, here I am, a sort of heroine, with something tragic and equivocal about me, doomed to drag along in my train all sorts of madmen and monomaniacs, like flies. It is not the Russian chauffeur who ought to be sent away, it is I who should go away. But go where?"

"You!" he cried, "go away! And what about us? What of me? Do you really expect me to believe that you have noticed nothing? No? Come now! That might be barely possible in Paris, but here! You said yourself a minute ago: they seem to be expecting something of me. Good God! You have finally got the better of all of us, we are at your mercy. '*An uneventful life, a little old lady with pink cheeks.*' You really like to make fun of us, don't you?"

She did not seem to hear him, although she kept her serious gaze fixed attentively on his face. And suddenly her voice rose, filled the silence with so pure, so heartbreaking a tone that he closed his eyes in spite of himself, better to feel the profound vibration in his breast.

"It is truc," she said. "I should have been more cautious since I had nothing to give. Oh, those are things you won't easily understand, I don't really hope to be able to justify myself! After all I was only thinking of God, I was simple and gay only for him . . . a child, a little child. . . . But only saints are children! But men, Dr. La Pérouse, all of us . . . men are sad, so sad! How strange! Just think, it has taken me years and years to discover it. . . . We don't notice because of habit, we don't see how sad men are. . . . Or, at least, I didn't want to believe it. I was like those idiots who affect a cheerful, clandestine manner when they talk to sick people. You feel like slapping them. Certainly there is the joy of God, plain joy—each one of us has his own idea of it. . . . But the great, the very great have the secret of letting it appear without harming their neighbors. I said to myself: What better can I do? I am as insignificant as possible, after all I can't make myself completely invisible! What is it that amazes them so? Because, you know very well, we distinguish easily in other people's attention what is given to our face, figure and our clothes—and what to the other, the privileged, the sacred part. . . . My God, I had no experience, no responsibilities, and not the least ambition either . . . I was simple, I was much too simple. The rest of you have lived, suffered, offended God, and I don't know what all! You have your regrets, your remorse, you are like old soldiers with their scars. . . . Our Lord never wearies of forgiving you; you are all dripping with the blood of the

Cross. What was I doing in that battle of men? I only succeeded in little things. And because I never attempt anything else people think that everything is possible for me, they expect wonders of me. Then, one day, naturally they want to put me to the test and I am not ready for any test at all."

"Please, please, be quiet," he said. "I had no right to put you to any test, I deserve your contempt."

"You do not frighten me," she replied, "that's the principal thing. Because I am absolutely sure of not despising anyone. Oh, no! I don't despise anyone. And even I myself, no matter what I did, I should never succeed in despising myself. Contempt is the poison of sadness, Dr. La Pérouse. Having drunk sadness, scorn stays at the bottom, a bitter black mud. And no matter how unhappy I may be some day, sadness won't find any room in me, ever. . . . You do not frighten me any longer, Dr. La Pérouse, neither you nor the others. I used to fear evil, not as one should fear it, no, I had a horror of evil. I know now that one should not have a horror of anything. To you a pious young girl who goes to mass and communion, seems pretty silly and childish; you take us for innocents. . . . Well, let me tell you, sometimes we know more about evil than people who have only learned to offend God. I have seen a saint die, yes, with my own eyes, and it isn't what you would expect, it isn't at all like what one reads about in books, you have to nerve yourself before such an experience, you feel your soul's armor cracking. It was then I understood what sin is. . . . Sin, why we are all in it! Some are in it for their pleasure, others for their pain, but in the end it is the same bread we break beside the fountain, swallowing hard, in disgust. You were certainly wrong to expect anything of me. . . . But I will give you what I have, the little I have, not more nor less. I said just now that you should be careful, that I would not bear your lies, that I would defend myself! I no longer want to defend myself, that's over . . . No one has a right to defend himself . . . God doesn't keep any of us like a rare bird in an aviary. . . . He gives up his best friends, he gives them for nothing, to the good, to the bad, to everybody, just as He was given up by Pilate: 'This is the man, take him!'— Oh, Dr. La Pérouse, how extraordinary, in that carnival of soldiers, Jewish priests and painted women—the first communion of the human race!"

She tiptoed to the door and opened it softly.

"How she sleeps, it's terrifying! . . . Dr. La Pérouse, do you think it would be safe to wake her now? I should like her to go back to her room through the hall and go to bed again until luncheon. That would give me time enough to straighten things out."

"You forget Fiodor," said the doctor.

"My God!" she cried. "It's true . . . I had forgotten he was there, saw everything, he will have turned the house upside down by now . . . But this poor house is always upside down, that's its natural state of equilibrium, it just won't stay right side up. I expect soon to be walking on my head. . . ."

She put her hand on his arm, and he noticed with an indefinable emotion—a cruel and delicious presentiment, the tender mockery in her eyes, her quiet smile.

"How wonderful, some day, to be lying stretched out on one's back in the earth, with one's arms crossed like everybody else, one's miserable bones a little dilapidated but nicely arranged in order! I love order so much, Dr. La Pérouse, perhaps too much! No one would dare to love it as much as I do."

"What—you are actually laughing! How can you—it's a miracle— When there isn't a soul here whom you can trust. Even . . ."

"Even you? Oh, but I can. I couldn't have an hour ago, because you didn't know then who I was. You thought me daring, stubborn, or even, who knows, consorting with angels? Whereas I am just a poor girl who is very much perplexed. Perplexed—there is no other word—big words confuse everything. Even if I had a seraph to help me, or the gift of miracles, I should still be perplexed. You see, Dr. La Pérouse, a good Christian doesn't care for miracles very much, because a miracle is God looking after his own affairs, and we prefer looking after them for Him. And so, I have committed one fault after the other. I have acted heedlessly. Now I shall have to extricate myself alone. You can imagine what help Papa would be to me! . . . Oh! And you couldn't help me either, Dr. La Pérouse, you less than anyone, we have said all we had to say, we have nothing more to say to each other. Yes, you and I, from now on, we are out of the game. . . . My God,—why are you crying?"

"Really," he said, "am I crying? Well, then, you mustn't look. They are tears of shame. Just think, for the last five minutes I have been searching for one moment, just one single moment of my life to offer you, that would be worthy of you. There is nothing, nothing I can find that isn't too filthy or too trifling. The whole life of a man wouldn't even fill the palm of a hand."

"What difference does that make?" she replied gently. "Only the present counts. And that reminds me, at the moment the most useful thing you could do would be to go and explain to Papa. Tell him that my grandmother was taken ill coming back from her walk this morning, that we put her to bed here, that he mustn't worry, that we are going to take her back to her own room. That will hold him until luncheon! After luncheon it will be my turn."

She stood for another moment in the open doorway as she said laughingly with a shrug of her shoulders:

"Bah, Dr. La Pérouse, what's the use of struggling? Our time has come."

"If I had waited for you, Mademoiselle," remarked the cook, "I could have whistled for my mushrooms. Fiodor has just gone to Verneuil, he'll find them at Jeanne Marchais'. As for Francine, I don't know what happened. She came back in a fury; you couldn't say a word to her."

She got up to close the door, came back and sat down again. Trying to appear calm, but in a voice that trembled with impatience to be convincing, to be believed, she said:

"What are we coming to? They're all alike here. No sense at all, and with the vices of millionaires. Nowadays gangsters and escaped convicts are taken into respectable houses, they're given good beds to sleep in. I keep wondering if you, Mademoiselle, are aware of the kind of crooks we have here? Only to mention one—that Russian is capable of anything!"

"My God!" cried her mistress, "enough! My poor Fernande, just look at me, do you think I am in any mood to discuss such nonsense? I am all in, my head is whirling, I am tired, tired, tired to death."

She shrugged her shoulders and continued with a smile that was so humble and so sad that for a second it seemed to efface the radiance of her glance, her pride.

"Capable of anything? Capable of nothing, I should say. Dear God, what liars they are! It is really discouraging in the end. You don't know who they are any longer. It seems to me they are only pretending to live, how do they ever expect to die, to be a real corpse, to die once and for all. Yes, one would like to teach them at least how to die like God's unhappy creatures, to die like men!"

She reached over and put her little hand lightly

over the cook's mouth: "Sh! be quiet! don't tell me any more horrors, Fernande, I am much more in need of reassurance . . . I'll tell you what . . . look me in the face without saying a word, just look at me with your kind blue eyes! Even when you are trying to be very crafty, your eyes are still too honest, they can't hide anything; they look as though they were freshly polished every morning. How happy your daughters —even the bad one who ran away with the road-mender—must have been to look at themselves in those eyes!"

Before the dumbfounded cook could move, Chantal kissed her on both cheeks and quickly disappeared. As she closed the door Fernande heard her lovely laugh that trembled a little, as she said:

"I'll explain everything later. . . . Now really . . . Oh well, what of it? I feel that I am good for nothing today."

4

"When, one day, you think yourself lost," Abbé Chevance had said, "it will be because your little task is almost done. When that happens you must not try to understand, you must not worry, you must just keep very still. Even prayer is sometimes an innocent ruse, a way of fleeing, of escaping like any other—a way, at least, of gaining time. Our Lord prayed on the Cross, and he also cried aloud, wept, groaned and gnashed his teeth, like all dying men. But more precious than all that is the moment, that long moment of silence, when all was accomplished."

How many times had he reverted to the subject with insistence, as though he were speaking, not of a possible peril, but of an absolutely certain contingency, as though he feared more than anything else for his beloved daughter a final, almost involuntary movement of defense, a last resistance. Was not that, perhaps, the lesson of his death, the hidden meaning of an end so humble, so abandoned that it had struck terror even into Chantal's heart? For she had remembered long afterward another equally strange saying: "I have despised fear too much," he had one day admitted. "I was too hot-blooded."

"What!" she had cried. "*You* talking like that! So now you want to admit fear into paradise too."

And he, with a pacifying gesture of his poor hand already red and swollen, laughed his silent laugh.

"Not so fast!" he had replied. "In one way fear is also God's daughter, redeemed on the night of Holy Friday. She is not beautiful to look at—oh no!—ridiculed at times, at others cursed, disowned by everyone . . . and yet, make no mistake about it, she is present at every death-bed—she is man's intercessor."

"How weary I am! God, how weary I am!" murmured Chantal as she mounted the stairs, letting the palm of her little hand slide along the cool wall. "I have never felt so weary. Poor Dr. La Pérouse was right, perhaps. There are days when one can neither give nor refuse anything, when one is tempted just to capitulate, to surrender, to beg for mercy."

She let herself sink into a low chair at the foot of her bed, then suddenly jumped up again quickly, in fear and disgust. She had caught herself in the very act of yielding to that overwhelming fatigue which sues for mercy. "No and no!" she said between her teeth. "No!" And she began pacing her room.

She wanted to throw herself on her knees, hide her face in her hands, disappear, go back into that marvelous silence which, just to think of, made her heart stop beating. But at the same moment an imperious order rose from the depths of her being, that part of self always on the alert to resist for another minute, another hour, a day (who could say) at all events, to await erect the fatal blow. She might restlessly come and go between bed and window, lift the curtain with a trembling hand, absently rearrange the cushions, or even whistle softly to herself the first bars of Debussy's *Arabesque* she loved so well, but she knew already that there was no issue to her struggle, that she had now advanced too far, had reached the point where unknown laws obtain, when the will is nothing more than a sling-stone at the height of its trajectory, ready to fall of its own weight again. What difference did it make? At least she would be a spectator of the inevitable fall. A stone falls, but a man suffers his destiny.

And, perhaps, had Chantal been confronted with some real, recognizable danger she would have been more affected. As it was, the very absurdity of the presentiment, so vague and yet so strange, completely absorbed her attention. Convinced that she would be struck unexpectedly by a blow that she would be unable to parry, she never gave a thought to defending herself, clinging only to that same stoic resignation which gives such dignity to the final atonement of the basest criminal, because his last steps toward death recall those initial steps toward life of a little child in a mother's loving hands, reveal some indefinable childish lordliness composed of terror, haste, trust, dazed surprise and a holy clumsiness. For he is not thinking of making use, one by one, of each minute of grace; his only concern is to circumvent any last tentative of the body, the terror, the revolt of the flesh, panic's demoniac madness or despair. And because of the effort he thus makes to destroy, to push back into nothingness those last seconds that uselessly prolong his agony, through this great straining toward oblivion, when he finally enters the darkness he has called upon, he is no longer alive.

Chantal could certainly not have given a name to that sort of consternation that had taken possession of her, nor to that impatience that she persisted in considering the sign of her weakness and cowardice. "Am I really frightened?" she asked herself. "Yet nothing has changed, nothing. Am I going to believe in premonitions too?" And she barely succeeded in smiling, a poor little anxious smile that implored, and tried to understand. "Why, of course!" she cried suddenly. "That's it! I must not try to understand. What for? Naturally Dr. La Pérouse upset me. He looked so terribly unhappy. I talked and talked—that never helps." She was idly fingering the thin tulle curtains and caught sight of her pale face in the window pane. "What am I doing here? Now I look like a rat in a trap. I gnaw the bars of my cage, it's disgraceful! I am free, free, free. All God's children are free." She hurried to the door, opened it, drew back, took a step forward again and remained trembling for a long time on the threshold. For a long time she stood breathing in the hot breathless darkness with disgust. Then, the same strange smile on her lips, gently and very carefully she closed the door, and defeated, came back into the room.

"Abbé Chevance was right," she said. "At a moment like this it is better to do nothing, keep very still. I would certainly only commit blunders. After all, I don't know what a great ordeal is, a real ordeal: this one has come suddenly, the lights have all gone out at once, I'll never find my way—but there must be a way! My God, by comparison, how happy I was only an hour or two ago! I would never have thought I could find myself so suddenly, so unexpectedly alone. Formerly, at least, I would have fallen on my knees, here or anywhere, at the foot of my cross. . . . (She clutched the handle of the window with her two little hands to prevent herself really from falling). At present I even have to pray to God with circumspection, cautiously. Very well then. I shall not budge from this spot until the light returns; I am not made to grope in the dark. I have to know where I am going."

"*Until the light returns,*" she said, but even as she spoke she no longer expected it to return, expected only the night, and it was the night she braved with her patient eyes: night and nothingness, and the fall, that soft swift downward sinking. . . . The illusion became so strong that she actually felt her muscles relax, her back bend, a deep rasping in her throat, and the air against her chest. The humble assurance that had inspired all the actions of her marvelous life, the certitude of having never been, on any occasion, more than a very little thing, vain and light, made to serve just for a moment, for the joy of a single moment, then to be thrown away without regret, now took on its full meaning. She had really been thrown away.

Suddenly the realization came to her that she had experienced this same vertiginous sensation before as she had watched beside her old master lying on his death-bed. And almost at the same instant the vision rose out of the darkness coming toward her with terrifying swiftness. First the soiled bed appeared, then grew larger, stopped abruptly quite close to her now, still swayed by an invisible swell. She could have touched the corner of the sheet hanging down, the gray blanket where the blood had left a dark violet stain. "Is it you?" she said sadly. "Is it you?" She felt neither curiosity, nor any fear. She simply found herself again at the same place, ready for the same struggle. Today, as yesterday, she could not expect any aid from her old friend, no word of consolation. She must simply remain steadfast and calm, as she had before, straight and watchful, her shadow hovering over the old master, incomprehensibly struck down.

She had barely the courage to raise her troubled eyes to the pillow and immediately lowered them again. The unbleached linen still kept, stamped in the down like the seal of perfect misery itself, the impress of head and shoulders. The bed was empty.

She had, in truth, expected nothing else. She had known that it was empty. She knew that it was written for all eternity that she was to arrive alone at the last turn of the road, that he would miss the supreme rendez-vous. She knew too that this mysterious bed, come to rest now so close to her, like a tiny ship still softly rolling on its anchor, on the surface of the darkness, was only a half-voluntary hallucination, an image hardly stronger than the others but that her imagination had seized as it passed. She accepted all this as a sign, probably the symbol of her humble destiny. Great ordeals were not meant for her, nor great joys, and what she called, for want of a better word, her anguish, to the very end was to resemble rather those deceptions of our childhood that are so like dreams. . . . And so, all her life she had been carefully, heroically watching over mediocre beings who were hardly real, over things of no value. And now she was going to keep watch for the last time over the useless remembrance of a dead man, beside an empty bed.

She took a step toward the vision, smiling. The image began to fade at once, disappeared into a milky shadow, vanished. In spite of the closed windows, the triple thickness of the white curtains, she could now hear Fernande's angry voice, the clanking of the buckets at the pump, a shrill laugh. She listened at first with a kind of weary surprise, almost incredulous, as though these noises came from a distant shore across an immense expanse of murmuring water. Then it seemed to her that each moment was irrevocably taking her farther and farther away from all these beings she had cherished. The thought that in an instant she would probably never again be able to do anything more for them, that she would have lost what was a thousand times more precious than their pitiful presence, the secret of their sadness, of their wretchedness, that the heavenly bond of pity between them would forever have been severed; that she would no longer be able to pity them, share their dark suffering, nor like a lightning flash pierce through it. She might have thought herself again the toy of some supernatural spite. The discouragement she had known during the last few weeks, the successive disillusionments, her struggles against her grandmother and La Pérouse, against herself, all seemed to her like so many traps set up in her path, obstacles against which she must spend her force, and be reduced to impotence, at the very moment she was to accomplish the unique work for which she had been born: the salvation of weak souls for whom she felt herself accountable to God. In choosing the commonest lot, a task equal to the least adept, the least enterprising, she had really only thought of her security and peace. "Give to God what is asked of little children," Abbé Chevance had told her. And he too had lived like a little child. With her he had laid a wager, maintained that challenge until —the ruse suddenly being revealed—he had sunk into death without a word, without a tear, become a man among men again, in a solemn renunciation.

Then those words *too late,* those two desolate words that contain all the sorrow of our kind, rose to her lips with a stifled groan, a hoarse cry that seemed torn out of a mother's breast. She saw herself carrying the old woman in her arms, against her heart, in the dust and dazzling heat of noon, under the prodigious sun. God had given her patience and strength enough for such burdens, and yet she had chosen the innocent game of divine grace, the daily task, humble joy fostered with such loving care, and that had been of no use to anyone, that no one had understood! . . . Thus too had Abbé Chevance worn himself out all his life on servile tasks, and had finally died abandoned and misunderstood by everyone, remained even for the daughter of his soul an enigma, a secret, almost a remorse. "I could have, I should have . . ." she stammered with dry eyes and flaming cheeks. "Yes, if it is true that they were expecting everything of me, then what have I given?"

She turned her head a little, listened again for the sounds through the closed windows with the absurd fear that she would never hear them again, as though it were possible for her little universe, which she had failed to save, to have been swept away in a trice, engulfed in oblivion. Oblivion . . . "Alas! I was all they had," she said. "God has forgotten them!"

The idea of this unavailing, eternal solitude which she had hardly dared conceive, suddenly broke down her resistance. She lifted toward the Christ hanging on the wall her avid gaze, and unable to turn away any longer from the ineffable spring for which she thirsted, she slipped to her knees and threw herself into prayer, her lips pressed tightly together, her eyes closed—as one falls, as one dies.

She had never before gone down into that strange world to which she alone had access, except gradually, imperceptibly; this time she felt herself plunging into it. She literally thought she heard deep waters closing over her, and felt her body sink under the immense, ever growing weight, whose irresistible pressure drove all life from her veins. It was like the uprooting of her whole being, so brutal and painful that the violated soul could respond only with a horrible silence. . . . And almost in the same incalculable fraction of time, light surged from all sides, covering everything.

"What was I looking for?" Chantal asked herself. "Where was I?" (She seemed to recognize one by one each familiar object, she felt that from now on she would envelop them, embrace them with that inner gaze that bathed in another light.) "Was it so difficult then to give myself into His hands? Now I am there indeed!"

For at present, the idea, the certainty of her impotence had become the dazzling center of her joy, the core of the flaming star. It was by that very impotence that she felt herself united to the still invisible Master, it was that humiliated portion of her soul that had plunged into the abyss of suavity. Slowly, with infinite precaution, she amorously completed the consumption of that scattered light; she concentrated its rays at a single point of her being as though she hoped to pierce the last obstacle and through the breach to lose herself in God. For another little moment the waters were still. Then the flamboyant wave began gently, insidiously to recede, scattering its foam everywhere. The pain appeared again like the black tooth of a reef between two columns of spray, but now stripped of all other feelings, reduced to its essence, smooth and bare indeed like a rock worn away by the waves. By this sign Chantal knew that the last stage had been passed, her humble sacrifice accepted, and that the anguish of the past hours, the doubts and even her remorse, had now been engulfed in the prodigious compassion of God.

She dared not move, nor even lower her wide-open eyes, fixed on the same point of the wall, a little below her crucifix. She felt plainly the fatigue of her knees, her back, the weight of the nape of her neck, that sort of hardening of the eyeballs that paralyzed her gaze. And yet her own suffering no longer belonged to her, she could no longer contain it; it was like an effusion, outside her own shattered, annihilated flesh, of the precious blood of another heart. "I possess nothing now," she thought with a joy, still naïve but yet august and solemn, and that she wanted to hug to her breast as though it had been the sublime fruit of her extraordinary union. . . . "If it were His will I could die."

It was less the expectation of death or her lucid felicity that made her soul fail, than the superhuman conviction of an annihilation so complete that she could no longer either live or die; so that if it pleased God to destroy a miserable little creature so perfectly dispossessed, he must needs share her death with her, take her heart's last feeble beat, the last breath of her mouth. Yes, she would receive death from those hands that could not close on anything any longer, held open by the nails forever. Like a child repeating, without understanding them but with reverent docility, the words that he receives, one by one, from his mother's lips, she would go forward step by step among the shadows of an Agony whose threshold no angel had yet crossed; she would gropingly gather each crumb of that terrible bread. . . . And at the same moment, the silence she longed for came and wrapped itself around her, covered her completely.

The image of Chevance, even his name, certainly seemed far from her thoughts at that moment. Yet by some unique prodigy, a movement of the soul as innocent and pure as those awkward movements of a child that ravish a mother's heart with love and pity, she vaguely feared that she had disobeyed, and turned toward her old master as a newborn baby whimpers in its sleep. What would he have said? What would he have thought? Would he not have stopped her long ago with one of his anxious smiles, so sad and so tender? Would he have allowed her to go on, along such a road? For, O wonder of wonders, it was not the leap of ecstasy that had carried her the last step of the way, on the contrary, it was the effort she had made to hold herself back. Now it was too late. She had gone too far into the illimitable Presence, she could only let herself slide like a runner at the end of his race. And while she had still thought she was refusing, being unworthy, the sublime gift, the divine Agony was already melting in her mortal heart, and she was being borne away in its talons.

Moreover, she scarcely dared distinguish this new prodigy from the simple prayers which had so often restored to her the meaning of her life, her equanimity, her secret. Many times, indeed since childhood, she had felt herself borne by her thoughts to the side of the lonely God seeking refuge in the night like a humiliated father, in the arms of the last of his daughters, slowly consuming his human anguish in the effusion of blood and tears, under the black olive trees. . . . Another woman tomorrow will go to the Cross, who at this moment while a cock crows, spies through a crack in the door a ray of moonlight that she mistakes for the cruel dawn. "What," she cries, "will this night never end? . . ." But all that Chantal desires is to crawl noiselessly as near as possible to that silent bending figure whose knees seem to her to tremble. Then lying at his feet, crouching on the ground she feels against her chest, against her cheeks the acrid coolness of the earth, that earth which with fierce avidity has just drunk the water of those ineffable eyes—eyes which having created the universe with a single glance, contain all evenings and all dawns. The breeze stirs over the miserable little hill. The rocky path with its muddy puddles follows the crest for a moment, then suddenly disappears, plunging into space. . . . A lighted window still shines on the hillside. Whence will the betrayal come?

The betrayal! It is of the betrayal he is thinking and she with him. It is over the betrayal that he is weeping, it is the execrable idea of betrayal that he vainly tries to cast out of him with the sweat of his blood, drop by drop. . . . He has loved like a man, humanly, man's humble heritage, his poor fireside, his table, his bread, his wine—the gray roads golden in the shower, the villages with their smoke, the little houses hidden in the thorn hedges, the peace of the falling evening and the children playing on the doorstep. He has loved all that humanly, after the manner of men, but as no man has ever loved it before, would ever love it again. So purely, so intimately with the heart he himself has made, just for that, with his own hands. And the night before, while the disciples were discussing among themselves plans for the following day, where they would sleep, what food they would take with them, like soldiers before starting out on a night's march—but still a little ashamed to have let the Rabbi go up there, almost alone, and for that very reason talking loudly in their strong peasant voices, clapping each other on the back after the manner of neatherds and horse-dealers. He, having blessed the first fruits of his coming Agony—just as he had blessed earlier that day the wine and the bread, consecrating for his people, for suffering mankind, his work, the holy Body—he gave it as an offering to all men, lifted it toward them with his holy, venerable hands, over the large sleeping earth whose seasons he had so loved. He offered it once, once and for all, while he was still in all the splendor and force of his youth, before delivering it up to fear, before leaving it face to face with hideous Fear, during that interminable night, until the remission of the dawn. And although he had, indeed, offered it to all men, he was thinking of only one. The only one to whom that Body really belonged, humanly belonged, as a slave belongs to his master, he having possessed himself of it by ruse, having already disposed of it as a legitimate possession, by virtue of a deed of sale in due order, faultless. The only one thus who could defy pity, walk straight into despair, make it his home, cover himself with despair as the first murderer covered himself with the night. The only man among men who really possessed something, was provided for, having nothing more to receive from now on from anyone, eternally.

What did Chantal see or not see at that moment—with her fleshly eyes—what matter? The terror that seized her remained completely lucid, unlike that which is born of dreams and with them disappears.

While ordinary anguish cannot be separated from a certain secret shame that steals our last strength and completes our degradation, this kind, while it tortures the soul, leaves it untroubled. The fulgurating pain was of such an intense purity and transparence that it shone far above the world of flesh. And yet, in this prodigious, unbearable coruscation that was the suffering of God himself, this extraordinary young girl recognized her faithful companion, the humble and sincere friend of her whole life—her own suffering. Just as she had accepted all the little familiar trials of every day, never sought but never refused—the mortification of some scoffing word, the spoiling of some carefully prepared dish—she gave herself ingenuously, she made once again the innocent gift of herself. None of the martyrs whom she loved had with more gracious abandon embraced the hatchet or the sword. Only a slight flush showed on her cheeks, while from the depth of her ecstasy, her arms and shoulders seemed to be trying to protect, to cover some loved presence, to be braving the fatal blow. . . .

What she saw only a few steps away—facing the God, betrayed, his love rejected, whose solemn breathing she could hear—was the strange, the incomprehensible creature who had renounced hope, sold the hope of mankind for thirty pieces of silver, and hung himself. She did not see him in the contemptible act of betrayal, when he was still only a half-starved, crafty, little Jew fingering the money in his pockets with his dirty fingernails, all his unwholesome flesh shaking at every clink of the centurion's sword in the scabbard, but at the hour when he had accomplished his destiny and was hanging forever a black fruit on a black tree, at the entrance of the shameful kingdom of darkness, punctual sentinel and incorruptible, whom pity will implore in vain, who will let no pardon pass in order that hell may safely consummate his horrible peace. Slowly the tree rises above the horizon, divides the sky into two equal parts, plunging the ghastly forehead into the clouds. She can see nothing now but the trunk, an enormous column covered with bark, as though the tree had folded over its fruit. And all those tears which she can hear falling on the stones will not restore a single drop of sap to that colossal gibbet.

Then, for the last time she listened to the ineffable lamentation, she gathered it into her soul as a diver fills his lungs with air. She was afraid to turn her head toward the marvelous vision fearing that she would be unable to tear her eyes away again before she had accomplished her task. No! She would accept nothing as long as she had still something to give! . . . The idea that she was accomplishing an act very different from the ordinary acts of her life never occurred to her, indeed no idea came to her. With the same simplicity with which she had so many times offered herself to sinners, with the same movement she went toward this sinner of sinners with outstretched arms; she offered herself to that impenetrable despair with a mysterious feeling that was neither altogether horror nor compassion, but a kind of holy curiosity.

She had taken only a step when, as furiously as it had grown taller, the gibbet now began to shrink, and suddenly stood there, within reach of her little hand, nothing but a twisted black olive tree. Its fork, very low down, was deformed by a great scar, an excrescence like the head of a pruned willow, covered with gray scales and a sort of lichen withered by winter. Although, now that the breeze had fallen, the silence on that deserted plateau was absolute, Chantal seemed to hear the laboring and cracking under the bark of the knotted but powerful limbs of the tree, and its deep roots. Then she saw the highest branches tremble and the vibrations passing from leaf to leaf, until the monstrous head, slowly breaking through its carapace of moss and bark, began turning around and around with hideous solemnity. . . . But what made Chantal start forward was not so much the enormity of such an uncouth vision, as the fear, only half conscious, that such a nightmare must mark the end of her ecstasy. With her eyes she measured again the distance from the obstacle and walked toward it.

"Where are you going?" said a very deliberate voice which she recognized at once. "It would hardly be seemly, would it, for me to let you go out as you are."

Abbé Cénabre was standing before her.

Abbé Cénabre had taken hold of the young girl's

arm and had not yet thought of releasing it, while his sad eyes rested on hers. His haughty countenance, slightly softened in these last few months by the added flesh of cheek and chin, and the worn look of his once magnificent forehead, expressed neither embarrassment nor surprise, but rather an extreme lassitude, not unmixed with disgust.

"I beg your pardon," he continued, "I hope you will excuse me—that is if you think it necessary? Is it really necessary?"

Chantal had stepped back a little and was leaning against the wall. Almost immediately she had regained her habitual poise, at least outwardly. She took a quick glance around the room, noticed the hollow imprint of her head and shoulders on the bed and quietly smoothed it with her hand.

"Oh, no!" she said with a slight shrug of her shoulders. "It is not at all necessary. What good would it do? I only wish it were over. Oh, God, how I wish it were over, once and for all!"

"I too," replied Cénabre after a pause. "It depends on you, perhaps." He gave a profound sigh. "In no way," he added, "does it depend on me. It is useless for me to give you the reasons—they are not worth knowing. Besides, such explanations would have no importance for you. It seems to me that you and I have gone far beyond ordinary conversations."

"Oh, there is no question of an ordinary conversation," said Chantal bitterly but in a voice as calm as his own. "It is a long time since I have forgotten what a normal conversation is like! And yet, nature gets the better of one—I should like to talk like everybody else, because in spite of appearances, I suffer like everybody else and perhaps even a little more. No matter what you think of me, I do not deserve this exceptional treatment."

"So be it," he said. "Moreover, it is only proper that you should know how I happen to be here and, I assure you, entirely against my will. The thing is doubtless no longer of great importance; it is enough, perhaps, that you should know that I am incapable of spying on anyone. Your father . . ."

"Pardon me," she interrupted, "I know all that already. The ridiculous part of my pitiful story is that everybody knows it better than I do, or at least boasts of knowing it. After all, I have only one secret, but this so-called secret is the least secret happening in this house. . . . It seems that I am not made for secrets."

"What secret?" asked Abbé Cénabre, still impassibly. "Ah! Mademoiselle Chantal, you have before you a man who is not like the other men around you, but one who, at least, knows by experience the weight of a secret. For the importance of a secret must be measured by its weight, the manner in which it weighs on your life. Well, I have seen how you have borne yours, with such admirable freedom. Even at this moment, your perfect composure is another proof that your freedom was not counterfeit. Forgive me for speaking to you less as a priest than as a man, and perhaps even an unhappy man. I believe firmly that this is the sort of language that suits you, fits the ordeal that you are undergoing. I have no rights over your conscience. And, moreover, as you know, on account of my poor health, my rather considerable literary work, my need for independence and solitude, I have been forced to give up, much to my regret, the cares and consolations of the ministry of souls. I admit that Monsieur de Clergerie has more than once talked to me about his rather naive apprehensions, of imaginary dangers. However, you have seen by my attitude toward you how much importance I attached to his confidence. I only listened to them through courtesy. A few moments ago I was involuntarily involved in a ridiculous discussion between your father and Dr. La Pérouse who seemed to have lost all control over himself, and made the most absurd and dangerous remarks about you. I know what indiscretions a man with the best intentions may commit, who entertains such incoherent, often grotesque, ideas about the inner life. And so, in order to avoid a greater evil I agreed to talk to you. May I add that the maid at my request knocked at your door several times without obtaining a reply, although she insisted that you were in your room. She said she felt something had happened to you, that you had fainted or were dead, and wanted to go in . . ."

Abbé Cénabre stopped abruptly, lowered his eyes and concluded coldly:

"The zeal of that young person seemed to me exaggerated. Moreover, she appears to be alarmingly well informed about everything that concerns you. Fearing a scandal I took the liberty of coming myself."

Never had this extraordinary man, whose tragic will was now at its highest tension, and which was to give way suddenly and only, as it were, taken by surprise, been more conscious of his power than at this irreparable moment when he was risking his last chance, gliding unwittingly toward his destiny. Although long ago he had closed his soul to any profound joy, having repulsed all joy as unworthy of him, as being the only deception capable of breaking his heart, he could not at this moment quite master a sudden access of intoxicating pride that now shone in his eyes.

Each word of that stark and terrible discourse, heavy with meaning, seemed to strike Chantal like so many blows, and the priest had every reason to believe that she was now at his mercy. At least whatever happened from now on, by this first brutal sounding he felt sure of remaining master to the last word of this interview which he had at first avoided and then put off, only to plunge into it headlong, at last, with unprecedented violence.

Insensible as he was to vulgar premonitions and indeed to any sort of superstition, this sudden, inexplicable anger, this unaccountable perturbation of his whole being over an obstacle in appearance so frail, failed to awaken any misgivings. He experienced a frenzy comparable to that which had driven him bodily against Abbé Chevance, had dragged him all one night at the heels of an old beggar, a prey to all the fury of homicidal curiosity. He had certainly, at one time, wanted to talk with Chantal, but that was when he still thought that the old dying priest had confided to her, that the admission had been torn from his dying anguish—anguish whose cause was known to him alone. That is how he explained the girl's singular reserve toward him, and the care with which she avoided him.

"According to Chantal, Abbé Chevance in his delirium never stopped talking about you," Monsieur de Clergerie had told him a hundred times. Cénabre found it sweet to think that so weak and defenceless a creature, so extraordinarily pure and incapable of betraying him, should guard something of that heavy secret and take this burden with her to the grave. "Naturally she doesn't know anything very precise. But still!" Cénabre used often to dream of that invisible fissure in the wall, that pale gleam of light in the tomb in which he had walled up his life. Now that gleam of light was gone, his solitude again intact. The very day after his arrival at Laigneville, after luncheon, while Abramovitch was spelling out a Sanscrit inscription in his impossible nasal voice, Cénabre had drawn the young girl gently toward the window into the bright light, his cup of camomile in his hand, looking at her with an expression in which she could have read (if she had dared) nothing but a sort of inexorable sadness. "Is it true," he had asked, "that Abbé Chevance talked to you about me before he died?" "Oh no," she had promptly replied, "that is one of Papa's ideas. And now he believes it. Our poor friend could scarcely speak at all, he had spat up so much blood, his mouth was full of clots. He simply pronounced your name several times with a gesture of his hand that we did not understand. . . ."

Yes, just now, every word of that discourse had been like a blow directed at her heart. Neither anger nor curiosity were apparent in this man speaking in such a tone! But he must have been watching her patiently for days and days, in silence, and had, she was sure, passed judgment—a judgment from which there was no appeal. Reproof would not have moved her as much, contempt would have found her prepared, and even against irony she would not have felt herself so defenceless. What troubled her profoundly was what amounted to a sudden, unexpected, heartbreaking revelation of her own misfortune, which she had always hitherto regarded as a simple ordeal made to her own measure, almost like a child's grief, her equal and the equal of the weak creatures with whom she had always lived, and who were so different from this impartial arbiter whose uncompromising attention, a sort of icy compassion, she felt weighing on her soul. What could she expect from him but strict justice? She could not justify herself to him or to anyone at this moment. And it came to her in a flash that she would certainly be lost at even the most indulgent interrogatory, for she knew absolutely nothing about her own experience, having lived too much only from day to day, from one hour to the next; one man alone knew her life's humble truth, having gathered it gradually and, as it were, bit by bit. But now he was under the ground, he had taken her secret with him. Yes, one man alone—at least he alone could have pleaded her defence. . . . At that moment Chantal had to make an immense effort to keep back her tears.

"I am sorry," she said. "Think of me what you please, I don't want to worry anybody. It seems silly to say it, and yet it is the truth—appearances are against me, I seem to be acting a part, a frightful part. But you will understand later that I could not ask anyone else the question I am going to ask you. And you must reply, because I have already waited too long to come to a decision. I shall decide today. I am sick of my lies of omission. What was I doing when you came into the room?"

"What were you doing?" repeated Cénabre.

His eyes wandered around the room stopping at each corner. Finally he let them rest calmly on the thin drawn face awaiting his reply in desperate suspense.

"For anyone at all, my child, I found you sleeping. Sleeping profoundly as one does at this season of the year, in such exceptionally hot weather. You had lain down for a moment on your bed and had fallen asleep. What could be simpler?"

He paused thoughtfully for a moment, pressing his lips together, then a strange smile began to play in the folds of his cheeks, spread slowly over his face, and disappeared.

"Appearances are never for or against," he said. "Appearances are nothing. That is, they are what we want them to be. And first of all they should not be feared, they are only dangerous to the weak. My dear child, I should certainly be loath to add another scruple to a conscience that I feel is already too prone to take alarm. I have only this to say to you: first of all, be what you are."

Chantal, her eyes half closed as though absorbed in a sort of inner vision, listened with prodigious attention. Her face, suddenly grown thinner, hollow, livid, took on little by little, and probably unknown to her, that hard, almost virile expression which, in her, betrayed, not only the premonition of a coming peril still uncertain, but also a determination to meet it face to face.

"My conscience is untroubled," she said, "I am not alarmed so easily. No. I simply do not understand, that is all. Oh, it is much simpler even than I can explain! If I must walk gropingly, so be it! But I . . . I cannot resign myself to hurting anyone. I have never tried to do any but the simplest easiest things, and instead of bringing peace to anyone I am the cause of disorder, or even perhaps an occasion of sin."

"What sin?" asked Cénabre.

"I really fear that they are being driven to despair," replied Chantal in her gentle voice as though she had just uttered the most commonplace words—"that I am driving them to despair. Have I then lied to them? What promise did I make them that I have not kept? My God, this is just what I have long been afraid of without daring to admit it, you see! It was such an absurd supposition. What can a poor girl like me have to do with despair?"

Abbé Cénabre seemed to hesitate a moment, looked toward the door and then faced her again. His motionless features might have been hewn out of stone.

"Don't worry about that," he said. "We never give what we think we are giving."

"But I gave nothing, that is the trouble!" said Chantal. "After all, what had I to give? God is just."

She was silent. And suddenly, with an abrupt almost brutal movement, but still smiling, that same painful smile:

"What do you mean?" she said.

"My dear child, if I were to answer that it would take us much too far. I came here to bring you the most insignificant message. And for the last few moments you have spoken as though I had been the witness or confidant of things I know nothing about, or that I should know nothing about. No, certainly! Where does your extraordinary assurance come from? Do you imagine that you see clearly into my intentions? Do you suppose that for a mere trifle I would break the resolution that I made the moment I arrived here? I may seem to you hard and inhuman. Nevertheless, I am doing something for you that no one else here is in any condition to do; I am giving you a warning that can be useful to you."

"I don't need any warning," cried Chantal in a trembling voice. "I cannot understand your language! I did not want to offend God, I only wanted to serve Him. Have I served God? Nothing else matters. And if you refuse to answer the only question that is worth asking, then I should prefer to remain silent. I have hardly enough strength as it is, I should rather struggle on alone. To be alone to the very end, to take the last step alone, I can easily imagine what that will be."

"I, too," said Cénabre.

For a moment Chantal looked at him with surprise and misgiving, then suddenly her pitiful face seemed to relax, her hands, which had been tightly closed, now opened.

"I can't stand any more," she murmured. "My head is whirling. What I am going to say is probably silly, but it doesn't matter! Please, speak to me gently. Don't hurt me. I impress people a little, in a way, I seem resolute, determined, but I am really good for nothing any longer, nothing at all. Certainly I don't think I ever lied to anyone; the trouble is, without wanting to, in spite of myself, I create an illusion. Even at this moment you are suffering from an illusion—even you, it is unbelievable! Yes, you are hoping to learn something from me. Nothing much perhaps, but something just the same. Oh, naturally, you are not thinking of the nonsense of La Pérouse, or that wretched Fiodor—they are crazy! You simply say to yourself that I must know more than appears, that an Abbé Chevance would never have bothered about a flighty, fantastical girl, and finally that I certainly have some idea of what took place here, in this room, ten minutes ago before you arrived. Well, the truth is, I haven't the least idea. When a drowning man is pulled out of the water, you don't ask him what he saw, and besides it is more likely than not that he didn't see anything at all. Alas! It would be nice if one could just let people talk, or else disappear as soon as anyone looked at you, crawl into one's poor little life like those little crabs that dive head first into the sand and disappear."

Cénabre interrupted her with an irritated gesture of his hand, and shrugged his shoulders. But he still stared at her sadly.

"Mademoiselle Chantal," he said, "your father sent me here to ask you to talk to Dr. La Pérouse who intends leaving us tonight, and who has been saying the most absurd things about your last conversation with him. I was anxious to bring you the message myself, for I am thus able to add some advice of my own: be sure not to give any explanation in the presence of La Pérouse, nor of anyone else. It is rather late to try to repair all your generous rashness! You should keep your secrets to yourself. I have learned too much myself without even trying to. Your secret escapes you without your knowing it; it is in the air you breathe. Be careful . . . "

He took a step forward, savagely, as though he

would have swept away at a blow some invisible obstacle.

"This mark of interest surprises you, doesn't it? Well, then let us suppose that our roads happen to cross today, that we meet as we pass by. . . . Ah, my child, I never realized how deeprooted is the spirit of the sacerdotal profession in us! It is difficult for me to forget that in other eventualities, and following the wishes of your father, you would undoubtedly have been confided to my care. What memories such a thought stirs in me! All the labors and all the thoughts of twenty years seem to surge up suddenly as though out of the earth, live again before my eyes. . . . Have you read my books?"

"No," said Chantal. "None of them."

"May I ask why?"

"Pardon me," she replied after a moment, but without averting her candid gaze. "Abbé Chevance did not permit me to read them."

"Ah, yes . . . Chevance . . ." repeated Cénabre in a dreamy voice (and it seemed to Chantal that at each hesitating step the tall black figure swayed a little like a man who, little by little, stops struggling against drowsiness and goes to sleep on his feet). Yes . . . Chevance . . . Oh! his was a very strange case. . . . But at this moment, verification becomes impossible—texts are missing, even testimony. . . . There are no more witnesses. Where is one to look? Besides what could they tell us? Everything is lost in an uncertain light. . . . I blame myself for my stupid violence toward him, the only evil action of my life, why did I drive him away? . . . My dear child . . ."

He fell silent, opened his eyes.

"Well then," he demanded curtly, "what have you decided? What are you going to do? We cannot go on with this discussion indefinitely. My presence here is becoming ridiculous and our interview has already lasted too long."

"It is not my fault," Chantal replied, "I have surely endured enough, you have not spared me. I don't know what it is you are advising. Your words tend rather to overwhelm me completely. My God! I don't ask for pity, but can't you—can't any of you try to see me as I am? For you it would be child's play. We have reached a point when I no longer ask to understand. It really doesn't matter. What is the use of going over the past, planning for the future? I am like those incurable invalids who are kept alive from day to day until our dear Lord decides upon their fate. Even Abbé Chevance no longer counts. What could he do for me? After so many blunders my wretched little life will finally seem to be as complicated as his death—and that was the death of a saint! So now the very best thing I can think of to do, is to remain quiet at any cost; I shall just let myself drift out with the tide, waiting for the next wave to rise, if it is ever going to rise."

She blushed slightly, hesitated, and looking straight into his eyes suddenly asked:

"Isn't it true? It will never rise again. . . . Oh, I have

certainly succeeded in wrecking my little ship; it couldn't have been done better. Here we are, all of us, stranded on the beach, I must seem pretty ridiculous to you."

Chantal tried again to smile, but unable to control any longer the sort of terror she had been anticipating all morning, she threw back her radiant head as though to drink in a final breath of pure air, swayed against the side of the bed, and grasping it desperately with her little hands sank forward on her knees.

"Calm yourself, my child," said Cénabre (his voice trembled but it was with a sort of scarcely contained rage). Then you haven't confided in anyone since Abbé Chevance's death? And how could Chevance have allowed you to remain in such complete ignorance of the true condition of your . . . your true condition?"

"My condition!" cried Chantal (tears were pouring down her cheeks). Do you really imagine that I used to be as I am now? Oh, no! I don't think I have ever been so weak and cowardly; everything gives way under me, I seem to be walking in a bog. If I go forward I shall surely sink in, and if I do not budge, I shall sink in anyway . . . My God! I shall go on all the same, I would gladly go in up to my eyes if it would be of the least use to anybody. But no matter what I do it seems that my suffering is now empty, empty, empty as a dream; my death itself will weigh nothing. I am an empty thing God has lost interest in. After all! What is there to my story? Hardly enough for a fantastic tale without even a moral! My grandmother, Papa, Fiodor, poor Dr. La Pérouse, this peaceful house, this lovely summer—how could I have succeeded in making such disorder out of all that? You know very well—you remember, don't you, how simple I used to be. I was such a simple girl! God would not have deserted me then, would he? It is because I have changed! I have changed, haven't I?"

"No," he said in his hoarse voice. "You were simple, it is true, and you still are. There are very few simple people. One should say of simplicity what the Jews said of Jehovah, 'No man can see His face and live!' "

Abbé Cénabre began balancing his head from side to side like a man preparing to lift a heavy weight, testing his strength. She watched him with stupefaction and although he continued looking at her he scarcely seemed to see her.

"What are you doing here," he began. "Why are you here? Yes, why? Who could have given you the absurd idea of living this ordinary life, coming and going among these people with the hope of remaining unnoticed? Unnoticed! You will drive them mad! And first of all what right have you? Indeed, I know what I am talking about, I do not speak lightly. What right has anyone to propose a problem without at least trying to solve it? And you will never be able to solve it."

"A problem! I!" she cried going white. "You too!

What problem? No, no, Abbé Cénabre, it isn't true, all I have done is to try to defend my life!"

She had got to her feet unsteadily; she forgot to wipe away her tears. Her mouth was trembling so that she could hardly pronounce the first words. But suddenly her expressive face contracted as though in reality she had gathered her strength, was defending her life.

"Haven't I the right to live?" she said. "Am I to be driven to despair? Is there no place for me anywhere?"

"Neither for you, nor for me," he said with affected calm, after a short silence. "You know too many things, and, I am afraid, you are ignorant of essential ones. In short, for different reasons, we both belong to those who cannot live in the open, and no shelter is safe if anyone else knows the road that leads to it . . . And whether we like it or not, we must sooner or later take men's curiosity into account, and their malice."

"Oh!" she cried. "Do you mean that we should lie?"

Cénabre could no longer avoid those proud eyes still shining with her recent tears; he looked into them thoughtfully.

"Lie! There are certain legitimate, honest retreats that the spiteful and fools might call lies—the last corner where those of us who ask for no other keeper but ourselves, find the axis of our lives, our secret appointed place. I am one of those and I trust in saying so I will not wound your conscience. My way of living

I think clearly excludes the least suspicion of any selfish motive. My existence is not unworthy of the priest that I still am. I simply avoid certain indiscretions. That's all. Please don't read any other meaning into those . . . the simple suggestions that I should like to see you profit by."

He was breathing heavily.

"At least if . . . if you are not able to protect yourself you should take the veil. I am not speaking as a spiritual director, you understand. I am speaking as a man, humanly."

"I feel that only too well!" she said. "You have human pity for me and nothing more. Is that what you came here to bring me? Is it for so little that you have broken your silence? Well, I prefer your silence. Neither my father, nor you, nor anyone will persuade me to go into a convent like those cowards who used to seek asylum in churches to save their miserable lives. Your advice, in any case, comes too late. It seems to me that I have nothing more to save—nothing."

She paused. Cénabre had just stretched out his powerful brown hand and seized her arm so brutally that she could hardly suppress a cry of pain.

"Nothing more!" he cried. "Do you believe what you say? Yes, of course. You are incapable of lying. But, human or not, my daughter, my pity is not first of all for you. Oh, but I'd rather not think of these other people here, they don't matter! And yet, just see what you have already done to them, see what kind of joy comes from you; are they not more to be pitied than before? It is a fatality that may appear mysterious, unjust, absurd, but, at least, don't blame me for pointing it out. There it is. We know it. No doubt that Chevance knew it too. One would have to be the most mediocre, inexperienced, witless of priests not to. Perhaps one may still meet, here or there, some somnolent . . . old priests. . . . Ah, but this doesn't interest you. The first duty of anyone who is your friend is to put you on your guard, not against anyone else, but against yourself alone. It is from you, from such beings as you, no less innocent, no less pure, as pure as fire. . . ."

Was he afraid to continue? . . . Or rather, it may be, those inscrutable half-living figures of an intolerable rigidity which sometimes woke him in the dawn, had suddenly filled the vague reverie that had been darkening his eyes like a great portico full of shadows. . . . For a time, for a long time, he remained motionless, rigid too, and yet seeming to be surrounded by movement like a black tree-trunk at the water's edge. Leaning a little to one side, his shoulders thrown back, his bent arms pressed tightly to his sides, he looked as though he were resisting with all his weight, holding on with all his strength, about to lose his balance like a wreck that has been jammed against the bank by the current and whose shadow can be seen wavering on the light sandy bottom. But Chantal's first words came to him as a shock, and his first reaction was a sort of painful moan whose sinister tone he had apparently realized too late for, growing suddenly pale, he slowly raised his hand to his mouth.

"I understand," said Chantal, "you don't need to say any more. I have heard that before many times from someone else. He too spoke of miracles and ecstasy . . . *A miracle, a sweet prodigy* . . . I know all that."

Cénabre shrugged his shoulders.

"You are mistaken," he said. "You did not understand. Besides what I said was not for you. It was for myself alone. I did not mean to speak."

"Oh! after all," cried Chantal. "That is too much! Are you accusing me of extorting words like that from you? Have I asked you for anything?"

"Extorted or not, they are said," he replied in the same gloomy voice. "From now on you may be sure that you can do with me as you please, with me and with the others. Yes, my child, whether you like it or not, that is what will wring your heart tomorrow. Whatever the gift may be that you have received, whatever its significance, its nature, you will have to bring yourself one day to share it, and that first partition is likely to be, for you, far worse than death, a sort of death, much worse than the other, a more terrible solitude. That too, I know. In what we call man's shameful passions there is a sort of gross deception, but it is not only sin that lies; another deception awaits you that I might have been able to spare you, or at least have helped you to endure!"

"I don't want to be spared," she cried with desperate violence, her whole being in revolt. "No! I don't want to be spared!"

"Yet the hour will come, my daughter, when you will long to be," he said, "and you will regret not having listened to the counsel of a friend. Yes, with bitter tears you will regret your childish defiance. No one else, do you understand, no one but me, is capable of helping you to see clearly into your own heart, see yourself clearly, as you are. If you will only consent to listen to me . . ."

He gave a terrible sigh, a sort of gasping sound that resembled the moan of pleasure. With amazement she saw his great shoulders tremble and the look of boundless fatigue in his eyes.

"I no longer need to see clearly in myself," she said. "It is too late. What difference does it make to me what I am or what I am not? I have been tossed into the wine-press; God will now take from me by force what I did not have the courage to give. There is nothing to stop Him now. It seemed to me a little while ago that His blessed pity had with a sad smile left me, and I feel sure that I will not find it again outside of paradise. Until then, you see, nothing matters to me, absolutely nothing. You may be able to describe the road I took to arrive where I am, tell me the reasons and the causes. But how would that help me? I could neither agree nor disagree. The nearer I come to the goal, the less I want to know what it is. God must have relieved me of that care. And to speak very frankly, at the risk of your thinking me very daring, even if I were to die in ten minutes, I should want to have Our Lord's permission first, like a child, no, not even—like an innocent little animal who takes his last breathful of air, his last drink of cool water, and walks to his death at the heels of his master. The master holds the leash, one only has to follow. . . . From now on what difference does it make whether I am sane or insane, a saint or a visionary, or even whether I am surrounded by angels or devils—nothing can take me any farther out of my path than the length of the leash! What you have just said, or rather hinted, might still have moved me yesterday, even tempted me. But at this moment . . ."

"Let us speak only of this moment, please," interrupted Cénabre. "Only the present moment interests me. It interests me prodigiously. Make a little effort, my daughter, forget what I have said. Consent to open up your conscience to me. Where does this premonition of your imminent solitude come from, this sadness that seems to me to have something strange about it, something equivocal . . . What makes you think it comes from God and not from men? Have you had a sign? Was there, perhaps, some particular event which, with a little reflection, may come back to you? . . . The death of Chevance, for example . . ."

"Hush!" cried Chantal. "I forbid you! If the choice were left to me, it is just such a death I should desire. And, moreover, what do you know of the death of Abbé Chevance? He, who had given so much, had let people take so much from him—*that*, at least, he kept for himself, that alone. He did not consent to share it with anyone, not even with me, his daughter. . . . And you would like, you . . ."

She paused, for he had turned deathly pale—if that sudden total transformation of a human face can be called pallor.

"Chevance . . ." he stammered, "ah, yes, Chevance . . . I have seen . . . I have seen him . . ."

He looked down at the ground and his hand spread open seemed to be fumbling for an apparition, too fragile, already fading . . .

"I saw him," he said, "like that, at my feet, begging for mercy, imploring me . . . Yes, weeping, he begged for mercy. He, Chevance! Nothing else matters. What good would it have done to see him die? What more would I have learned, can you tell me?"

"At least," said Chantal in a trembling voice, "you would have learned not to take advantage of a wretched girl's simplicity, to tempt her beyond her strength."

"Beyond your strength?" he repeated with a bitter laugh. "We are always tempted beyond our strength. And which one of us has been setting snares I should like to know! For the last hour haven't you been getting out of me everything you like? Very well then! Take the rest, take everything, take the whole truth. Are you afraid?"

"My God!" she answered, very white, "I am only afraid for you. Do with me what you please. Treat me as a thing not intended for you but which belongs to you now, just the same, because it is of no value, because you were the last one to come along—it belongs to the last comer . . . and that's the end of it."

"Let us not go any further," said Cénabre after a pause. "You must understand, however, that for the last quarter of an hour you have been playing, like a child, with a secret that is much too heavy for you. Besides I never refused you that secret—you nor anyone else. From the very first I resolved to give it to anyone who would ask for it. I am not an actor. But admit that, even before I opened my mouth, you knew everything. Chevance had spoken. Oh! don't think I mean to accuse him of disloyalty! With you, Chantal, he was the only living creature who has ever seemed to me worthy of consideration, that particular kind of consideration one accords oneself. He was simply delirious, and you overheard him in spite of yourself. Why lament over the past? I regret nothing. It had to be like that. It doesn't give me the slightest pang, nor any consolation either, nothing can ever trouble my peace again. But how I should have regretted leaving you without having seen you as you are, without having spoken to you in this language which you are probably the only one capable of understanding—understanding in the particular way I mean. In anyone else I should have met only indifference or anger."

"I know you perfectly," he went on, "I have spent my life poring over beings like you. I could retrace, line for line, the drama you are living today, predict its end, for it is today, at this very minute, that your destiny is being consummated, I know it. It was inevitable that we should meet like this, in this way, once and for all. Who could tell what the spectacle of a holy man's death, and his last dying ramblings would inspire in a heart like yours! I was the obstacle that had to be overcome, the intolerable secret thought, the inner stumbling block that poisons even prayer, and that this interview has brought out into the light, torn from you. For, you see, I am a man like other men. I live in a peace that you cannot possibly imagine because your nature is all warmth, all passion; I live in a silence more favorable, more in accord with the deepest needs of my nature, than any kind of harmony, heavenly or not. What is the difference? You and I live in harmony with ourselves, that is enough. I don't ask you to envy my tranquillity, it is right that it should horrify you. Supernatural life always finds its consummation in suffering, but that knowledge has never deterred saints. Neither Chevance nor you can give me back God, and yet, at least to judge by appearances and all your useless torments, your lack is greater than mine."

His voice trembled ever so slightly on the last words, while an inscrutable smile played over his features, settling finally in the bitter lines around his mouth in a sort of tragic grimace. Only then he lifted his eyes altogether. And at the first glance, before even the thought had had time to take form, he realized the enormity of his mistake. For the second time he had confided himself in vain, confided himself uselessly to Chantal as he had to Chevance before, in one of those frightful accesses of cold fury before the will has had time to perceive the danger.

With a lucidity mixed with shame, Cénabre could now read clearly all those pitiful images that flashed like lightning across the girl's face, torturing, one by one, her child-like heart. It was as though he were rapidly, furiously, turning over the pages of a book, or rather the leaves of a record, to the last one, the one on which was written the final judgment without appeal. For the curiosity of Abbé Cénabre was of the kind that even anguish cannot overwhelm, that survives anything, everything.

But now suddenly this curiosity had been deceived. Chantal's thin little pinched face expressed nothing but so humble, so mysterious a resignation that he was overcome with a sort of terror. The words he was about to say died suddenly on his lips.

"Forgive me," said Chantal. "It is not true that Abbé Chevance talked to me about you; he died, you see, without any last wishes, without any confidences, modestly, so modestly, the way one would like to live . . . But I should have understood sooner . . . should . . . I . . ."

She was silent.

"Very well," replied Cénabre roughly, "let's say no more about it. What is done is done."

"No," she said. "I still have a favor to ask of you. You can't imagine how cruel it is for me to think that . . . this—well, that what you called your secret has been taken from you by surprise . . . stolen from you. Yes, stolen. Now I should like . . ."

"You want me to give it to you?" said the priest. "Very well then, take it. It is yours. Of all the people I know there is no one else to whom I would give it so freely. You have not, then, stolen anything from me. Peace be with you."

He looked at her, looked at her from head to foot, with a sort of fierce pity.

"What are you going to do with it?" he continued. "It is nothing. Or rather a second ago it was nothing, nothing but a very ordinary secret. What will it become in your hands? Whatever you touch is straightway transformed into something that resembles you, marvelously qualified to torture you."

"I!" she cried. "You can't believe that. Whatever I touch is destroyed, turns to dust. You said something so true a while ago, so exact. More than anyone else God is lacking to me. I have called God, you see, I was waiting for Him, but I had not searched for Him enough; I did not rush forth to meet Him. And now I would be poorer, much poorer than you, if you had not given me—miraculously given me this—this thing to keep."

She walked slowly over to the window, opened it wide, took a deep breath of hot air and came back to him smiling.

"What a summer!" she said. "One finally looks at the sunlight with a bitter hatred, as an enemy. It will make the winter seem even darker."

"Yes," he replied just as calmly. "That is the way things are. We hate the night and the day is just as hard to endure."

She blushed.

"I shall go downstairs with you," she said after a pause. "Thinking it over, it seems to me better to speak to Papa today. All this talk of La Pérouse is ridiculous. You must be fair; I cannot be held responsible for everything that happens here. Don't you think they would do just as silly things without me?"

They had left her room and were going together along the darkened corridor. With her even step barely faltering on the polished floor, she walked a little ahead of him. And they had almost reached the stairway when she stopped suddenly and turned, facing him. He saw in a flash her distorted face, her altered features, and put out his arm. But when she felt that consecrated hand touching her she gave a sort of sorrowful moan, tore herself from his arms, and turning about, collapsed silently against the wall.

For a moment, a long moment, he hesitated, twice started toward the stairs, listened. Then, suddenly making up his mind, he lifted the light body without any effort, carried her back to her room, laid her on the bed and stooped to listen to her heart. Chantal opened her eyes.

"Don't move," he said in a low voice. "You have had a slight syncope. It is nothing. Do you want me to call anyone?"

She shook her head, and as she turned it on the pillow he started to take away his hand that had been resting there. But she caught it in her own, and raising it to her lips, kissed it.

5

"I SAW Chantal," said Monsieur de Clergerie. "She is not coming down this evening. I am sure a good night's rest will fix everything."

The windows of the dining-room had been opened onto the ancient park that was now growing dark. The thirsty lawns, where night had already painted all the burnt patches with a purplish ink, encircled by the pale gravel walks, looked like an immense pond of stagnant water lost in the autumnal mist.

"Dear friend," Clergerie continued in a low voice when the door had closed behind Francine, "I am not taken in by your friendly deception. It is perfectly evident that your interview this morning was not as insignificant as you pretend. But, alas! It is the habit of all those who care for me the most to think, first of all, of sparing my feelings."

"Well," said Cénabre, "I did not think of it this time. As a matter of fact, I don't think I ever have."

Monsieur de Clergerie raised his eyes toward the priest in amazement.

"What!" he cried. "What has come over you? You have always been the most sincere, the most discreet of friends— I might almost say the judge and arbiter of my life. . . . Are you going to let the caprices . . . Go away, Francine," he shouted shrilly as the red-haired maid appeared in the doorway again. "Put the tray on the table and leave us! I won't take my linden tea tonight."

When she had disappeared he turned to Cénabre apologetically:

"You must excuse this display of irritation. That girl is always peeping through keyholes. Since she accused my Russian chauffeur of certain irregularities, everywhere I go I see her looking at me with teary eyes and a little smile of absurd complicity."

He kept nervously folding and unfolding his napkin.

"Please answer me . . . say something. I can't tell you how the silence here in this house is getting on my nerves. Here I am all alone, or practically. . . . For I cannot hope to keep you much longer. Yet to go back to Paris in the middle of this heat would kill me. Will I ever be able to get through this abominable summer without another attack?"

"My dear sir," said Cénabre, "I too have an urgent need of rest, of calm. The little phrase that seemed to upset you just now was not meant to be offensive. I have never tried to spare anyone's feelings and no one has ever spared mine. Believe me, I am perfectly willing to talk to you about Mademoiselle Chantal with complete frankness, only I am afraid I should only worry you uselessly. No doubt you have found the natural conclusion to the discussion I am trying to avoid when you say: 'A good night's rest will fix everything.' "

Cénabre let his words hiss through his teeth with abominable precision, while his long fingers absent-mindedly stroked the tablecloth. But Monsieur de Clergerie rebelled:

"Oh," he said bitterly, "you too think I am a much too indifferent, timid father! . . . But, after all, nothing has really happened! Has anyone noticed anything different or out of the ordinary? It seems to me that my daughter is just the same as she was yesterday, as she was last winter—perhaps a little less easy and gay, that is all. Naturally, all this stupid business about Fiodor, my inevitable intervention, my advice, the knowledge that has thus come to her, alas! of a certain malignity that she was too pure ever to suspect—all these trifles together constitute quite a drama for a young girl . . . an innocent drama. She is so terribly pure! Let's be reasonable. This anxiety I speak of has developed around her without her knowing it. It has been nurtured by us, by all of us."

Cénabre drummed softly with his closed fist on the table.

"You must remember," he said, "that I have only intervened at your request. And also you are strangely mistaken if you think that I feel any anxiety. Anxiety about what?"

"Dear friend, we are all familiar with your extraordinary strength of character, your perfect control over your nerves, your will-power that is equal to any emergency. Must I not therefore take seriously your evident signs of impatience this evening? Why deny it? A mysterious misunderstanding is estranging us all. Mr. Abramovitch was the first to go, our dear Espelette has followed him, La Pérouse is visibly changing. After several strange conversations that have upset me terribly, he made a scene today that was even more extraordinary."

"Dr. La Pérouse seems to me half crazy," said Cénabre, rising. "What difference does it make to us?"

"One moment, my old friend," implored Clergerie. "You don't know everything. I have not been able to speak freely. I have been waiting for a favorable occasion. If I were to take literally certain statements of La Pérouse. . . . Well, in short, La Pérouse has reported the most amazing things about Chantal, about my servants, especially Fiodor. He says that he knew the Russian when he was with Madame Artiguenave, and believes him capable of any dishonesty . . . even of a crime. He was on the point of insisting on my discharging the wretched man. It may have been foolish of me to get angry, but I am, you know, an old liberal, and not ashamed of my opinions. I hate anything that smacks of abuse of authority. Moreover, I cannot condemn without first hearing him, a former servant of Baroness de Montanel, one whom she particularly recommended to me. Nevertheless, the precipitous, not to say incorrect, departure of La Pérouse has surprised me enormously and has left me in a dilemma. What am I to think of his incoherent remarks? When you talked to my daughter, did she . . ."

He was afraid to go on, made a vague gesture and turned toward the open window with a look that betrayed suspicion and bewilderment by turns. The silence was so complete that he heard the priest's regular breathing, and listened to the imperceptible rasping sound just as the pyrotechnist, having lighted the fuse, watches the little sparks spluttering among the stones.

"I am beginning to find all this gossip very stupid," said Abbé Cénabre, as calm as ever. "But it seems to me that you are dangerously ignorant of the character and habits of Dr. La Pérouse. I think he is a pretty fair judge of the matter under discussion."

He gave a hard throaty little laugh. Monsieur de Clergerie literally felt his temples oppressed by the weight of that forbidding gaze, in which, to his astonishment, he thought he detected an inexplicable anger.

"You could very well have found out for yourself," continued Cénabre, "and long ago. But it is too ridiculous to suppose that I should have talked to your daughter about something that concerns no one but yourself."

"Yes, of course, of course," agreed Clergerie in despair. "This is, after all, a dream, a bad dream . . . Psychiatrists are astonishing! They would sacrifice anybody's reputation to their hypotheses." Suddenly his worried face lit up with a silly smile. "Historians too, alas! . . . But we, after all, seldom hurt the living, the dead are all we need for our work. Dear friend, tonight, before dinner, I made a drastic decision—a decision that I think you will approve . . ."

He put his elbows on the table and rested his chin in his trembling hands.

"Baroness de Montanel is passing through Paris tomorrow coming from La Bourboule on her way back to her château of Lérinville. It would hardly be proper for me to see her there, as in a few months, in a few weeks, we shall make that estate our common home. But I have decided to, as it were, hold up my fiancée, as it were, on the road. I shall probably see her at Madame Marais-Courtin's. That is why, dear friend, I am taking the eleven-nine train tonight. I shall be back tomorrow night. So you see my absence will not be long. I pray God that these few hours will be enough to convince the Baroness of the urgent necessity of hastening our marriage at all costs! The presence of an intelligent woman in the house . . . with her poise, her tact, her exceptional understanding of a girl's heart which her delicate works prove, in short with her charm—she will be sure to set everything right again. Oh, I don't doubt, dear friend, that I shall, as usual, be maliciously accused of trying to escape my paternal responsibilities. However, I once accepted those of a husband, and I don't want to risk the same deplorable misunderstanding that spoiled my first marriage and ruined my health."

While de Clergerie was speaking Cénabre had gone slowly toward the door. There he made an abrupt about-face as though not so much to put an end to his host's stupid monologue as to stop some secret inner debate of his own. A sort of mild gleam lingering in Cénabre's eyes seemed a sinister omen to the unhappy Clergerie, who had by now reached the end of his endurance.

"Should I go?" he said in a toneless voice. "Because of . . . of these extraordinary circumstances would you excuse my leaving you alone for a day? I admit that the sudden disappearance of Dr. La Pérouse has painfully shaken my nerves. No matter what I do, I cannot help holding my daughter responsible for an . . . incident which will . . . which is in danger of compromising the success of a treatment begun two months ago and never interrupted. For, after all, you must admit, that counts!"

"That certainly counts," said Cénabre. "Of course you must go. Perhaps you will succeed in bringing La Pérouse back with you, which is the only thing that interests you in the least! Alas! I personally cannot blame an invalid's attachment to his physician; I knew something very similar once myself, and bonds forged by hope are the hardest to break. . . . Well, then, do not break them! It's simple."

He began to laugh as he had laughed that winter night, that frightful night last winter. . . . But this time he pressed his closed fist hard against his mouth so that Clergerie heard only a strange smothered chuckling, very painful to his pride.

"You are wrong," he said. "But there is no use trying to justify myself. The future, the near future . . . will see to that for me, and I know you well enough not to misunderstand the friendly intentions back of your apparent severity. Perhaps you are right. Perhaps La Pérouse has acquired too great an ascendancy over me. It is the fault of all of you. A neurotic manages his own life so badly! All my hesitations, my anxiety, my perpetual apprehensions must inspire in a simple strong man like you less interest than pity. But after all, one word from you would bring me peace. If it is true that my fears are vain, what can I do to overcome them?"

"Vain?" replied Cénabre. "No. I think they are useless, not vain."

He came up to Clergerie and put his hands lightly on his shoulders.

"Just let me add this: your daughter does not know, perhaps, where it is she is going, but wherever it is— that is where she is going. And wherever she goes, you will go. The decisive moment has come for all of us— how each one of us extricates himself will depend entirely on his strength and his luck."

With these enigmatic words he departed, leaving Monsieur de Clergerie gaping.

Had he really said them? Or were they not rather an inner murmur, just as vague, just as deceptive as those mysterious images which, during the entire course of the peaceful conversation, had kept taking the place of the real things before his eyes, or like a translucid vapor, had kept insidiously obliterating all contours and reliefs, transforming that country drawing-room, so orderly and calm, into a small unstable universe of superimposed planes like the shingles of a roof. While, with a painful tension of his whole being, succeeding in maintaining a firm, even imperious expression before the increasingly agitated little man, Abbé Cénabre had felt himself more powerless than ever to shake off his monotonous reverie, as though forced, in spite of himself, to carry on a now useless debate with himself, interrupted a thousand times, a thousand times resumed. Moreover, for a long time now he had found it singularly difficult to follow other people's rhythm, always lagging a little behind each word, each gesture, dragging along an invisible load, a dead weight, the obsession of something left unfinished . . . what was it? Sometimes by a prodigious effort of will he thought he had overcome this strange lag, found his lost equilibrium again. Vain hope! Even solitude only dissipated temporarily this fundamental disquietude, or rather, even alone, he was always obscurely conscious of it, and would begin to desire the presence of other people again, like a stubborn gambler who refuses to admit himself beaten. With Chantal a few hours ago he had tried with all his might to restrain the dangerous, dubious words capable of betraying him. But they seemed to come out of his mouth of themselves, and to form into orderly ranks like well disciplined soldiers. And they were the very words that an instant before he had tried without success to formulate for himself, for his own relief, his deliverance. In the same way the warning he had just given de Clergerie came as a surprise to himself, he had not distinguished it from his other trivial, prudent words until too late. He even wondered now if he had really uttered it. He said it over to himself in a low voice as he went upstairs to his room; he repeated it again leaning out of the window overlooking the quivering park . . .

What a night! The odor of hot bark and resin, the odor of the centenarian trees as vigorous and musky as animals, had killed all the more fragile perfumes distilled by the delicate alchemy of day, and now, fostered by darkness, floated slowly, heavily, like a thick fog, warm as living things, and left on the tongue a taste of sweat and blood . . . "What silly impatience drives me, either out of boredom, or bravado, or for the sake of some unconscious revenge, to risk my so hardly-gained peace of mind?" thought Cénabre. "Is last winter going to begin again? Why am I unable to live with other men? Who prevents me? What madness?"

Once more, but half-heartedly, he went over the stages already traversed, and once more the vulgarity, the insignificance of the episodes disgusted, sickened him. Try as he might he could find nowhere in that tranquil regular life of a writer, man of letters, laborious scholar, anything to justify a fatigue so profound, so fundamental, or an exhaustion so serious that it seemed to be irreparably undermining, not only his moral equilibrium of which he used to be so proud, but even the free exercise of his mental faculties. He had been a taciturn boy, ashamed of his birth and his poverty, already resolved to outdistance his happier rivals by his solid merits, his precocious earnestness and peasant obstinacy; then a little later a diligent student, a scrupulous seminarist, an apparently irreproachable priest; he seemed to have known no other passion than the austere ambition of a scholar. The only really fruitful joys that belief had ever given him were those of curiosity—entirely occupied with the problem of that supernatural life whose reality he no more thought of denying today than he had before. Yes, today as formerly the theories of rationalism, the ridiculous, ostentatious dream of psycho-physiology, or even worse the psychiatry now in fashion, exasperated him by their coarseness and their poverty. So that the only problem that had ever interested him remained the same, would always remain the same. He was perfectly free to pursue for years and years to come, until the very end, the researches and observations that had made him famous. Even the constraint of a watchful, suspicious authority, the necessity of ingeniously adapting himself to it, and of avoiding its carefully prepared traps, had marvelously preserved him from narrowminded dogmatism, had served merely to discipline and make more supple his somewhat rough genius. What was it he still desired? At no time had he known the heartbreaking anguish of a sudden rupture with the past—that is with himself. Faith which in him had never been more than a habit, although a profound one, had faded gradually and when he had felt the final shock of realization and the inevitable recoil, he was already profoundly engaged in doubt or indifference, and closing his eyes had felt himself falling like a stone. It had, after all, only depended on himself to take his place quietly again, once the ordeal had passed. Yes, undoubtedly. But he had confided in Chevance!

That was his first mistake, or rather his only mistake. That imperceptible deviation from the road he had so carefully mapped out had distorted all his calculations ever since. Why? Who could tell? For in that mad step he had wanted to see—longed with all his might to see—nothing more than a negligible imprudence. Yes, it had been only a cry of pain, the involuntary call for help torn from a man not so much by terror as surprise, and that another ear had overheard by chance. What he could not admit, without indeed compromising that sort of peace so dearly bought, so fragile, was that by that cry in the night he had done much more than give his secret to an old indigent priest, he had revealed himself to himself, had for once, once only, known the profound voice of his nature, the cry of his entrails that even the prodigious cunning of his deception had been unable to stifle. He believed that he was thinking only of Chevance. With morbid attention and childish care he kept reviewing each detail of the scene, like a meticulous author who will go back over an important dialogue twenty times, but Cénabre made only one actor appear. Chevance alone came and went, talked and wept in a pathetic monologue. The other presence remained silent, Cénabre refused, probably without design but through an instinct of defense, to risk uttering such a cry again, even in a dream.

At present, at this hour, his last interview with Chantal returned to his memory, slowly entering it at the same painful point, and his familiar anguish was thereby so strangely increased that he hardly recognized it. And it seemed to him that with his new avowal he had allowed the most precious part of his being to escape, a warmer richer blood. He felt literally thc lucid exhaustion, the sensation of luminous weakness that always follows a great loss of any bodily substance. And at the same time the images, hardly distorted, half-way between delirium and dream, that were like the phantoms of his own meditations, began again before his eyes their strange, transparent round, their silent mournful glidings. . . . He was not delirious. What had worried him for weeks now was the extraordinary sensibility of his overworked brain that made his abstract constructions take on the high relief and movement of living things. He finally tore himself away from the window, threw himself on his bed and closed his eyes. But his head on the pillow was soon soaked with sweat and he got up again, went back to the window and leaned there shivering.

What a night! . . . The tops of the pines were hardly blacker than the dark backdrop, where a single star was slowly vanishing. Everything that the terrible sun had been able to pump out of the arid earth had slowly risen, inhaled by the dusk, had formed an invisible cloud a thousand feet above the earth, and the eye could just discern toward the west its glowing edges, still coppery from the setting sun. A drop of rain fell on Cénabre's hand—hot, heavy, perfumed like a drop of spikenard, the very essence of the vanished day.

Leaning out a little he could see the window of Clergerie's study that was still lighted, and suddenly he heard the crunching of the gravel under the little man's brisk and, at the same time, hesitating step, heard his nervous cough. A door opened, the automobile motor began to purr, stopped, then after a human groan that rent the night, purred again. And almost at the same moment the beams of the headlights shot out, swept the sky, hesitated a second, then the two interminable antennae, turning majestically around, plunged suddenly, and disappeared.

Why did Abbé Cénabre begin to make a mental calculation? He could not have said. Moreover he gave little heed to the figures that seemed to appear of themselves. He calculated that the station was not more than eight hundred yards away so that Fiodor's car should be back within five minutes. He drew out his watch. And at precisely the fifth minute the wandering lights, as though keeping a mysterious rendezvous, appeared at the top of the hill, while the poplars lining the avenue as they were lighted up all together, looked wan and tremulous against the black velvet screen. . . . "I'm rid of that idiot for a day at least," said Cénabre in a low voice. And it seemed to him that he experienced an inexpressible sense of relief.

It was then, it was at that very moment of oblivion, of remission, as he closed the window again to relish more completely his recovered feeling of solitude, that the strange thing began to happen in him, made each nerve quiver, ran insidiously along the marrow of his bones, and then began to glow in his mind with a steady, unendurable brightness. To efface, to crush this coruscating spot, he could not suppress the idiotic gesture of raising his hands to his forehead, pressing his head between his large palms. But that first movement of surprise was gone in a flash—the shock had been too severe, too unexpected for that energetic, indomitable man not to react with all his strength. And while the lower faculties were in complete rout, reason's imperious call to order reached the brain, and stayed the fatal moment. "Another attack like the one of last winter," he thought. "Am I going mad?"

He hurried to the window, opened it again, stared out into the night. He could hardly resist the temptation of throwing himself into that darkness, of stretching out his arms and falling, of losing himself at last with his hated secret. And yet that was not the way he had wanted to die that other time, when he had pressed the muzzle of the revolver to his forehead. Now it was only the flesh that longed for nothingness, for rest—or rather longed for nothing at all. He was fleeing, fleeing before an unknown danger whose cause was outside himself. Or, rather, he was trying to escape.

Now, with his clenched fists he shook the guard rail with stealthy, vicious blows as though he wanted to tear it out of the stone. This crude expense of force relieved him. Still trembling all over from the terrifying attack, his face haggard, his mouth bitter, he began, one by one, to regain possession of the ideas and images that the sudden explosion of terror had scattered like dead leaves; he tried to reason with these poor fragments saved from the disaster as a sinking ship lights its last flares.

"But what happened?" he stammered. "Nothing. I heard nothing, saw nothing, thought nothing. It was as though I had been hit in the back." And indeed, he had to restrain his impulse to turn around, to face it. No matter how ardently he wished to see in this sudden attack simply an attenuated return of the former one, he could no longer deceive himself. The anguish had not, this time, risen slowly in himself at the end of an interminable rumination, a perilous examination penetrating to the quick of his soul. This time the blow had come from without. Yes, outside himself, outside his power to control, an event had just occurred, he did not know what, perhaps he would never know—yet as real, as certain, as any he had seen with his own eyes. What was it?

There was no use letting his eyes wander from one humble witness of his strange adventure to another, from the flowered chintz of the wall to the massive bed, he could discover none of those phantoms whose presence he now so much desired, because his pride could master them, or, at least, meet them face to face. On the contrary, he had a growing certitude—evidence that was a thousand times more absurd than any phantom and more humiliating to his pride. It seemed to him that he was no longer master of any of those secrets that the most ordinary man is able to defend against other people's curiosity. Of course, he had received no proof of this evidence. Yet he could not question it—it had blazed with a furious glowing light. And light is the exact word, for from the first shock, that complete dispossession of himself had had its physical sign which even his reason could not deny, which it accepted with a kind of desperate resignation—a flood of light had entered him and he had closed his eyelids not to see the effulgence on his pale hands.

At that moment anyone but Abbé Cénabre would have called upon madness as a relief, or else have fallen on his knees. But his powerful nature still refused to surrender, or it is probable that the idea never even occurred to him. He only thought of being his own deliverer, of freeing himself through his own efforts, he was prepared to engage in that mournful gamble in which he himself was the stake. For years he had been familiar with that secret, impenetrable life, his strange genius occupied with animating his dream personages, its saints, men and women—so that he was very far above the surprises or the terrors of an uninitiated spectator. The image of Chantal, her last words, and that humble kiss—these three recollections had never ceased to float above those fantastic apparitions, and he was now convinced that it was at that same already wounded place in his brain—there and nowhere else—that the conflagration had been kindled. "Strange little girl," he thought, "I shall see her again tomorrow. I shall know . . . I shall explain . . . I shall . . ."

As he murmured these words to himself, he threw his coat over his shoulders, started for the stairs, and calmly groping for the banisters, descended with his heavy, even tread. Still groping, he mechanically let down the bar and shot the bolts of the entrance door, felt the gravel crunching under his soles, went forward into the darkness, a tall figure magnificently calm and poised, although in reality he was already emptied of all his strength, ready now either for pardon or despair. All the energy and pride he had left, he would squander his last reserves, throw them away with both hands, as it were, with magnificent indifference, in order to keep erect another hour, two hours, the entire night, resolved to spend the time, minute by minute, until dawn. For he could no longer endure the idea of going back to his room, of going on with the silent sickening struggle. "It will be over tomorrow," he thought. "Before then I shall have worn out my nerves. . . ." Tomorrow!

He strode straight ahead like a blind man, guided only by the pale glow of the freshly white-washed wall of the dependencies, both hands pressed flat against his chest, like a wounded man who has turned his back on his assassin and taken a few steps in bewilderment, a knife in his heart. Stumbling over the border of some shrubbery he staggered, fell on his knees, got up and, feeling nothing, went on again, wholly absorbed in his thought, which was scarcely a thought, just as a corpse is not quite an object but is not a person either—a solitary image outside life's bustle. And yet he would willingly have believed that this mental concentration was rather the harbinger of his deliverance, for he felt the lie within him loosening; by a sort of inner immobility he was, to a certain extent, escaping from that fearful constraint, patiently, heroically endured for so many months. The mysterious but certain event, of which he had just had the premonition, without yet in the least knowing what it might be, was none the less of that order of events that reverse the course of adversity and never fail to be auspicious, even when they are sure to consummate a ruin already long awaited with intolerable suspense.

Like a dying man who once has felt deep in his

breast, against his heart, the first chill that is the herald of his agony, longs for its return without suspecting that in that instant he has irreparably offered himself to death, the miserable priest, having reached the end of his strength, defended himself no longer, gave himself up, worn out by five months of a struggle that, without his suspecting it, had been nothing but a ludicrous challenge to his own nature, a useless wager from the moment the first blow had been struck in the edifice of his imposture, when he had let his secret escape. For hypocrisy is only a vice like the others—weakness and strength, instinct and calculation—for which we make allowance, while such a total lie, an integral part of every one of our acts, if it is to be maintained to the end, must espouse completely our life, embrace its rhythm. Let the least disaccord creep in, and attention is aroused, the will stiffens, conscience levels its steady gaze at the weak point. What will could sustain such an effort for long? Abbé Cénabre did not suspect that his own had just snapped. He did not suspect it because that magnificent will had yielded too late, after having worn out the resistance of a brain already marked with an old taint. He had thought that his insupportable burden was growing gradually lighter, when it was he who had let his hands open, was sinking.

He did not, moreover, this time commit the same folly of calling for help. There was no one whose presence he desired. The sudden sensation of solitude that had formerly seized him when God's name had come unprompted to his lips, and which had increased ever since, had been fading gradually during the last weeks. The ever narrowing circle was closing around the pitiless priest, so that it was useless for him to try any longer to find his way. He was perfectly unconcerned. His blindness was that of a man beyond danger, already lost. A few weeks before while walking along the shore between Ollioules and Toulon he had said to the village doctor whom he had met by chance at the inn, and who listened to the horrible aphorism without understanding it, repeating it to Father Domange at the first opportunity: "There are certain conjunctures in a man's life when he feels God only as a hindrance, a last obstacle to be overcome."

At this moment it was really against such an obstacle he was advancing with half-closed eyes, trying to forget that vague light he had thought he saw a moment ago coming through his trembling hands, as though he had been so inwardly saturated with it that it overflowed. Where had it come from? How had it entered his breast? By what breach? His reason might be tottering, but could he really be deceived by such a crude hallucination? Yet he could not completely reject it, nevertheless, because the terrible pang it had given him was marvelously in keeping with that new, unexpected certitude of his vulnerability, the conviction that he was pierced through and through and henceforth incapable of concealing any lie, delivered over to what all his life he had feared more than any danger, men's curiosity, the cruelty of human judgments. And so, less with the idea of escaping from the mysterious light than hoping to recover his secret so suddenly lost, the lie that was his security, he turned his back on the high house glowing faintly in the darkness, and directed his steps instinctively toward the night. Suddenly as he walked around a clump of yews his chest came up against a living body, and instead of crying out in startled surprise (for he had reached that stage of nervous apathy when the exhausted body no longer reacts to fear) he gave a dismal groan.

"How you frightened me, Abbé!" It was Fernande, the fat cook, who spoke in a whisper. "Didn't you see me, Abbé Cénabre? You came straight toward me," she added with asperity, "I really thought you saw me. The night isn't as black as all that—in ten minutes the moon will be up."

Cénabre could hardly make out the face turned toward him, but he was aware of a sort of urgency and terror that caught, for a moment, his wandering attention.

"What do you want with me?" he asked roughly. "What does this exhibition mean?"

To ward him off she had put her hand against him, and he felt that she was trembling.

"The dear God has sent you," she said simply. "I'll tell you . . . but no . . . there isn't time, you'll have to take my word for it. . . . Here is the master gone away! And what is a poor woman like me doing mixed up in such things! This infernal house is a nest of rats, Abbé. . . . Well, as true as God is my witness, there was a man in Mademoiselle Chantal's room, I saw him with my own eyes!"

"And is it for that you stopped me?" said Cénabre in disgust. "The storm has affected your brain, my good woman. You ought to go to bed."

"Go to bed?" she returned scornfully. "That's all very well to say. Ah me, many's the time I've done that, when I should have kept my eyes and my ears open! If I've made a mistake today, well, so much the worse for me. I'll never be able to look you in the face again. Yes, Abbé, you'd have the right to despise me! Think what you please of me, now, but don't let me go up there alone! I've tried twenty times and I just can't do it. What is it to you? Just to the stairway, Abbé Cénabre! You can stay on the stairs and listen for me if I call."

"Let me go!" he commanded in an oddly tremulous voice. "You have chosen a bad moment to try to frighten me, my good woman. I have another burden to bear tonight."

Had she noticed the scarcely perceptible change in his voice as he said these last incomprehensible words? Before replying she looked more closely into his face, silently, questioningly:

"Well now, it's no time to be losing our heads! I never get excited for nothing, you may be sure. The chauffeur was drunk, Abbé, cold drunk. . . . The filthy ether was coming out of his eyes, you would have said a real devil. He beat up Francine, I found her lying flat on her stomach on the bed spitting blood, her mouth all covered with it . . . "Look out for Mademoiselle Chantal!" she says, the poor thing! And not another word could I get out of her. She'd not sell her darling for anything. Then when I heard the master's car coming back I looked for the Russian everywhere. Vanished! He's capable of going through keyholes, the monster! I thought—since I hadn't lost sight of the stairway—he must have stayed outside in the fresh air. Only, you see, I'd forgotten. You can get upstairs through the little store room just by putting a leg over the window sill . . . Oh! Abbé Cénabre, just a second before I met you, I . . . I . . ."

"I'll come with you," Cénabre said quickly and his voice had suddenly grown gentle. "Walk slowly. Possibly it will turn out to be only a dream. I must husband my strength."

He gave a deep sigh and followed her with his customary tread, measured and calm. But when they reached the flight of stairs, she could restrain herself no longer and started up them at a bound, leaving Cénabre behind. For another moment she could still hear his panting breathing like the whimpering of a child, then nothing. She had reached the room, opened the door and darted in. The light burst forth, and at the same time her shriek:

"Abbé, Abbé, they are both here, they are here!"

She ran to the balustrade, leaned over but, still dazzled by the light, she could make nothing out in the dark chasm . . .

"Abbé . . . Abbé . . . you will have to help me, no one must come and find her. At least we must put her on her bed . . . Mademoiselle Chantal is dead!"

There was a silence. Then an unrecognizable voice came up out of the darkness.

"Please try, first of all, to calm yourself. What are you trying to say? What is it? Your voice echoes frightfully, I cannot hear you."

She came down a few steps having first instinctively closed the door, shutting in the light and the two dead bodies. The darkness seemed blacker now, and the cook groped blindly, confused by the curve of the banisters, leaning with her whole weight against the wall. Two steps . . . three steps . . . five steps . . . And suddenly she felt the priest's hot breath on her cheek.

"Are you blind?" he said. "The night is not as dark as that. . . . What were you saying up there . . . Are you losing your wits? Mademoiselle de Clergerie dead! How did it happen? Who killed her?"

The cook, as though fascinated by that voice coming out of the darkness, standing motionless, not daring to turn her head, received each word full in her face with his hot breath.

"The madman," she said at last. "Yes, Abbé Cénabre, the Russian. . . . He killed himself afterwards, naturally. And now there he is barring the entrance with his great demon body, so floppy and heavy, I'll never be able to budge it alone. . . . And he still has his filthy revolver in his hand, he's still capable of harm, the filthy beast."

She shuddered with disgust and went on in childish supplication:

"No, Abbé. I don't want anyone to find her there, it would be terrible, imagine! If you won't help me, I'd much rather see Mademoiselle Chantal anywhere else, poor darling, she'd be happier in a corner of the hedge, yes, even in the grass like a dead bird. Russian or no Russian, the house itself was no good for her, I know."

She smothered a sob, then suddenly frightened, was silent. The night seemed emptier than ever all around her tear-drenched face. She could not even hear the priest's breathing any longer. For a second she thought she could make out the contour of his face close to hers, his roving eyes, the pale glint of his skin, but the voice came from the other side of the stairs to her left. It seemed to be coming out of the wall.

"Will you kindly give me your hand," said Cénabre. "I fear I cannot take a single step unassisted."

She felt her arm seized with convulsive force. At once he began climbing the stairs, slowly, heavily, as though he were pushing a tremendous weight with his forehead. And when, after the door had been opened, the light struck his face, frozen in an anguish that was more than human, the poor woman, in spite of her terror, could not suppress a cry of pity.

"My God," she cried. "Don't you bother. I can manage by myself. Just help me put the darling on her bed. Lord God! her poor little head is nothing but one big wound. You take her under the arms, Abbé . . . it makes me feel sick too. I haven't the strength all alone."

"One second, excuse me . . ." said Cénabre calmly. "Give me a second or two. For the moment I cannot help you; I cannot even see you, Madame Fernande."

On her knees beside the miserable body lying on the floor, the cook was trying to hold up the shattered neck in the crook of her arm, but the voice of Cénabre, in spite of her dazed horror, gave her such a start that with a somewhat ridiculous, instinctive movement, she got to her feet as though to honor that sovereign grief which had just spoken in a voice more imperative than death itself.

The priest, standing on the threshold of the room, took in the scene at a glance like a man who knows what he is looking for, and having found it, will not be put off. Now he was looking down at the body of Chantal as it lay stretched out on the floor, his expression so grim that it sent a chill through Fernande at first. But coming nearer, coolheaded as usual, she noticed that the look she had thought fixed on the little victim was in reality floating above her, looking at nothing.

Then the cook shrugged her shoulders, and lifted Chantal up bodily in her arms. When Cénabre heard the lamentable burden bounce on the bed, he gave a painful groan and took a step forward.

"I had to, excuse me, there was no other way," said

the poor woman covered with confusion. "Light as she is I could hardly make it, my arms are broken. Dear God, one would like to carry her on one's knees like the Holy Sacrament! Anyway, poor darling, she is still with us, with you and me, she can be content. Tomorrow, ugh! it will be all over the papers and tongues will begin wagging! You'll never get it out of my head, Abbé, that it is the death she wanted—no other—just this one! You couldn't ever humiliate her enough, she wanted nothing but scorn, she would have lived in the dust. That Russian was surely the wickedest of us all. So she would have wanted her end to come from him. . . . She never thought like you and me, the poor angel. . . . And now people will be shaking their heads, and gossiping, they'll say she was crazy or worse. . . . She will have renounced everything, Abbé, everything I tell you, even her death."

The priest remained standing under the harsh light. No human wisdom, not even the genius of compassion, could have read in those still features anything but the death pangs of a prodigious will, carved from within, marked with the sign of the eternal. For a moment, a long moment, the balance swung between the dead girl, still living, and this living man, already dead.

"Will you come nearer, Madame Fernande," he said finally in a whisper as though husbanding even his breath.

He turned his blind stare toward her and suddenly she thought she saw his mouth relax, the heavy lines of his cheeks disappear, the whole face darken. But he moved his shoulders like a man taking up his burden again, and almost at the same time she heard these astonishing words:

"Madame Fernande, do you feel equal to reciting a *Pater?*"

"Yes, Abbé Cénabre," she said humbly. "*Our Father Who art in Heaven, hallowed be Thy name . . .*"

He had put his hand on her arm; she felt it growing heavier and heavier.

"Repeat it, please," he said gently. "I cannot."

"*Our Father Who art in Heaven,*" she began softly with her accent of the province of Auge.

"PATER NOSTER," said Cénabre, in a superhuman voice.

And he fell forward on his face.[1]

[1] Abbé Cénabre died the 10th of March 1912, in the sanatorium of Dr. Lelièvre, without having regained his reason.